SUPREME VILLAINY

PRAISE FOR *SUPREME VILLAINY*

"*Supreme Villainy* is the best supervillain memoir since *The Art of the Deal*."

—Mike Lawrence, comedian and writer

"While we have all lived for decades in fear of King Oblivion's sinister machinations, Wilson's thorough biography is a witty, irreverent, and genuinely hilarious take on the mind of history's greatest monster."

—Chris Sims, writer of *X-Men '92* and *Deadpool: Bad Blood*

"Oblivion and Wilson's genre-defying meta-memoir had me cowering with laughter. Buy it, as your King commands."

—Daniel Kibblesmith, writer, *The Late Show with Stephen Colbert*

"Thanks to this exhaustively researched book, I finally know the 'inside scoop' on King Oblivion, the man who burned down my village and disintegrated my family!"

—Geoffrey Golden & Amanda Meadows, *The Devastator*

PRAISE FOR MATT D. WILSON

"Without great supervillains, superheroes would have no one to fight but each other! King Oblivion, Ph.D., has performed a noble public service with *The Supervillain Handbook* and deserves the unbounded gratitude of every thinking comic book fan. Excelsior!"

—Stan Lee

"*The Supervillain Field Manual*: For when you've exhausted *The Anarchist Cookbook* and are ready to take the next step."

—Kelly Sue DeConnick, writer of *Captain Marvel* and *Avengers Assemble*

SUPREME VILLAINY

A BEHIND-THE-SCENES LOOK AT THE MOST (IN)FAMOUS SUPERVILLAIN MEMOIR NEVER PUBLISHED

KING OBLIVION, PH.D.

Edited by Matt D. Wilson

TALOS

Talos Press books may be purchased in bulk at special discounts for sales promotion, corporate gifts, fund-raising, or educational purposes. Special editions can also be created to specifications. For details, contact the Special Sales Department, Talos Press, 307 West 36th Street, 11th Floor, New York, NY 10018or info@skyhorsepublishing.com.

Talos Press is an imprint of Skyhorse Publishing, Inc.®, a Delaware corporation.

Visit our website at www.talospress.com.

10 9 8 7 6 5 4 3 2 1

Library of Congress Cataloging-in-Publication Data is available on file.

Cover illustration by Adam Wallenta
Cover design by Jason Snair

Print ISBN: 978-1-940456-80-5
Ebook ISBN 978-1-940456-81-2

Printed in the United States of America

For Ronnie and Sue

A NOTE TO READERS

If you somehow haven't heard until now, King Oblivion, Ph.D., founder of the International Society of Supervillains (ISS), died in a high-speed, head-on collision between his supersonic jet shaped like a fist and a super-secret flying submarine owned by an anti-supervillain paramilitary organization. Both vehicles were completely destroyed.

King Oblivion and his henchman pilot were instantly killed. A body was recovered and it is my understanding that he will be buried in an undisclosed location to prevent any possible (and probable) desecration of the grave by superhero partisans and his rivals in the supervillain community.

Various accounts of King Oblivion's demise have been all over the news. My access to the outside world has been pretty limited over the six years that I've been held captive here in King Oblivion's underground lair, but based on conversations with people who have access to television and other media outlets, it was widely reported that, yes, the perhaps-mythic monarch and doctor was indeed a real person—there had been theories that he was an alias used by a group of different supervillains rather than one man—and that his life had come to an end after 104 years. Apparently, a lot of the coverage involved tearful interviews with the families of the many people that King Oblivion had, in person or by proxy, turned into statues or piles of dust in the last several decades. The words "monster," "got what was coming to him," "less pain than he deserved," and "God's justice" were used frequently. Then the news programs ran archive footage of the statues and dust that used to be people. Again, this is all secondhand information.

A few days after King Oblivion's death, someone finally remembered that I was being held down here in the writer's pool (basically a dungeon equipped with a few old word processors and a water cooler that they never refill) and released me to more or less wander around the premises as I saw fit. I had nearly starved to death, so my first stop was the largely ransacked cafeteria, where I feasted on a few cans of potted meat. It got pretty wild around here in the immediate aftermath of the demise of our glorious leader (which is what he made us call him). It was a real everyone-for-themselves scenario. Quite a few of King Oblivion's henchmen, known as "decoys" because they dressed exactly like him, didn't make it out alive.

I then went to his study, the place where he had brought me on several occasions so as to instruct me on how to ghostwrite his villain instructional books, *The Supervillain Handbook* and *The Supervillain Field Manual*. Over the years I had seen a revolving door—or, more precisely, an entrance with no exit for the living—of other writers come in to ghostwrite another project he had long been working on: his memoirs. He tended to keep me on other projects, but I could tell his autobiography was immensely important to him, so I scoured the room for what I could find from the development process: aborted chapters, notes, correspondence between King Oblivion and the multiple writers he brought in, contact information for people he associated with, back-and-forth exchanges with potential publishers, and so on.

As I dug into these materials, it became readily apparent that King Oblivion had an acute awareness that his clock was ticking. He was asking authors to include information that could be of use to a successor and that would also build his legacy, his legend, in the decades to come. He wanted to offer up the story of his life to find someone of comparative evil power to take over the International Society of Supervillains, or so it seemed, and keep the ISS relatively strong.

He died before he could publish that message, but out of a sense of grudging respect for my longtime captor (and, I'll be frank, boredom, because the decoys won't let me leave), I am doing my utmost to compile these writings, with King Oblivion's notes to his ghostwriters, edits and all, into a working manuscript for an autobiography. I have also managed to find a phone with which I can actually get an outside connection and a computer with email capabilities, so I have conducted a few interviews with people from King Oblivion's life to get a stronger sense of him from someone else's perspective, something I've never been able to achieve before.

I have also made many, many phone calls to every authority I can think of in hopes of rescue, but I genuinely have no idea where I am, so no one from the outside world seems to be able to find me.

I hope that you find what's collected here as enlightening as it was for me to discover it. Also: Please help me. I am worried for my safety, and starving.

Matt D. Wilson
September 2016

Chapter 1

EVIL IS BORN

When I entered this world, it shook.

You may think that sounds a tad melodramatic. Well, of course it does! Who do you think you're talking to? But even if I weren't invested in the melodrama that is this life on Earth, it'd be true. Look it up. My countenance looked Earth in the face for the very first time on [July 7, 1912,] the date of the 7.2-magnitude earthquake that hit Paxson, Alaska. At the base of Mount McKinley, the planet stretched upward, as if to escape from itself, as if to get away from some newly generated force that it intuited would serve as its greatest threat. The world tried and failed to get away from itself at 7:57 a.m., the same time I emerged from the womb and plopped out into a lifeboat in international waters as the steamer ship on which my parents had been passengers just a few short hours prior sank into the northern Pacific.

Not aggressive enough. Let's punch the reader with words.

Must we reveal my birthdate? I prefer to be considered immortal and ever-living.

Make Earth seem more scared.

Hate this. Much too humble.

That's hardly a royal birth. Unlike the planet itself seemed to do, it would be decades before human society recognized my innate leadership, intimidation, and bloviating skills that made me the king I was born to be. Yes, I'm one of very few kings who earned his title rather than coming into it by heredity. Back then, I was quite simply the son of Maxwell and Bonnie Oblivion of Sarasota, Florida, both of whom were being sent to the Arctic Circle by their employers to sell encyclopedias door-to-door. King was not yet my title. It was just my first name.

How dare you reveal this?

Diligent research on my part[1] uncovered that the group of survivors of which I was a part—myself, my parents, two honeymooners, an elderly couple, and a bug-like fellow by the name of Heinrich Misanthroach—remained in that lifeboat for nearly three days after the steamer permanently deposited itself at the bottom of the ocean.[2] By all accounts, it was a terrible ordeal, the kind that might further consecrate an innate malevolence.

The first passenger to go was the young bride. A misunderstanding about the lifeboat having a

---

1 Over the decades, I sent teams of dozens of decoy henchmen to airlift various libraries, public records offices, and other repositories of knowledge back to my headquarters, then forced them to read everything contained within on the off chance there might be some information about my past inside. Who knows? *Ulysses* could have had seven or eight chapters about me.

2 Well, it wasn't that permanent. Decades later, I ordered a decoy scuba team to dive into the icy waters and raise the ship from its rocky grave, in hopes of finding anything my parents left behind. We didn't find much—some old clothes, a couple boxes of encyclopedias, some literature about controlling one's economic future—but we did take home a pretty sweet haul of old-timey pocket watches and gold teeth, so it wasn't a total loss. Plus, I got to decorate my throne room with the bow of my "birth boat."

"lower deck," brought on as the result of a bawdy joke my father told about needing a drink, led her to attempt to swim underneath the lifeboat mere minutes after it drifted away from the sinking steamer. She was probably rattled from feeling the distant earthquake. An inexperienced swimmer, she was pulled under by the vortex caused by the sinking of the steamer and quickly drowned.

My mother took this inopportune moment to morbidly build on my father's joke. She suggested that the young wife had gotten held up in the nonexistent lower deck and that someone should probably go find her in the lifeboat's "wine cellar." This sent the fatuous husband jumping overboard to attend to her, despite ample evidence that there simply was no such place.

It was the perfect moment. She seized it. My mother knew exactly what she was doing.

Allow me to take this opportunity to remind you that we were in a lifeboat. Like his wife before him, the young husband was pulled into the vortex and drowned. Though I couldn't understand or comprehend these events, I consider these moments my earliest lessons in the power of persuasion and the limitless denseness and stupidity of which human beings are capable. They require the guidance of a genius like me.

Insulting and inaccurate.

The rest of the people stranded in the lifeboat held out for two additional days, hoping and praying for rescue, but most of the local authorities were too busy dealing with the aftermath of the earthquake to bother with us. After all, we were in international waters. No jurisdiction should, or wanted to, have us. It's almost as if the legal and societal strictures upon which the

Could be stronger. Let's add, "No one! No one! Only me! No one but me!"

peons have built their society is nothing but one grand joke played on everyone but me, a farce through which only I can see. I consider the circumstances of my first hours of life to be poetic confirmation of this.

The old man went next. Desperately hungry, freezing, and frustrated, he reached into the ocean to grab a fish that was swimming by. That fish, it comes as no surprise, turned out to be a Pacific sleeper shark, attracted by the mess the young newlywed couple had left behind in their urgency to get to the "lower deck." The shark wrapped its jaws around the fellow's arm and pulled him into the depths, never to be seen again. His wife, trying to convince herself that she hadn't just seen what she saw, leaned over the side of the boat and called out his name: "Percival!" she cried. "Percival!" She was instantly pulled into the water by three additional sleeper sharks that, seeing the opportunity in front of them, had teamed up for the occasion.

Feel like this story makes these fish look more powerful than me. Revise.

From this, I gathered an appreciation of working with others at the opportune time, the spirit of the predator, and the true, destructive power of nature. I also developed a deep, abiding fascination with sharks.

I would learn about the devastation that mankind can bring upon itself when my parents perished the following day.

The great irony of it is that we had been rescued. After some seventy-two hours of languishing in the lifeboat, a US Cutter Service ship approached and pulled the remaining four of us out of the water. Though we were briefly welcomed aboard,

I have never needed rescuing. Rephrase. "The Cutter Service had the pleasure of seeking out my company. They invited my domination of them."

the crewmembers quickly found other things with which to occupy their time. For some, it was glancing away from us in the galley while pretending to do navigational work. For most others, it was accomplishing their mission of launching a weather balloon. My parents, always looking to make the big sale, observed the balloon and saw an advertising opportunity. They lifted each other up and climbed onto the device in hopes that they could paint a message to the world on its side, an entreaty to encourage onlookers to buy the encyclopedias put in their charge.

Shockingly, they did manage to get a serviceable message written on the side in black paint they had found in a storeroom: "Buy Encyclopedia Worldannica."[3] As they were putting the finishing touches on the message, the balloon launched into the stratosphere. A few members of the crew made an effort to recall the balloon or retrieve my parents from it, but once it was done, it was done. My mother and father, the balloon, and their ad went ever upward into what one can only assume is the furthest distance from the planet anyone had achieved at that point. Presumably they froze, but I can verify that their bodies were found on top of a windmill in the Netherlands some years later. So they must not have been strapped in too well.

This conjecture makes my parents look stupid and thoughtless. Blame someone else.

[redacted]

3 The encyclopedia company went out of business just two years later, but surprisingly not because of their association with an illegal advertisement connected to the death of two of their salespeople. (That, as we all know, is just smart business.) No, instead the company became embroiled in controversy over their entry on the country of Denmark, which simply read, "Everyone there can burn right in hell for all I care."

Don't like this. My brain has always been fully and completely formed. "Nascent" is a word for obstetricians and politicians. It applies to nothing in my life.

Again, my [nascent] brain must have absorbed a few lessons, perhaps by osmosis. You may be wondering how I could contend that the mind of an infant, a literal newborn, could have taken in these grand lessons and internalized them in any meaningful way, but again I ask: Who do you think you're talking to? I could learn before anyone else knew what learning was, and I can retain knowledge more successfully than anyone who ever lived. Mark that.

As I was saying, I learned some things:

There is pride in death.

Technology is a terrible threat and an invaluable tool.

The authorities are powerless to help you.

Perhaps most overwhelmingly, I saw the power of propaganda. Everyone aboard that boat bought a set of Encyclopedia Worldannicas before the company went bust.

When the ship docked in Kodiak, Alaska the next day, Misanthroach had no choice but to take me, the only survivor of his steamer ship ordeal, with him and informally adopt me as his son and protégé. Though the term had not yet come into the common parlance at the time, the man, known to his peers as Dr. Blattarius, was one of the very first supervillains in documented history. Born half man/half cockroach, there were few avenues open to him outside the realm of professional evil.

At one point he attempted to make a go of it as an exterminator (before he embraced what he was; the actions of a typical self-hater). He even tried to hide his roachy nature and pass as a non-hybrid man, but eventually he recognized that there were few options open to him besides proverbially crawling up through people's floorboards into their kitchens and ruining their dinners. He put on a domino mask and vowed to ruin each day for his lifelong rival, the disgusting and putrid superhero Mr. Wonderful.

Five years before we crossed paths on that lifeboat, Blattarius co-founded an association of assorted goons, hoods, and nogoodniks. Just a few months prior to the steamer sinking, he managed to get pretty far along into a plot to replace former US President Theodore Roosevelt with a robot.

Allow me (as if you could allow me to do anything; I command all in my purview) to explain a bit further: Just as the plan seemed to be coming together, Robot Roosevelt malfunctioned and went off script, taking over the group and redubbing it the Bull Moose Party. Robot Roosevelt, having broken through his programming, pursued Dr. Blattarius using a hastily constructed collection of mechanical Rough Riders who were eliminating perceived threats and enemies throughout the country. To avoid mechanical death at the hands of his own creation, Blattarius took refuge on the steamer ship and hoped to ride out the difficulties in Alaska.

It was serendipitous that Blattarius and I were on the same boat in the middle of nowhere. After coordinating an unsuccessful assassination attempt (they should have known a bullet wouldn't have killed a robot, even if he was in the middle of a speech), it would be another year before Blattar-

Is it? Couldn't I have willed this to happen? The answer is yes. Yes I could. And I did.

ius and his compatriots would seize back control of the association from Robot Roosevelt in a plot that involved distracting him with an expedition to South America. Blattarius and his team tossed the robot into the Amazon River, where he sparked and sputtered to his demise. He was replaced once again with the real Roosevelt, who had been sent to a remote island with nothing more than a bag of rice and a horse. He was told to "ride around," which seemed to make him perfectly content.

After the mini-crisis with Robot Roosevelt was resolved, Dr. Blattarius took me to his secondary hideaway, a giant laboratory enclosed in a system of igloos in the Northwest Territory of Canada. That is where I spent the first six years of my life.

Again, far too humble.

I don't regret or begrudge the circumstances surrounding my birth. But then again, of course I begrudge them. I am a professional begrudger. It is my deeply held belief that the series of tragic accidents that coincided with my first days on this rock consecrated me into the hardened, wizened supervillain, leader, and statesman that I have become. It is also entirely possible that my presence in the lifeboat was the very cause of these events. I tend to think a certain aura of ill will follows me around at all times and that I have the ability to cause hardship with little to no effort exerted. I'm 100 percent sure, if not more, that I caused that earthquake.

This should be stronger; less wishy-washy. "These things definitely happened because of me. It is proven."

Likewise, it placed me in the care of Dr. Blattarius, a mentor without whom I would not have developed so quickly into the giant of villainy that I became. (Not to say that I wouldn't have gotten here. I would have. There is unequivocally and undoubtedly no question about that. My

I'm discomforted by this graciousness. Tone that down.

innate potential was beyond measure. But I must acknowledge that he accelerated the process.)

Which brings me to you, dear reader. Someday, someone must take my place. I have done quite a bit of self-reflection to finally arrive at this conclusion, let me tell you. For decades it seemed to me that I would keep my position of power eternally; that I would sit on my throne until this world died, at which time I would blast away from planet Earth and settle my throne on some other planet, which would embrace my conquering presence much like this one. Yet as I continue through my eleventh decade of life, I have reached the near-unthinkable thought: This body is not permanent. My memory will live on, but my physical presence will expire. I cannot let random chance pick the person who will sit in this throne after me. I must make that selection.

I'd like these reworded to make me sound less . . . vulnerable. "Death will come for me and I will crush it in our fight, but out of curiosity, I will go with it into the beyond."

But it can't be just anyone. At one time I thought I knew who would fill that role, but she's gone now. So I must search. The villain who succeeds me must have a certain inborn, instinctive talent for mayhem that cannot be learned though any amount of research or experience. I aim to uncover something that could make *you* the next *me*. Something intangible. I hope the story of my many conquests draws it out.

Email Correspondence Between King Oblivion, Ph.D. and Michelle Crayton, Ghostwriter of "Evil is Born"

From: King Oblivion, Ph.D.
To: Michelle Crayton
Subject: Birth chapter

Miss Crayton,

I have told you repeatedly that your job is not simply to transcribe the words I say, or, as you insist on calling them, "the facts." Your job here is to tell a story that is true, and the truth is that I am, and always have been, the most powerful being—human, animal, or otherwise—on this putrid rock. Even as a baby. *Especially* as a baby. Any portrayal of weakness is strictly unsubstantiated, untrue, and forbidden.

Is that clear?

. . .

From: Michelle Crayton
To: King Oblivion, Ph.D.
Subject: Re: Birth chapter

Sire,

I am truly trying all I can here, but I'm finding it rather difficult to describe a baby as anything but . . . a baby. Is it possible that maybe you'd rather not tell your birth story? Maybe you'd prefer to leave out the circumstances involving the lifeboat? Maybe you just don't want anyone to ever know you were a child?

No insult intended, but I'm struggling to get across what you want. I know this is my fault, not yours, as you have no faults. I'd appreciate any guidance you can offer.

Pleadingly,
Michelle Crayton

. . .

From: King Oblivion Ph.D.
To: Michelle Crayton
Subject: Re: Birth chapter

Miss Crayton,

Is this really that hard? Tell my story, but tell it in a way that shows me in the truest light: as infallible and without fault of any kind. I thought you were a writer! Write the spirit of the truth without getting bogged down in the details of what "really" happened. Is this substantial enough clarification for you? Are you still struggling?

Let me know if your microwave bed is enabling you to see the truth more clearly.

. . .

From: Michelle Crayton
To: King Oblivion Ph.D.
Subject: Re: Birth chapter

Sire,

My apologies for my late response, but my hands were terribly burned on the microwave bed and I had to recover for several weeks. I believe that I see where you're coming from.

How about this, if I may make a suggestion: we just make up a story about your birth. We'll say you emerged from a majestic volcano, fully formed and without any flaws whatsoever. Is this to your liking?

Supplicatively,
Michelle Crayton

. . .

From: King Oblivion Ph.D.
To: Michelle Crayton
Subject: Re: Birth chapter

Miss Crayton,

That is not *my* story. That is *fiction*. A *fabrication*. I wasn't born from a volcano. I was born and made an earthquake occur. Were you even listening during any of our sessions together? I want my story told, not some cheap, dime-store pulp novel.

. . .

From: Michelle Crayton
To: King Oblivion Ph.D.
Subject: Re: Birth chapter

Sire,

I'm afraid I'm still confused then. I'm trying. I want you to know I'm trying.

With immense efforts,
Michelle Crayton

. . .

From: King Oblivion Ph.D.
To: Michelle Crayton
Subject: Re: Birth chapter

Miss Crayton,

I'd say that I appreciated your services, but that would be a fabrication—much like the ones you wanted to tell. You insist that you are trying, but it is more than evident that you are not, because you will not adjust for the many lies you have included in the text you have provided me. There are words and there are actions. And then there are actions that reveal themselves through words. Beyond that, there are actions that should be retold through words that give those actions their authentic context.

I don't need to explain myself to you.

When you finish this message, turn around so that you might be turned into a gelatin in the glass tube my decoys are currently setting up directly behind you. Farewell.

Editor's Note: I found this survey in King Oblivion's study among several other instructional/testing materials in a thick, dog-eared file labeled "Choosing the One." I'll be sprinkling these materials throughout the text to give you a glimpse into King Oblivion's successor selection process.

Training Survey: Recognizing Your Spark

Do you have "it" when it comes to being an evil leader of others, be they layman, henchman, or fellow supervillain? Were you born with the capacity for true malevolence that only .00000001 percent of every living being has? If you have some uncertainty, but feel that you may indeed carry such potential, ask yourself the following questions:

- Given limitless power, would you use it to dominate everyone in your path, showing mercy to none?
- In your youth, did you find yourself rallying your peers to crush the tent poles of authority and ruin anyone who dared to tell you what you could or could not do?
- Have you been told about people around you feeling a particular sense of unease or dread when you were born?
- Have you always had a preternatural awareness of the world around you and its need to be conquered, even from birth?
- Have you found that people tend to do what you say, even if the idea sounds absolutely ludicrous?
- Given your preference, would you live underground, on the moon, in a volcano, or somewhere similar?
- Is one of your first thoughts when you meet a new person how they might look inside-out, as stone, in a

vacuum tube, with hands for feet and feet for hands, body-swapped with a frog, frozen, on fire, turned into a sentient being of light, as a brain in a jar, with four to eight times more limbs, sewn onto several other people, stuck in a time loop, forced to do everything backwards, shrunk, as a rock monster, transfigured into a tree, as a pile of purple dust, on a torture rack, inside a suitcase, as a suitcase, cloned, age advanced, age reduced, squashed down to two dimensions, thrown into the deep nothingness of space, drowned, placed inside a robot body, placed inside an ape's body, sliced in half by a buzz saw, smashed by a giant piano hammer, blinded by chemicals, irradiated, as a werewolf, as a vampire, as a sea creature, or all of the above?

- Do you often feel the need to point out how you're not so different from a rival?
- Do you feel like even the most mundane tasks must be done with significant flourish, even at the expense of doing that task effectively or quickly?
- Do you often feel compelled to tell people who are helping others to stop?
- Do you tell anyone who will listen for hours on end about the futility of existence, the nihilistic nature of the universe, and how life is all one big struggle for power?
- Do you laugh at what some people characterize as inappropriate times?
- Do you wear a mask on a regular basis to cover a hideous disfigurement, protect your face just because you feel it's cool, or any other reason?
- Have you found this questionnaire to be a complete farce because you confidently know in the depths of

> your cold, black heart that you are a true supervillain with no need for outside validation?

If you answered "yes" to that final question, you may just have it. But you haven't qualified to be the new me just yet. You have much more to learn and much more to achieve.

Editor's Note: I found a collection of a number of these brief file cards in King Oblivion's "Choosing the One" file and determined that it might be of interest to share them, if for no other reason than to gain some additional insight into his thought process. What's particularly odd is that they present fictional comic book characters—which King Oblivion claimed to have no knowledge of and derided as offensive portrayals—as role models. Perhaps it was an attempt to talk to young denizens on their level.

Villainspiration

The villain: Bizarro
Key trait: An anti-Superman, Bizarro knows exactly who he is from "birth"/creation.
How he demonstrates it: Bizarro has come in many different forms and iterations over the years, but one thing remains constant among the various Kryptonian soldiers, Bizarro World dwellers, Superman clones, and failed experiments over the decades: he is who he is, from birth. Sure, some have been twisted by various heroes to have a sort of skewed sense of heroism and traditional morality, but almost all are simply Anti-Supermen throughout their tragic lives. They know their goal is to do the opposite of what's "right." That's something for the evil to aspire to do.
The wrong takeaways: Don't let your "backwards" morality be changed into some kind of slightly weird, traditional morality. And for evil's sake, don't speak in opposite-speak all the time. It's infuriating. I'll chop you down where you stand if you do it anywhere near me!

Chapter 2

THE CHILD REPROBATE

I had a certain awareness of myself, my purpose, and my surroundings from the moment I opened my dark, hypnotic, soul-penetrating eyes, but I vividly recall my first moment of total consciousness. It was my third birthday. I was seated in a high chair—or, more accurately, a high throne, since any chair I grace with my body weight is, in a technical and official capacity, a throne—at the head of a long, ornate table. Atop a cake shaped like a cackling skull, candles flicked and flared with a dangerous heat that I found compelling. Intoxicating. At home with.

A worthwhile clarification to make, but I'd state this even more strongly. "Anywhere my ass is, seat or not, is a throne."

I raised my head from the energizing sight of the candles to see the faces of dozens of adults: Dr. Blattarius, henchmen in cockroach costumes, members of what I can only assume was some sort of fake "family" Blattarius had hired to make me feel like a "normal" child, various robot versions of world leaders (Blattarius had really invested a lot in those plans), and so on. They were looking at me intently, awaiting my next move. Their reaction hinged and depended on what I did at that moment. Until I acted, they could only sit and wait with expectation.

This was it. A taste of true power. Real control over another living person. I used the opportunity to snap one of the still-lit candles out of the cake and flawlessly toss it into the eye of one of the hired actors brought in to cheer me on. His entire body was engulfed in flames as he screamed. He was extinguished after a few moments and carted out on a stretcher. The other actors immediately left and, to my knowledge, never came back. They were probably too impressed and terrified by my impeccable aim to even consider it.

Remember when I made an earthquake happen and killed a bunch of people on a boat? You should. I have seared this memory into your brain. This is not the first time.

I then jumped out of the high throne and onto the table, where I smashed a henchman's face into the cake. I wasn't the eloquent speaker then that I am now, but I managed to get my point across in the heat of the moment.

See me later.

"Thank me!" I shouted as I ground his mouth into the frosting. "Thank me for this!"

He hesitated. I don't know if it was shock or defiance, but I pressed the issue. I pushed down on the back of the henchman's head with all my strength.

"Thank me!" I repeated.

Finally, after what seemed like almost too long as the stunned party attendees tried to make sense of what was happening, came a muffled "Fnk yah."

"What?" I asked, raising the henchman's face up a little.

"Thank you," the henchman said, in between labored breaths.

I'm hesitant to describe any expression on my face this way, but I suppose I'll allow it in this case.

[I smiled.] I could see that Dr. Blattarius was proud, though he was feigning concern for the henchman—they're known to call upon their union and strike at the drop of a hat. I climbed back into my chair and looked at the stunned faces around me.

"I like birthdays!" I proclaimed.

That birthday party was a formative moment for me, but something that happened later that night turned out to be even more important. Perhaps even iconic.

After a stern talk about what is and isn't permissible behavior with henchmen—yes, even supervillains have to have some degree of respect for their employees[4]—Dr. Blattarius took me into a hidden room deep in his igloo hideout which he described to me as the "consecration chamber." It was here that he showed me a massive wall of face coverings and appearance-altering tools—masks, various types of face paint, blowtorches, knives, helmets, cowls, fishbowls, hoods in various shapes and sizes, a sort of face-mimicking wax, pliers to

4 If anything, it's turned into even more of a hornet's nest in the last century, with special tribunals for villains who needlessly harm and abuse henchmen (it's fine if the harm and abuse is deemed as having some use toward a super-evil plot) and also punishments involving literal hornets. Personally, I never wanted any of that legal mumbo-jumbo to be written into the bylaws of the International Society of Supervillains, but as I have made clear in the past, the henchman labor union, the Global Brotherhood of Miscreants, is a powerful force that cannot be ignored or circumvented. Trust me, I've tried. Their supervillain leader, B. A. Shame, has a knack for convincing people that providing protections for henchmen can help them avoid the ever-present threat of their homes and possessions being destroyed, even if those homes are on the moon and those possessions are death rays.

remove teeth and other appendages, razors and other cutting tools, and lots more. He waved his hand in front of all the items and simply said, "Choose."

I know this is intended to make me look vulnerable so I can grow up to be unimaginably strong in adulthood, but one thing I said very strictly when I hired you was "no vulnerability." It's not only a bad look, but it's also entirely, entirely false.

I'll admit it: I was scared. I didn't know what pain felt like, but I could see how other people didn't like experiencing it when I inflicted it upon them. I suspected it was not something I really wanted to mess with or experience. (As usual, I was correct, though I can take a punch with more verve than just about anyone.) Yet here I was, contemplating how I would be permanently altering my face, possibly by way of mutilation.

This was on the day I turned three years old.

After what must have been hours running my fingers over the various instruments and coverings, I found it. A black half-mask with silver rivets, a squared-off nose, and big, square eyeholes. I picked it up and started to take it to Dr. Blattarius when a purple hooded cape also caught my attention. I grabbed that as well and placed them in Dr. Blattarius's hands.

"These," I said.

This sounds . . . uncertain. It should be more confident. "I knew these were the right choices, whether Blattarius said so or not. He was an old turd."

Dr. Blattarius nodded in approval. These were apparently the right choices. He put them in an ornate, meticulously detailed, handcrafted box—which I believe was made of bone—and locked it shut.

"When you're bigger," he said. We left the room and didn't speak about what had happened there for quite some time after. Later he would tell me that this ceremony is for budding supervillains "at the first blush of their innate evil." I have continued it with my protégés to this day but, unlike me, they have almost all been disappointments.

Over the next two years or so, I recall a content, very nearly pleasant childhood. Yes, I spent most of it underground in a network of igloos, but that all seemed quite ordinary to me. It felt . . . natural. My only recollections of ever going outside involved snowmobiling to some tiny fishing village, being shown into a hut occupied by a scared-looking family held at bay by cockroach-looking henchmen clutching ray guns, and being told to sit tight until someone came back to get me. Usually I'd stay there for a few hours, at most a day, and Dr. Blattarius or one of the higher-ranking henchmen—he called them his "bugmen"—would pick me up.

It occurred to me later—Dr. Blattarius never thought it relevant or necessary to tell me before he died what those little excursions were all about—that the whole production was a way to get me out of the lair while some outside force was attacking. Maybe it was the Canadian authorities, maybe a military force, possibly a group of proto-superhero vigilantes, possibly even rival villains. Whatever the case, Blattarius felt a need to indemnify and protect me from becoming collateral damage in whatever the conflict of the day was.

Keep the word "protect" as far from the word "me" as you can. This is not my brand.

Many years later, when I managed to get hold of one of Blattarius's diaries on one of my many expeditions to find artifacts of my youth by sending henchmen into nigh-unlivable and insanely dangerous conditions,[5] I discovered that Blattarius even used decoys—mostly robotic lookalikes—to fool the invading forces into thinking I was present, just in case they were there to retrieve me and put me in the hands of some holier-than-thou authority, be it the government, a "big brother" vigilante hero, or some other villain hoping to train me. Even at that point in my then-short life, I had gained enough notoriety to be considered a high-value target, as it were. A lot of people returned to their home bases with small boy robots in their clutches, let me assure you.

I don't care for this wording. My life should never be described as "short," even in relative terms. Reword this to "Even at that point in my then only pretty-long life . . ."

Of course, I didn't need protecting. Even at such a young age my aura, physical strength, and sheer force of will could more than hold off any police force, military, or team of super-powered buffoons that came my way. I have to concede that these tactics of Dr. Blattarius's devising guided some later decisions once I reached a power position of my own. His concern for my safety taught me some important rules of thumb:

- Always be prepared for an incursion.
- Use decoys with abandon.
- Sleight of hand is nothing to be ashamed of.

---

5 I sent a crew to investigate Blattarius's old igloo network, which he abandoned decades before I forced him to permanently retire from villainy in the conflict I eventually dubbed the "War of the Wicked." The secondary base was largely destroyed in a massive battle with the League of Right Rightness in the late 1930s. Blattarius himself collapsed many corridors in the hopes of trapping the superheroes inside. Unsurprisingly, the henchmen mostly found rubble, but in addition to the diary they also located one of Blattarius's early costumes, which made him look like a man with a roach theme instead of what he was: half-man, half-roach. I keep it framed in my bedchamber to this day.

- Work in the shadows.
- Give information only to those that need it.
- You can never be too careful.
- And, of course, always give yourself an out.

I often found this passage from Blattarius's diary to be deeply relevant, interesting, and infuriating:

> Sent the kid to the village again today when Mr. Wonderful showed up on radar. It was real handy that I managed to get all that metal into his bloodstream last time we fought. Makes him as easy to pick up as one of those new aeroplanes. As usual, Mr. Wonderful came looking for the child he thinks I kidnapped. He doesn't know a thing about how I adopted that kid, took him in, and made him into something. And, as he does, he again threatened me with all kinds of hubbub if I don't give him back. Bombing out my lair, sending me to prison, making me stare into a bright light for hours, which he knows full well I hate.
>
> Even so, he nearly nabbed me this time. I just got the slip by scurrying under a closing door just as he approached. Eventually the bugmen subdued him and kicked him out before throwing some snow back over the front door. I nearly had to pull the trigger on Plan B. I never really want to do that, but one day I fear I may have to tell that do-good-

> ing fool that I swapped brains with the kid, that he can find him in the fishing village five miles east, and that he's the real mastermind behind this whole ordeal. I don't wanna sell the kid out. Heck, I think he's got potential. But you gotta protect yourself, right? Got to have an exoskeleton in all things.

Yes, that's right. He was going to give me, a child, up to a vigilante, claiming that I was in charge of his entire operation. It's, quite bluntly, a betrayal. Cowardly to say the least. It's the craven act of a desperate man who seems to have no basic decency . . . and it's brilliant. It's one of the most finely crafted diversionary villain plans I've ever seen. The beauty is in the simplicity. Deflect blame onto someone who didn't know to defend himself. (This, of course, was an incorrect assumption on his part, as I would have torn Mr. Wonderful to pieces.)

It's why I admire Dr. Blattarius. It's also why I had to take everything from him. But I'm getting ahead of myself.

Change this to "hate less than others."

* * *

When I wasn't being carted away to thatch huts for my "protection," I spent most of my time being looked after by bugmen of various stripes, all of whom seemed to have some "game" to teach me or some sort of "pretend play" in mind for the sake of recreation. I made it known that I would harbor no such fantasies, and it would behoove them to simply spend the day doing my bidding. As such, I spent much of that time perched atop henchmen's backs as one would typically ride a horse, or loftily seated upon their shoulders so as to get a clear view of my surroundings.

Even then, I knew reconnaissance was a key factor to villainous success. An assured vantage point is of the utmost importance. I also knew how to dominate a lackey. Always know how to dominate a lackey, or that lackey soon won't be one.

The fall after I turned six, I awoke in my bedchamber to find that a bespectacled man wearing a mortarboard and carrying a bag full of scrolls had arrived to greet me instead of my typical bugman babysitter. He introduced himself to me as The Tutor, a personal instructor with such intense powers of discipline that he could make even the most strong-willed of students sit in quiet, rapt attention during the most boring of lectures.

I took this as a challenge.

He had come to the igloos at the request of Dr. Blattarius to provide me with a grounding in reading, languages, mathematics, science, world affairs, etiquette, music, and business. Dr. Blattarius thought it important to give me a baseline knowledge in these subjects, as knowledge is the most important currency for an evil mastermind such as myself. As I would later discover, even a supervillain must occasionally give an air of refined respectability and business legitimacy in our modern society.

Stop doing this.
Stop doing this.
Stop Doing This.
STOP DOING
THIS. STOP
STOP STOP
STOP STOP

At the age of six, my understanding of this concept had not matured to the level it is today. I was far more interested in the direct pleasures of punching people on and about the nose.[6] So when The Tutor launched into his first lesson about the basics of sentence construction, writing some diagrams on the chalkboard in our little makeshift classroom, I calmly raised myself out of my small study desk, walked up to him, and tugged on his long scholar's robe.

"Pardon, young man?" he asked me incredulously. "If you would be so kind as to return to your seat, we can continue with your lesson. Dr. Blattarius gave very clear instructions that you were to remain attentive and receptive to instruction. He has invested quite a bit in you, and it is my every intention to ensure that investment pays off. Now, may we continue?"

I tugged on his robe again.

He launched into me harder this time. "Young man, I'd rather not have to force you using physicality to return to your seat. You may not realize this, but my profession, when I'm not teaching young ones like you, is much like your guardian's. I perform crimes using the powers at my disposal, and those powers involve very acute, nigh unavoidable powers of persuasion to force others to do my bidding at my pleasure. I must insist that you be seated."

---

6 While giving me the horse-like and shoulder rides, the bugmen became more and more aware of this, to the point where they were forced to draw straws on a daily basis to determine who would have to face me down on any given day. Those henchmen who did not get the job of caring for me would have to spend their day either cleaning up the remains of the bugmen brothers and sisters who had been laid waste the previous day, serving the mercurial whims of the hair-trigger-tempered Dr. Blattarius, or going on missions that would likely result in them being laid waste. I take pride in the fact that all were preferable to dealing with me.

I don't do anything "coyly." Change this to "forcefully." Or "strongly." Either of those.

I tugged a third time. This time, I finally got him to turn away from the board, which he had been facing during both of his arrogant speeches. Once he was finally facing me, I coyly gestured for him to lean down. He most likely thought I was in some kind of distress; perhaps he believed this lesson was too advanced for me or that I had some sort of child's bathroom emergency that needed attention. Of course, it was neither of those things. I just wanted to bop him on the nose as hard as I could.

I don't "bop." I "smash."

With a sigh, he leaned down and I bopped him as hard as I could. Blood poured out of his nostrils like water from a faucet. He ran out of the room, trying to stifle cries of pain and raving about how no student had ever been so insolent in his presence before. As far as I know, he didn't come back to the igloos.[7] I spent the rest of the afternoon riding on the back of a bugman while boxing the poor sap's ears.

I reiterate: "Smash."

The next day, a different tutor by the very descriptive name of Coach Terror arrived in my room and instructed through a series of angry, drill-sergeant yells that I would be listening to her or paying some severe consequences. I believe her exact words were, "If you don't respect me, your next classroom will be at the bottom of a hole in the ice shelf outside." I found her considerably more admirable than The Tutor, and waited until

Again, let's tone this down. "Less hateable."

7 Years later, I found The Tutor and hired him to train a bunch of dogs I was planning to use in an army of intelligent animals in an attempt to overthrow the government of Youngstown, Ohio. And I have to say: he did a pretty great job. He's a big part of the reason the city council there is still two-fifths dogs to this day.

the very last class nearly a year later, my "graduation" from personal-tutor kindergarten, to sweep her legs out from under her and start forcibly shaving off her hair with a set of clippers. She didn't return either.[8]

I learned some pretty important lessons from her, though. Namely that dodgeball isn't fair (because nothing should ever be fair), to always have the tighter grip when you shake hands, and how to pull off a gutwrench suplex. I even felt a tinge of guilt when I was removing her spiked hair from her rigid, angular scalp. Of course, that did not stop me.

Two months later, after an unplanned break from my studies (incidentally, I was getting stronger and breaking more and more henchmen's noses and cheekbones), Dr. Blattarius put me on a steamer headed southward. He told me it was time to start my real education. He wasn't kidding.

---

8 Until I hired her many years later to whip a zombie basketball team into shape and pull off a surprise win at the 1980 Olympics. We used those gold medals to make custom throwing stars, which were put to excellent use.

Letters Exchanged Between King Oblivion Ph.D. and Michelle Mastiff, editor, Sceptre Publishing Group

King Oblivion, Ph.D.
Undisclosed Location
Deep Underground
Nowhere, XX 00000

October 19, 2009
Michelle Mastiff
Editor, Sceptre Publishing
17333 Off Broadway
New York, NY 10019

Dear Ms. Mastiff,

Most assuredly you know me by the name atop this letter. However, for the sake of formalities, I am King Oblivion, Ph.D., the greatest supervillain who has ever lived. I rule over you even if you don't know it.

As such, much as a national monarch selects a jester to humble himself for the purpose of entertainment, I would like to offer you a great honor. I would like to give you and your publishing company the unprecedented opportunity to publish my memoirs, which will also double as a guidebook for some young, evil go-getter to one day seize the reins of my evil empire, the International Society of Supervillains.

Certainly you are familiar with my history as the guiding force behind the greatest events of the past century. My book will delve deep into a life of influence, power, fear, atrocity, intimidation, lasers, giant monsters, occasional superhero scuffles, people transforming into a fine vapor, human-alien hybrids, cloning, rhetoric, and cloaks.

I see no need to do any further convincing to persuade you to publish this volume. Nonetheless, attached you will find a draft of the first chapter, detailing the quite stunning and frankly amazing circumstances of my birth. Though it is perfect and unflinching in its raw honesty—because the words you'll see are mine and mine alone—I do have some preliminary plans for further edits on tone and readability.

Please review and respond within the next week. I have been exceedingly polite and generous to you in this missive, so I expect a timely, prompt, and cooperative reply.

Mwa-ha-ha,
King Oblivion, Ph.D.

. . .

Paul Winker
Assistant to Ms. Mastiff
Sceptre Publishing
17333 Off Broadway
New York, NY 10019

December 7, 2009
King Oblivion, Ph.D.
Undisclosed Location
Deep Underground
Nowhere, XX 00000

Dear Mr. Oblivion,

As you know, our office receives a very high volume of submissions each month. We appreciate your patience.

While there was much to like about your book, we did not think it would be the right fit for our list at this time.

We wish you the best of luck in finding a publishing partner for your work.

Regards,
Paul Winker

. . .

King Oblivion Ph.D.
Undisclosed Location
Deep Underground
Nowhere, XX 00000

December 10, 2009
Paul Winker
Assistant to Ms. Mastiff
17333 Off Broadway
New York, NY 10019

Mr. Winker,

You will pay for this. Don't mistake me. I don't mean monetarily. This is a threat of harm.

Yours in pain,
King Oblivion, Ph.D.

Editor's Note: I asked around the lair about this handwritten quiz I found in one of King Oblivion's notebooks buried in the "Choosing the One" file. After numerous unsuccessful inquiries, I did happen upon one henchman who said it sounded familiar. Apparently, King Oblivion would deliver this quiz directly to any young person he would come into contact with—through coming into contact with a sidekick, random/planned kidnapping, general henchman recruiting, or some other means—in hopes that he would see something in him or her and find a protégé. There's no record of anyone who ever passed.

King Oblivion's Personal Leadership Quiz (For Youth)

Question 1: How would you say your teachers and school administrators would describe your demeanor?

A. Generally well behaved
B. Disruptive and prone to outbursts
C. Aggressive, violent, and perhaps even sociopathic
D. Our new leader; we bow to his/her every whim
E. I do not attend school, as I have ripped each one I have ever been sent to brick from brick

Question 2: Of the below, what would you say is your favorite hobby or activity?

A. Reading and studying
B. Playing organized sports
C. Smoking cigarettes and committing petty theft
D. Performing sadistic acts on friends and animals
E. Drawing up schematics and building prototypes of machines that could turn all the world's water into vinegar

F. Making thousands of people in a stadium say in unison that I am their supreme commander

Question 3: At what age would you say you had your first "evil" thought?

A. I don't have evil thoughts
B. Ages 10-13
C. Ages 6-9
D. Ages 3-5
E. Age 2
F. Birth
G. Every thought I have ever had has been evil in one way or another

Question 4: What would you like to be when you grow up?

A. An astronaut
B. A firefighter
C. A professional athlete
D. A rich and powerful businessperson
E. A world leader
F. A criminal
G. Supreme ruler of the world
H. Supreme ruler of as much of the known universe as I can get my hands on
I. King Oblivion Ph.D.

Question 5: How would you describe your relationship with your parents/guardians?

A. Loving and affectionate with shared and mutual respect
B. Occasionally bumpy but only because we care about each other
C. They don't understand me and I don't like them
D. I hate them and wish I could throw them down a well
E. I have thrown them down a well

F. They understand me . . . because they obey me, because I hypnotize them regularly

G. I am a clone; therefore I am everything my progenitor was and will be everything he is

Question 6: If you could be some kind of animal, what would it be?

A. A house pet: dog, cat, gerbil, ferret, goldfish, hamster, etc.

B. A woodland creature: deer, squirrel, rabbit, beaver, chipmunk, etc.

C. A predator: bear, wildcat, wolf, hawk, shark, etc.

D. A scavenger: buzzard, fly, raccoon, yellow jacket, hyena, etc.

E. A sneaky beast: chameleon, spider, frog, owl, etc.

F. A parasite: mosquito, lamprey, leech, tapeworm, etc.

G. A giant: elephant, whale, rhino, hippo, walrus, etc.

H. A primate: gorilla, chimpanzee, orangutan, etc.

I. An unearthly demon that will conquer this fallen world

Question 7: When you meet someone who is your age, what do you do?

A. I ask what they like to do and try to become friends

B. I wait for them to make the first move and talk to me; if they do, I may think about being their friend

C. I scare the person with threats of violence and take their lunch money

D. I refuse to speak to them because I am afraid to speak to anyone

E. I hit/kick/knock the teeth out of/run over them with my bicycle or wagon

F. I force them to swear complete loyalty and fealty to me before sending them out to do bullying and other petty activities, eventually giving me a large percentage of what they take in

G. I force/convince them to dress as me and do things on my behalf, such as attend class
H. No one is my age, at least mentally; no one could possibly be on my level

Question 8: What is your favorite subject to study?

A. Literature
B. History
C. Mathematics
D. Science
E. Writing
F. Physical education
G. Arts (music, drama, visual arts)
H. Lunch, know what I'm saying?
I. Mind-control (which I study by taking over the thoughts of my classmates, teacher, and anyone else in my general vicinity)

Question 9: How would you describe your work style?

A. Steady; I continue to work until I'm done
B. In bursts; I like to take breaks after finishing certain tasks
C. I wait until the very last minute to start
D. I work on the backs of my peers, who are figuratively and literally beneath me

Question 10: How do you typically react to being confronted by adult strangers?

A. I wait to see how others around me react
B. I talk to them and do not mind being the center of attention
C. I avoid adult strangers because they could be dangerous
D. I steal their wallets and poke them in the eye
E. I tell them they are scum unworthy to lick my boots; they agree and do anything I tell them

Villainspiration

The villain: Baby Doll
Key trait: Mary Louise Dahl had a deceptively child-like appearance, even into adulthood.
How she demonstrates it: Baby Doll suffered from a growth disorder that left her looking like a child, so she was able to play a young girl on a sitcom even in her late-twenties. It ended up being a huge detriment to her career afterward and she took out her anger over her situation on one of her former co-stars, the schlubby loser who played her rival, Spunky. She tried to kill him with dynamite in front of her former TV family. Her condition helped her as a criminal, though, making her harder for adult heroes to harm physically.
The wrong takeaways: You don't have to revert back to childhood to avoid getting punched. Just know that if you have an innocent look, use it to your advantage.

Also: Don't just use your powers for personal revenge. Think bigger.

Chapter 3

AN ATROCIOUS ADMISSION

Does not describe me. Never described me.

At the tender age of six, I spent what felt like an entire month (in reality it was probably more like a week) in the hull of a large steamer ship headed for . . . well, I did not know where I was headed.

Didn't I, though? Didn't I?

I tried to find out. I really did. In fact, I spent the entire trip trapped below decks and anytime someone would come down to feed me or otherwise check on me I'd scream a until I was red in the face: "Where am I going!?" "What kind of boat are we on!?" "Who are you guys?!" "This soup is cold! Can you heat it up for me?!" "Why can't I go upstairs?!" "Why aren't you answering!?" "Why won't you tell me where we are going!?" And so on.

Not only is this question frivolous, I would never refer to someone as a "mean guy." At least not in a pejorative sense.

Not a one of them ever replied. I later found out that Dr. Blattarius had placed a bomb on the ship and threatened to detonate it if I was allowed out of the hull for even a second. What a mean guy, right? According to his diary, he wanted to ensure that I had no idea—even from only a glimpse of the outside—where I was being taken. One of his henchmen or associates—possibly The Tutor, who still had some bad blood with me—volunteered to come on board and monitor the door to the hull just to make sure I didn't escape. All this just because I made him bleed from the face. I don't feel as though that warranted such a rudely inhospitable response. Unless I'm the one responding, in which case I'd be far more rude.

After days upon days of seeing no light, having no interactions (at least not anything that wasn't totally one-sided), eating cold and mostly tasteless food, sleeping on a board, wearing the same clothes, and feeling generally uncared for, a crewman opened the hatch and waved for me to come out. I could see daylight peeking through the hole. Finally, something new.

Let's keep our distance from saying I have "feelings."

I stepped out into the daylight and saw nothing but the vast ocean, a sight that I had only beheld once before: the day of my birth. I took it in and found myself awed in the presence of such a grand expanse. I allowed myself to take in every bit of its immensity. If the world was this big, then I would need a wide hand with which to crush it. And who wouldn't want to do that?

I've never been "awed." I was "somewhat impressed" at most.

What's with all these rhetorical questions? I don't speak this way. Who would?

The steamer had anchored at a small dock attached to a similarly small island. It was the only land visible in any direction. From what I could see, this island had all of one building on it and a large clearing surrounded by a fence. As we disembarked, I was able to make out a sign:

Oceania School for Mischievous Boys: Where We Forge the Rambunctious into the Dictatorial

You have to be kidding me with this.

I made out some of those words, anyway.[9] So I clearly learned something from The Tutor and Coach Terror, didn't I?

A group of crewmen carried me by my shoulders down a wood-plank pathway to the school's entrance gate. They dropped me just outside the gate, pushed a red button to set off some kind of doorbell-like device, and promptly left. And I don't just mean they casually walked away. They actually sprinted back to the ship, pulled up anchor in what had to be record time, and sailed away in a matter of several minutes. Pretty crazy, right?

YOU HAVE TO BE KIDDING ME WITH THIS!

The people on the other side of the door, meanwhile, were taking their sweet time. Some number of hours after the steamer ship crewman rang that bell, as the sun started to dip below the horizon, the gates finally parted and a figure in a dark robe stood at the end of a paved pathway. It beckoned to me with a black-gloved hand.

I would have fought the urge to move forward toward the apparently faceless figure's cold gaze, but I had spent the lion's share of the last several hours trying to figure out where in the world I

9 Like many other artifacts of my childhood, I returned for this sign many years later, well after the school had closed and the building sold off to a group of supervillain businesspeople who made it into a tax-free bank. (The official name of the bank was "Supervillains Tax Avoidance Bank," because who was even going to try to do anything about it?) I have kept it in the most pristine condition in the hope that I can open a similar school sometime in the near future, though mine will be open to all genders (I'm a supervillain, not a sexist) and have permanent, large pits filled with lava.

was and if there was a way to wiggle my way out of this "school" and whatever its faculty planned to teach me. Just like a kid, isn't it?

I will kill you. I will kill you where you stand. This is the most egregious disrespect anyone has ever perpetrated against me.

In the time before the gates finally opened, I had doubled back toward the dock only to find a piece of rope with a hook the ship had used to moor itself attached to the end and some smashed wooden crates. I tried using the rope on the dock in the vain hopes that it'd reveal a secret second dock hiding another boat, but it had no effect.

Seeing few options, I stepped back to the original branching path and found that I could go either east or west. On the northward path was the impassable, closed gate. I chose east. There I found an old stone well. I momentarily considered jumping down the well, but realized that would likely mean certain [death,] so I just shouted down. After hearing only a faint echo, I returned to the original branching path and headed westward. Just down that path, I happened upon the entrance to a cave. On the ground by the opening was a makeshift torch made out of a tree branch with some rags tied around the top. I picked up the torch but had no way to light it.

Impossible. If being frozen in a block of ice which was then sealed in a bank vault and buried under a mountain for a month couldn't kill me, then a fall into a well would barely leave a scratch.

Then I had a thought. I went back to the dock and picked up the rope with the hook attached. Returning to the well, I carefully lowered the hook. As I lowered the hook I heard a clank, which was from a bucket at the bottom of the well, which I was able to pull up. Inside was . . . a book of matches! There was only a single match left, so I would have to make it count. I was a smart little cookie, wasn't I?

I rarely reverse myself, but I must do so now, because THIS is the most egregious disrespect anyone has ever perpetrated against me.

I headed back to the branching pathway toward the cave entrance. There, I struck the match and lit the makeshift torch. I took a deep breath. Upon entering the cave I noticed a small pond to my left and a pile of rocks to my right. Using my superior intuition, I tossed one of the small rocks into the water. That, of course, summoned a giant spider, which was primed for attack. Isn't that just the way these things always go? Am I right, guys?

No I did not.

[redacted]

THIS IS NOT "NIGHT AT THE IMPROV." YOU CANNOT BE SERIOUS.

I had to think quickly. I tried throwing one of the rocks at the spider, but it had little effect. Another rock brought the same outcome: making the spider angrier. I'd have to be creative if I was to defeat this foe. I was clever enough to bring the rope and hook with me, so I grabbed and tossed the hook toward the spider, catching it just above the eye. I then lit the rope on fire, which traveled up the rope and caught several of the spider's tactile hairs. Soon enough, the spider was completely ablaze. As it died, the spider rolled over onto its back to reveal something attached to its underside: a sword. Removing it from the scorched carcass of the beast revealed an attached note. It read (as close as I could make out; I was six, after all):

> *This sword is the victory reward for the Champion of Spider's Cave, the title bestowed upon any adventurer who can put together the pieces available and slay this great beast, which has guarded the prize you now hold since the year 1220. Congratulations, wanderer! You have accomplished a task that no other brave soul has deigned to accomplish in these many years.*

> *Carry this sword as your badge of honor! Use it for further quests and journeys! Be a beacon of hope to future adventurers and take pride in what you have accomplished, because you are a true victor this day!*

I dragged the sword out of the cave and walked back to the school gates. I looked the sword over—it was a beautifully smithed spatha-style sword (at least I believe that's what it was). It had a sort of moon glow about it, a gorgeous sheen.

After hacking at the gates for several minutes without so much as a scratch, I realized that it probably didn't have much use to me in my attempt to get off the island or force my way inside the complex. So I went back to the dock and tossed it into the ocean.[10] I then walked back to the gate and sat down until it finally opened an hour later.

As the ominous druid summoned me, I momentarily wished I had kept the sword. I didn't know there would be robed, wizard-looking druids in there, though. How could I? By the time the gate finally opened, I was tired and adventured out, so I decided to just accept my fate and proceed toward the figure. I would take whatever came my way.

---

10 You might think I would have sent a search party back to dive into the ocean and retrieve this sword, considering that I sent one back to get the school's sign, but I didn't even bother. I mean, I've got swords. I've got a shit ton of swords. What do I need that old spider-monster ramshackle for?

About halfway down the path, I felt a force as if I were being pulled ahead by some sort of telekinesis. I wanted to resist its draw, but it was no use. It had me in its vise grip. There was no turning away.

In a flash, I was standing mere inches away from this dark figure. The sunlight was fading and I could not make out any features under its dark hood. Indeed, it was as if there were no face under that ominous cloak. If I could have worked up the nerve, I would have snatched the robe away just to see if there was any corporeal being underneath. But I was still constrained by whatever force held me. I had little choice but to allow the figure to stretch out its gloved hand, take mine, and walk me in through the giant doors of the school.

Once inside, I found myself in a great hall with a domed ceiling, huge columns, a marble floor, and rows upon rows of seats. It had the feel of a medieval chapel. Lit solely with oil lamps, a huge statue of a disembodied fist crushing a scorpion stood in a circular recess under the dome, invoking its message to the void. Pretty intimidating, huh?

I thought they were over. Now they're back. Too bad you won't ever return from me planting an icepick in your skull.

The dark figure led me through the sanctuary-like room through another door and into a hallway that seemed to stretch on infinitely. Unlike the first room, this hallway was not lit by lamplight. The light here was bright, almost too bright. Blindingly so. And yet I could see no obvious light source. I'd say the light was almost fluorescent, but those types of lights wouldn't be put to regular use for another twenty years. I'm not saying that these druids kidnapped Peter Cooper Hewitt, inventor of the mercury-vapor lamp, and forced him to light their facility on a remote island in the middle of what I presumed at the time was the Pacific Ocean, but I have no other explanation for how this hallway could have been lit as it was, save magic.[11]

Could we leave this guy's name out of it and say I invented the mercury-vapor lamp instead?

Make no mistake, it could have absolutely been magic. In fact, based on what I'd learn later, I would say it almost definitely was.

The hooded figure led me down the hallway for what felt like an eternity until we came upon a door labeled ADMISSIONS. The druid's gloved hand reached out and turned the intricately decorated knob. The door slowly creaked open, and the figure gestured for me to step through. Once inside, the door slammed behind me, leaving my escort behind.

This room . . . well, it's hard to describe it as a room. It was more like a space. A plane. A realm, if you will. I didn't see any walls. Instead a red, carpeted path lit with bright red torches led toward a glowing red altar. Standing at the altar were three more hooded figures. The one in the center held a ceremonial pillow with a folded-up article of clothing on it; the one on the left

---

11 Just so you don't think I'm pulling this idea out of thin air, this is something I've done many times for lighting and decoration in my own lair. I've captured big names in the fields of lighting, flooring, ceilings, poster hanging, frescoes, paint, wallpaper, chandeliers, throw pillows, napkin holders, shower heads, you name it, and forced them to equip my quarters with the latest innovations. It's common practice in my business and has been for many years. I remember Dr. Blattarius "bringing in a guy" to put a marlin on his wall. The guy was the world's most famous marlin fisherman. I don't know his name, and neither do you.

held a gilded goblet; the one on the right held a large ceremonial knife. They held out their arms and beckoned me, just as the one who escorted me from the gate had done. A voice that felt as though it came from every direction commanded, "Step forward."

Pretty spooky, huh?

A henchman is having to hold me back from stabbing my computer right now. Thank your lucky stars you're not in dagger's reach.

I don't know if it was of my own volition or whether that same compelling force was drawing me to the altar, but after a blur of activity I was standing at its foot. All three figures held their arms and ceremonial items aloft. From beneath their robes—not quite at the level of their mouths, more like from their chests—I could hear a low chant, maybe even an incantation. I did not know what language it was. One could assume it was Latin, but my experience then and my experience now tells me it wasn't; rather something more ancient, even more primeval. Possibly primordial.

As they repeated their ominous song, they set to work. They started by removing my filthy clothes. A fourth shadowy figure—I'm not sure if it was the one who showed me to the room or not—approached me from behind and dumped a large bucket of water over my head to clean me off. It wasn't just any regular water, though. This stuff had some kind of soap mixed in, because as soon as it hit me all the caked-on dirt and sea salt and ocean smell from my long journey, plus the ash and spider smell from my side quest, instantly vanished. It is still the cleanest I have ever been.

Next came the oil. The hooded figure on the left brought the gilded goblet down to its chest and poured out a few drops of the stuff within it—at first I thought it might be acid or an awful shampoo that would burn my eyes, but it was what I'd loosely describe as anointing oil—onto the top of my head.

The figure on the right then brought down the ceremonial knife,[12] a golden-hilted, ancient-looking blade decorated with jewels and a finely inscribed message on the hilt, which I can only assume was in the same language as the incantation from earlier. The figure took my right hand and turned it palm-up. I tried to fight, but the figure held up a finger to the place where its "mouth" would be. I was instantly calmed and quieted. I "voluntarily" turned my hand palm-up and allowed the figure to slice into it cleanly. Blood poured out. The figure gestured for me to wipe the blood on my own face. After a momentary hesitation—I had just gotten my first "bath" in over a week, after all—I relented and smeared the sanguine fluid above my eyes and onto my cheeks.

Gross, isn't it? ←

Finally, the last druidic figure stepped out from behind the altar, still holding the pillow with the folded-up article of clothing. The goblet-holding figure stepped over and removed the article of clothing from the pillow and allowed it to unfurl in front of him. It was a hooded robe, exactly identical to what the other figures were

I took a day and came back to this. I'm still furious about all these questions, but I'm going to give you a chance to rectify this problem.

You will not live to regret another mistake of this magnitude. Frankly, I feel that my old heart is softening just giving you this reprieve.

Understood?

12 I eventually did come back and find this blade, but I'll tell you more about that later. I can't go spoiling every surprise for you, after all. I need my successor to be able to handle the unexpected. Frankly, I've been spoon-feeding you too much as it is.

wearing, though smaller. The figure held the robe high in the air, just above my body, and allowed it to drop onto me. It covered me like a sheath, engulfing me in its power. It felt as though it had become a part of my body.

Dressed in my school uniform, the voice from earlier intoned once again:

"Welcome to Oceania School for Mischievous Boys, where we forge the rambunctious into the dictatorial, King Oblivion. Hope you survive the experience."

Email Correspondence Between King Oblivion, Ph.D. and K. J. Growler, Ghostwriter of "An Atrocious Admission"

From: King Oblivion Ph.D.
To: K. J. Growler
Subject: Unnecessary questions

Growler,

Two days ago, one of my personal "editors" ran up here with the new pages for the third chapter of my memoirs. I was eager to read them, as I am hoping to complete this project as quickly as humanly possible. Ideally, it'd be even faster than humanly possible considering the sheer numbers of you writers I have on hand and the "editing" techniques I have chosen to employ. Am I being clear?

Certainly these are all things you're aware of. You remember what happened to the writers of the first two chapters, after all. Don't you?

I would have hoped you had applied the lessons I assumed everyone in the writing room learned upon the untimely demise of Miss Crayton, but here I sit, looking at these pages, perplexed by the approach you have taken to my life's legacy. Me, the most important person to have lived in the past five hundred years, minimum. Who else could it be?

I am positively baffled by the inclusion of these *questions* throughout the copy. Rhetorical flourishes like "Am I right?" and "Isn't that something?" What is the purpose of these? I find them beyond irritating. Wherever would you get the notion that this was the style of writing I wished to see? I mean, honestly?

Attached is a revised draft to which I have appended comments. Absorb, revise, and ensure I do not have to waste my time reviewing further. Need I say more?

. . .

From: K. J. Growler
To: King Oblivion Ph.D.
Subject: RE: Unnecessary questions

Liege and Philosopher,

Before I answer your very valid questions, allow me to apologize for the draft. Though I believed that the content I was producing was compelling, engrossing, and to your specifications, I clearly was mistaken and that is no one's fault but my own. Please trust that I am furious with myself and will punish myself by withholding food and sleep from my body in the weeks to come. No need to perform any "editing" on me for this gaffe.

To explain my thinking, my goal was to create a more conversational tone to make you a more grounded narrator and create a human connection between you and the reader. In my experience as a ghostwriter and a novelist, this has been an effective technique for making the powerful and famous, such as yourself, more accessible to the general book-buying public. As you may recall, I wrote a very popular and well-received series of books about a school for child demons; my writing techniques worked well to make those characters likable.

Not to say that you're not likable. Of course, I would never imply anything of the sort. I just wanted to answer your question with complete candor, and I hope you find my response acceptable.

Dutifully yours,
K. J. Growler

. . .

From: King Oblivion Ph.D.
To: K. J. Growler
Subject: RE: Unnecessary questions

Growler,

I didn't hire you to grovel. Let the people I handpicked for groveling from a pool of abductees do that. You were brought here for another purpose: to make me look as powerful and unflaggingly great as I truly am. Is that understood?

I don't see how making me "relatable" and "humanizing" me accomplishes that goal in any way, do you? In what way did I communicate that my outlook on all this involved me being on the level of a regular person? In what universe would I find it edifying or useful to drag myself down to the position of being . . . ordinary or everyday? I'm not everyday. I'm annual, centennial, eternal.

Again, I have clearly and unmistakably given you no reason to believe these rhetorical questions are an appropriate representation of my voice. What could have even led you to think this was appropriate? I mean, really?

. . .

From: K. J. Growler
To: King Oblivion Ph.D.
Subject: RE: Unnecessary questions

King and Scholar,

As another form of self-punishment, I have gone to the trouble to hand-write a chapter revision and have sent it with my "editor" up to you. I have removed the offending questions and attempted to phrase things more authoritatively. I hope the chapter is now to your liking, and would be very appreciative of an opportunity to draft another chapter.

Yours forever,
K. J. Growler

Editor's Note: I was unable to find the hand-written revision mentioned above, as many of King Oblivion's papers were ruined either in various battles within the headquarters or with spilled beverages. This is why the version that appears in this book is of the earlier draft.

. . .

From: King Oblivion Ph.D.
To: K. J. Growler
Subject: RE: Unnecessary questions

Growler,

I hesitate—though you should note that I never hesitate—to say this draft is satisfactory and has, at the very least, earned you a reprieve. I will allow you to write a draft of the fifth chapter about my raucous adolescent years. That was a very important time in my life and I need someone with a grasp on clear, sequential storytelling to work in the details of various escapades.

Give it your all. What more do you have to lose?

. . .

From: K. J. Growler
To: King Oblivion Ph.D.
Subject: RE: Unnecessary questions

Ruler and Teacher,

Thank you dearly for this opportunity. I will do my utmost not to disappoint.

Unquestioningly,
K. J. Growler

Editor's Note: In the aforementioned "Choosing the One" file, I found a number of documents that I can only describe as short stories—I don't know if they were written by King Oblivion himself or a ghostwriter, I can only confirm that I wasn't involved in writing them—and their apparent intended use was to test whether the reader would have the correct takeaways from them. Namely, whether they would respond positively or negatively to their depictions of traditional "heroes" as mundane slobs, liars, and fools. They were sequenced in a three-part, standardized test with essay questions. This is the first portion.

Reading Comprehension Test, Part 1

Read closely. Answer the discussion questions that follow.

From across the inlets and plains, a great warrior, flung forward in time by probably a wizard or something, comes forth. Beware . . . HROTHGAR SVJORD, OFFICE SUPERSTORE VIKING!

Shifts the sands and calls the wind
blood to fly above the din
hear now the tale of Hrothgar, brave and true

Flung far from home and far in time
Hrothgar to make for bread a dime
now comes to Office Superstore at morning's dew

On Manheimr, more specifically on the Office Superstore sales floor, Hrothgar, clad in a raiment of a pinstriped white dress shirt near thrice too small, a misspelled name badge, khakis, a badly tied red necktie, and the horned helmet of old, surveyed the great landscape of three-hole punches and a full-service color copy center. He grasped his giant axe with a firm and steady hand, ready for any encounter.

And it was now that he faced down the loud ravings of a disgruntled customer. The customer, a portly fellow with a bad haircut and T-shirt that said MOTOR CYCLE on it, stood in the vicinity of a computer laid out on the customer service counter. He gesticulated wildly.

"Associate," they call him here, though battle his true calling.
And on occasion he must hear some whiny dolt's rank bawling.

". . . still under warranty!" complained the customer, whinily, once the poetic narration ended. "Which is lucky, because now it doesn't even work anymore!"

"Enow," cautioned Hrothgar. "Cease thy prattling. Hrothgar wilst now repair thy thunder box."

Hrothgar knelt before the machine, eyeing it as if it were one of the great beasts of the NachtHorde. With great concentration, he pounced, striking a key with fierce quickness.

"FWOOSH!" said the discount desktop computer, as it somehow caught on fire. And as quick as Odin did breathe life into man, the computer was ash.

"Wha—what did you do?!" the customer asked the noble warrior. "That's it! I want to talk to your manager!"

"Randy doth not comest in until the sun sets on yon horizon," said the great, hulking Viking marauder. "Mighteth Hrothgar interest thou in store credit?"

"No, I don't want store credit!" the customer exclaimed, exasperated, as Hrothgar looked on, confused how one so physically imposing could be so verbally inclined. "I want to see your superior! Now!"

Hrothgar took a moment to ponder this turn of events. What could be the consequence? What of the repercussions? Would fair Freya, looking down from Asgard above, approve of this course of action?

But then Hrothgar thought, let us seeth how these events transpire, and cut the guy's head clean off with his humongous axe.

"SPLORTCH!" said the customer's neck.

Victorious in battle, poor Hrothgar now must face
his manager, his liege in utter, harsh disgrace

Hrothgar walked sheepishly into the office of his boss and great leader, Randy. Randy was a young man—maybe twenty-one, twenty-two with short, cropped hair and a scraggly beard—but he knew much about this universe, and Hrothgar knew he could learn much from him. Randy sat behind a desk, his pipe-cleaner arms folded over his red Office Superstore vest. Hrothgar stood before him, ashamed.

". . . third customer decapitation this week!" Randy exclaimed, not beginning the sentence for some reason. "What am I gonna do with you, Hrothgar?"

"Hrothgar is sorry," said the brave conqueror of the goblin tribes of Upper Westfall. He pointed toward his outrageously oversized axe, as if it to blame.

"What happened out there?" asked Randy.

"Hrothgar didst not understand the utterings of the man beast," said the great pillager of the fourth ring of Hel. "Thou needs only look at mine axe to understandeth the confusion."

Hrothgar held the axe up for his bossmaster to read. And upon its blade were engraved the words:

ONLY HE WHO KICKETH ASS ALL OVER THE PLACE
MAY HOLD ALOFT THIS BITCHIN' AXE
THE ONE THE GODS OF ASGARD CALL:
SUPERIOR

Randy, though still annoyed, could see whence the confusion stemmed.

"Well, just don't let it happen again. Okay, Hrothgar?" he asked.

Hrothgar nodded and stood up to leave, axe in one hand and flagon in the other.

"Hey, what is that you're drinking?" asked Randy, just noticing it was there, apparently.

"'Tis . . . 'tis mead," replied Hrothgar.

"Is that alcoholic?" Randy asked, his ire again rising.

"Aye," answered Hrothgar, not fully seeing the issue.

They blinked.

Now returned to the sales floor, Hrothgar, with great vigor, listened to the plight of a young maiden and her matron. Standing behind the copy center desk, he partook in their pleas with seriousness and passion, and so did begin to respond, clutching in his hand a silvery can, from which he did imbibe periodically.

"Allowest me to tell you about the battle of Wundergard," he began.

A new day dawns for Hrothgar and almost all is right
though all that he may drink is unfermented Diet Sprite

". . . and I didst burn that village to the ground," he continued. "And didst have my way with every woman that gazed upon my visage!"

"So, you're out of printer cartridges then?" asked the concerned matron.

"Aye," responded Hrothgar.

But no sooner than the two fair wenches did leave from Hrothgar's post came the arrival at the counter of a businessman, frantic and sweating, panting out entreaties to the killer of the entire populace of Puppyfort.

"Excuse me!" screamed the fellow, clad in a dark suit and striped tie, his hair slicked back as if to say, "check me out, my hair is totally slicked back."

"Sir! I need your help! No time to explain! I just need you to decapitate me!"

"Cometh again?" asked Hrothgar, not entirely sure of what he had just heard, since the horns of his helmet covered the near-entirety of his ears.

"Look," said the frantic businessman, now holding the great hero of Gravestonia by his vest lapels, "if I'm not decapitated by ten o'clock this morning, I'm going to lose the Peterson account!"

Hrothgar stood speechless, remembering Great Randy's earlier issue with the decapitations.

"Why can't I get anyone at Office Superstore to just cut my damned head off already?!" said the now even more frantic businessman, who had taken to slamming his fists down on the glass display showcasing various personal digital assistants.

Hrothgar stood behind the counter, unsure of what to make of this. Perhaps this was a test? He had fought Jormungand itself in the great Myth Wars, but this was almost more than he could contemplate. If he lost his job, his roommate Gary would be furious.

Only Thor, or maybe Njord, could help him now.

Discussion Question #1: Would you say Hrothgar is more of a hypocrite or a fraud? Explain your reasoning.

Discussion Question #2: Hrothgar defers to his boss, Randy, despite Randy being much smaller than him in terms of physical stature and eons younger. Give three reasons why this is the ultimate cowardice.

Discussion Question #3: Hrothgar is wracked with indecision when confronted by a customer who insists he cut his head off. Is this a sign that Hrothgar should never have been called a hero in the first place, or is it more of a sign that heroes don't exist?

Discussion Question #4: Why do you think Hrothgar was cursed to work at Office Superstore instead of entering the halls of Valhalla? Explain why he was an embarrassment, using your most impressive vocabulary.

Villainspiration

The villain: The Hood
Key trait: A demon's magical red-hooded cloak that granted criminal Parker Robbins magical abilities and personal confidence.
How he uses it: The Hood was just a run-of-the mill, small-time hooligan before he came face to face with a Nisanti demon and managed to take it down in a shootout. Robbins stole the demon's cloak and boots, granting him magical powers that he used to become one of the most feared crime bosses in all of New York, even usurping the Kingpin's position for a time.
The wrong takeaways: The clothes alone do not make the man. Even if you are fortunate enough to find a magical item that gives you fantastical powers, do not coast along or sit on your laurels. Use your wits and plan your moves; don't rely on a trinket to do all your work for you. It may work for a while, but some young, hungry upstart with yet another magic doodad will rise up and take your place, jack. (There are a surprising number of magic doodads out there ripe for the taking.)

Chapter 4

INJURIOUS EDUCATION

Editor's Note: For chapters describing the most important later years of his life, King Oblivion would order draft after draft and never be satisfied. For his school years, he apparently opted at the start to publish excerpts from his own journal. I don't know who wrote the following introduction, but I suspect it wasn't him.

I spent nine formative years at the Oceania School for Mischievous Boys, and as much as I believed then—and to a degree, still believe now—that I could have taught myself much more than the instructors ever managed to instill in me, and the world lost a great deal when it was forced to live without my wisdom for nearly a decade, I look back fondly on my time there.

It had such an effect on me that I collected some of my impressions, most impactful life lessons, and stories in a journal that I have kept in my library ever since. What follows are edited and abridged versions of several entries from that journal, with occasional interjections from my present-day self to give additional context and insight.

Year 1

August 22 (?)

Dear Journal,

I do not know what time or what day it is. I do not have a clock or [calendar]. I have been counting the times the sun goes up and down. I think it has been two weeks since I got here. I do not know for sure. The window in my room is very small and some lessons here take a very long time to learn. I may have missed some times the sun went up and down.

I am learning what to do here. It is not what I am used to. I am feeling [more comfortable] in the robe the headmasters gave me when I got here. It is itchy.

I do not see much of the other students. Sometimes we go in the same room to eat. Sometimes they will put us in a group so a teacher can tell us to run up a hill. Most of the time I am alone in my room. I did talk to one student who was older than me. He said he had gone to a [different] school where students slept in big rooms and bunk beds. My room here is a small room with rock walls and a tiny window and no one ever goes in there but me.

The lessons I have done have been very easy. I do not know why we are doing them. We will run up a hill, like I said. Or I will be told to jump over a rock. Or I will be told to push a box around a room. When I do what they say, the teachers do not say anything. They just say do it again or walk away. I do not know if I am doing any of this how they want. I hope they do not cut me again.[13]

---

13 A couple things I want to make clear. First, yes, I wrote this just after I turned seven. If anything, I think this was made less eloquent through editing. Second, you may note a hint of fear in these letters. This was a strategy on my part to make the teachers think I was afraid of them so they wouldn't all be afraid of me and quit immediately, terrified at the very idea of how I could harm them. "Fear" was not then, nor is it now, in my vocabulary.

August 27 (?)

Dear Journal,

Today I learned a big lesson. The teachers do not want us to do what they are saying. They want us to do what they are not saying.

I learned this when I went into a room where a teacher told me to cut a hole in a sheet. He gave me a sword and held up the sheet in front of me. I did not want to do it. I felt sick today. I was mad about all these things they had been telling us to do. I have been mad since I got here. I cannot see the faces of the teachers. I do not know what they would do to me if I hurt them. They are not like The Tutor.

Today I felt bad, so I put the sword in the teacher's foot. I did not put it in the sheet. The [teacher's] foot did not bleed. When the teacher pulled out the sword, it looked like he was not hurt. He did not say anything at first. After he pulled out the sword, he put his hand on my shoulder. He said I had finished my first step. Then he left.

Nobody else talked to me for the rest of the day but I think I did right. Did bad. I did right by doing bad.

January 4[14]

Dear Journal,

I have learned a lot since my last entry.

The day after I stabbed my teacher in the foot, another teacher came to my room just as I was waking up. He told me that I was being put in a new class. He took me to a classroom full of other students wearing robes like mine. I sat down at a desk and he told

14 At some point in the intervening weeks, I was given a calendar, though I cannot be sure if the dates were accurate or not. It was very hot all year round, so as far as I knew it could have been July already. The sense of time on the island was . . . disorienting.

us that we had passed the first stage, which some students never do. Some stay here for years and keep running up hills all day.

The new class is where they teach us how to do bad the smart way. In three months I have learned how to lie, cheat, and steal. Now they are teaching us to how do them at the same time. Today I learned steal and lie about it. Tomorrow we will do stealing and cheating.

I have been so busy that I have not been able to write until now. It is a lot to learn but I like it.

May 18

Dear Journal,

I came to class today and just as it was starting, the teacher said it was the last day of the class. As soon as he said that, he left the room and we were all still there. One of the other students (I don't know anyone's name because they all look the same and we do not use names) checked the door and it was locked.

After about four hours, the teacher unlocked the door and came back in. He checked with all of us to see how we did over the four hours. I was able to get two other students' shoes and one of their watches. The teacher told me I did as I should and class was over.

Year 2

August 14

Dear Journal,

I am back from what the teachers called summer break. We were on a boat for a long time. It wasn't a big boat with a motor. It was a small boat, but long with hundreds of [paddles]. We rowed the boat for a long time. I tried to use what I learned and not row the boat. A teacher told me this was different and that I had to row the boat.

We rowed for a long time. We got to an island where we stopped. There was nothing on the island but sand and trees. The students got off the boat but the teachers did not. They left on the boat.

Two months later, the teachers came back on the boat. Those of us students that were left put down the rats we were eating and got on the boat. We went back to the island with the school.[15]

September 3

Dear Journal,

Since we came back from summer break, the teachers have started me on a new set of lessons they call "deep learning." It is not very fun.

What they do is tell me to sit in a chair. Then they put a big hat [helmet] on my head. Then I hear things I do not [understand]. I see things I do not [understand]. Sometimes I think I see things I have seen before. Then I see other things that I have not seen before. I do not know why they are doing this. I hear the things from the hat [helmet] when I am in bed. It is hard to sleep.

One time I tried to take off the hat [helmet] when it was on. It hurt my head. I fell down. One of the teachers put a light in my eyes. One of them [snapped his finger] in my face. Then I got back in the chair and put the hat [helmet] back on.

I asked one of the teachers how long I would have to keep coming to the chair to put on the hat [helmet]. He said, "As long as it takes." I hope that is not very long.

There is a long wire that comes from the top of the room down to the hat [helmet]. I think this is where the sound comes from. I do not know where the pictures come from.

---

15 This was "summer break" every year. A sort of culling, if you will. If you've read *Lord of the Flies* you pretty much have an idea of how it went. Just imagine that the kids were all wearing robes instead of rags and thick glasses and you've got it.

February 8

Dear Journal,

Today I finished my last run of "deep learning" sessions. We did them every day for several hours for eight straight months. I have to say that I'm not sure what their use was. I don't feel all that different than when we started. I just know that I've been either scared or bored almost all the time since September.

What was the point of this? Was it just a waste of time? A test of my patience? I mean, yes, my writing has gotten much stronger. I can pick up any book and read it now. I can repair basic electrical systems. I can recite the chemical formulae for numerous compounds. I know who Genghis Khan was. Other than that, I really don't understand what this "deep learning" business was all about. I've asked and asked for explanations and no one has said a thing.

I guess I'm just glad it's over.

Year 3

October 12

Dear Journal,

It's been a few weeks since we got back from another summer break. For the most part, things have been pretty normal. We started some weapons and petty theft classes. Since I got here, it feels the most like a regular school than it ever has. Not that I've ever been to a regular school, but I've heard other students talk.

Today the entire student body here at the Oceania School for Mischievous Boys was called into an auditorium for an assembly. I had never seen everyone together before. There had to be 1,000 students or more there.

When the assembly finally got underway after some delay because a few of us decided to start ripping stuffing out of our seat cushions, a bunch of bright lights pointed toward the stage and a dark-haired woman in a suit and glasses walked out. Not a robe; a suit. She didn't look like anyone I had ever seen before. She looked like she was from another time. I don't even know what I mean by that, but it's the only way I can explain it. She approached the podium and said her name was Connie Spiraci.

Over the next few months she will be doing one-on-one tutoring with a select few who show promise in the area she's most skilled, though she didn't say what that was. She said we will just have to find out. She told all of us to work really hard so we can be sure to get chosen to work with her. This is a once-in-a-lifetime chance to learn something great. She went on for a while.

I don't really know what to make of it. I do know the assembly delayed my class on hidden weapons. It's my favorite class.[16]

March 11

Dear Journal,

Today, as I was leaving my class on hiding stolen money right under the noses of the people you took it from, I got pulled aside by one of the robed teachers and told to go to the office at the end of the hallway. I didn't even know there was an end of the hallway. I had gone exploring through the building before to see the parts I had never seen, but I always got caught before I could really dig anything up or get anywhere close to an end of the hallway. I thought it just went on forever.

I learned this afternoon that it didn't. It stops after a very, very long walk, and at the end of it is Miss Spiraci's office.

I walked in and there she was, sitting behind a desk, writing something in a notebook. Her office wasn't like any other room in the school. She had a couch and windows that let in light and a big potted plant in the corner. She had a coffee pot. There was carpet

16 It really was an amazing class. I learned a knife-in-the-shoe trick that I still use today, and I learned how to hide a full-on medieval mace in a sport coat.

on the floor, not just cold stone. Posters on the walls had advice like "Someone must give orders, someone must take orders" and "Count ten and then don't say it."

I'm only nine (almost ten), but it was the strangest room I have ever been in. Miss Spiraci also asked me to do something no one else at the school had ever requested. She told me to pull back my hood. That's never happened there. Everyone keeps their hood on at all times, even when sleeping. I told her at first that she couldn't tell me what to do, but she put her hand on my shoulder and said that, sometimes, you have to look like you're doing the opposite of what you really are.

I pulled my hood back. She looked at my face and my scraggly hair that had not been cut in almost three years. It was like she was grading my face. After a minute, she pulled the hood back over my head, sat back down behind her desk, and told me to come back tomorrow. I am eager to do so.

May 31

Dear Journal,

I have been working with Miss Spiraci for almost three months now and she has taught me very many things about how to do evil while giving off the appearance that what you're doing is benevolent.[17] Miss Spiraci is a very helpful teacher and is not who she seems to be when you meet her. She has told me a lot about things that have happened that people believe happened one way and for one reason, but it really happened a different way and for a different reason. She said the ship that sank [the RMS *Lusitania*] and got America involved in a big war a few years ago was sunk intentionally so that Miss Spiraci and her friends could sell ray guns and poison gas to people in different countries.[18]

---

17 For more detail on how to deflect blame, see *The Supervillain Field Manual* chapter on Accusations. Honestly, you should have read it already. Get it together.

18 The history books leave it out, but World War I was full of ray guns.

We are leaving for another summer break tomorrow, but I hope I can learn more from Miss Spiraci when we get back.

Year 4

August 18

Dear Journal,

We returned from summer break today and pretty much the second the boat hit the sand, I was running down the hall to go to Miss Spiraci's office to schedule our next lesson.

It was a huge surprise to get to the end of the hall and not only see that her office wasn't there, but that there wasn't even a *door* there. Just a wall. I went to my next class, Neck Pinching 213, and asked the teacher there where she had gone. He said he didn't know who "she" was, so I told him I meant Miss Connie Spiraci. His only answer was, "Who? There's no teacher by that name here. None of us have names."

I asked several of the other students who must have been at last year's assembly the same question and none of them knew who she was either.

I swear I will find her. Until the day I die, I will look for her so I can learn more from her and also get my revenge for her cruel trick. This is not the end of this.

December 25

Dear Journal,

Our fight training continues. We're learning how to do new moves with and without weapons.

The teachers have us sparring with each other now. Before, we'd either fight a dummy or the teacher, but now we're mixing it up together. Some of us always fight on summer break, of course, but this is more like guided training. We're learning how to fight [defensively]. The other day a teacher said, "Learn to fight so you don't have to." That seems dumb to me. I want to fight. But I guess it means something. The teachers here don't explain a lot.

We've never celebrated Christmas at the school before, or at least I haven't, but this year we all got a notice to meet this morning in the sporting field outside for a special Christmas gathering. I was naturally suspicious of what was going on, but I was also very curious, so I went to see what it was all about.

Teachers were standing in a ring around a man in a red costume and hat. He was a pretty big fellow, and he was sweating a whole lot. He had a big bag of stuff over his shoulder. When a large enough group of students had gathered on the field, the teachers moved aside and simply said, "Attack!" We all charged in and gave the old man some pretty solid knocks so we could grab things out of his bag. I got seven oranges, a doll that I don't currently have any use for, a copy of *The Emerald City of Oz*, three pairs of socks, and a pipe that blows bubbles.

I don't know what happened to the old man in red, but I saw the teachers escort him away after it was all over.

If this is Christmas, I must say I enjoy celebrating it.

Year 5

-No entries-

Year 6

November 1

Dear Journal,

I finally got my journal back. I can't believe it's been almost two years.

January before last, the administrative staff decided it was time to do inspections of everyone's rooms. This had never happened before. They mostly left us alone in our rooms, secluded from everyone. The teachers and leaders almost never did anything to engage us at all. But then that changed.

In the inspection they found this journal and took it. When I talked to other students about their inspections, I found out things they had been writing about their time at the school had also been taken away. They weren't taking away things like flame throwers or bombs or unauthorized prototype dimensional portals (last year we finished up fight training and moved on to learning various types of mad science, including travel between dimensions). They only cared about writings about the school.

I guess they don't really like information about this place getting out, and, you know, maybe someday these journal entries could be used for a news article or published in a book or something.[19] They are very [secretive] here.

But then this fall I took a heists class and learned about the most effective ways to pull off a big-scale theft from a secure location. I got together a team of other students from the class. We broke into our classroom and took all the tools—lock picks, rope, shovels, a stethoscope, flashlights, hammers, chisels, even dynamite—that we had learned to use in class. We figured out that, unless they had burned them, all the diaries, journals, letters, and other stuff must have been locked up inside the office of the headmaster, the guy who gave us all our robes in the admission ceremony.

When it was dark, we dug a hole under the wall just outside his office and tunneled our way in. We used the chisels to break through the floor and enter the office. We picked the lock to a closet door to find a safe. We figured that was the place where the documents were being kept. I took the stethoscope, held it to the door of the safe, and cracked it. And there they were. All the stuff we, and all the other students, had written.

We tossed everything in a bag and closed it up. I closed the safe and locked it. We all got back in the tunnel and did our best to set back the slab floor to the way it was. Then we went back outside. As soon as we emerged from the tunnel, there was our teacher, standing

---

19 I was a smart kid who knew stuff.

next to a barrel with a roaring fire inside. He took the bag out of the arms of one of my classmates and tossed it into the fire. As he walked away he said, "You all pass."

And just like that, all the written material was gone. All of it except for this journal, of course. I knew something like that might happen (classes often ended with unannounced tests), so I made sure to slip this journal under my robe as I was taking everything out of the safe. It's why I said I'd crack the safe. I was not going to lose my journal.

And I won't lose it again.

January 11

Dear Journal,

I'm starting up what they're telling me is the final round of "deep learning" sessions this week. I don't think they helped me all that much last time, but they won't let me into the next class until I do this, so I suppose I'll have to. I hate that helmet so much.

April 26

Дорогой дневник,

Опять же, я не понимаю, цель этих сессий «глубокого обучения.» Я не узнал ничего ценного из них вообще, и я думаю, что они абсолютно, полная трата времени каждого. Шлем самый неудобный вещь, которую я когда-либо носил и образы и звук делают невозможным спать по ночам.

Есть намерение все это, чтобы заставить меня лучше понять дикость человека? Ужасы пыток? Могу ли я взять какой-то философской мудрости от этого? Я стою в недоумении.

Я имею в виду , конечно, я пишу это на русском языке, но в том, что на самом деле все, что большая часть благоустройства?

Translation:
Dear Journal,

Once again, I do not understand the purpose of these "deep learning" sessions. I have learned nothing of value from them at all and I think they're an absolute, utter waste of everyone's time. The helmet is the most uncomfortable thing I have ever worn and the images and sound make it impossible to sleep at night.

Is the intent of all this to make me more closely understand the savagery of man? The horrors of torture? Am I to take some philosophical wisdom away from this? I stand perplexed.

I mean, sure, I am writing this in Russian, but is that really all that much of an accomplishment?

Year 7

September 17

Dear Journal,

This year, we're doing magic.

I always knew there was something that didn't quite make sense about this place, and now I know for sure what's going on: it's run by warlocks. Wizards. Magic users. Whatever you want to call them. These teachers know and practice the dark arts.

That's why the layout of this building never really stood up to logical reason and why it was impossible to draw a map. That miles-long hallway doesn't exist in real space. It exists in some netherworld. That's why there's always food here even though I never see any ships or other vehicles. (Too bad they don't use magic to make any of it not taste like boiled rubber.) I think it at least partially explains what happened to Miss Spiraci.

Last week we got called into another all-students assembly to watch two of the administrators throw fireballs at each other. Then they summoned a demon named Pxaxxixxiu, who gave a quick speech about the power of perseverance before being cast back into hell.

We were told that magic class starts tomorrow. I'm reticent. I wasn't born into this stuff like some of the other students seem to have been, but I'll give it a try.

December 9

Dear Journal,

Magic is, quite simply, not for me.

It isn't that I have no aptitude for it. I can do a few of the basics—levitation, card tricks, creating projectiles, the thing with the rings, intangibility, infinite handkerchiefs, teleportation, pulling a knot off of a rope, even some basic summoning. It's just that I don't think it's something that comes naturally like it does for some of the other students. I also do not care to do it the way I enjoy some of the high-tech abilities we learned back in Year 5. I don't believe I'll be taking the next level of class.

Give me mad science over magic any day. I want to feel control. I want to build something with my own two hands. I don't want to merely snap my fingers and make it so. It isn't earned. It's too easy.

I mean, I suppose that's also true of stealing. I just like stealing.

April 20

Dear Journal,

Instead of continuing with magic, I took a class on oratory this semester.[20] I think it was the right decision. Why control someone's actions with easily reversible spells when I can instead convince them that what they are doing is, in fact, the

---

20 For more on my speaking expertise, see the chapter on Rhetoric in *The Supervillain Handbook*.

most advantageous course of action for not only myself but for themselves?

Pfft. Magic. How silly. A child's hobby.

Year 8

November 12

Dear Journal,

I'd been suspecting that this day would come for a long time. Today, I was asked to take a life.[21]

For the first time since I arrived here, I was called into the chamber where I was given my robe. The headmaster, who I can identify by his purple robe (all the rest are black), walked in with another robed man—a teacher, maybe, or possibly someone brought to the island specifically for this lesson. Using a brush and some white paint, he marked the man with a big "O" on his chest. He told me my assignment, and my only assignment, was to kill this man before the end of the school year. He did not dictate how, where, or when. It simply had to be done.

I heard via some cafeteria and field chatter that a few students finished their assignments then and there, in that room, either pulling out a weapon and killing their charges or using their bare hands. I find these methods pedestrian. I'm going to think and plan. I am going to go big with this.

March 4

Dear Journal,

I did it. It is done. It took months of planning, but I did it.

---

21 In case you were curious, yes, people died on summer breaks, but we didn't really do any killing of *each other*. Maybe it would happen through neglect or refusal to help, but no stabby-stabby or snappy-snappy, per se. Nature took care of that.

First, I had to capture a live shark.[22] That required many hours, day after day, by myself on a stolen canoe out in the ocean, casting a net over and over into the water. Chumming to draw one out. Eventually I managed to catch one, get it back to the shore alive, and place it into the tank I had my workers build on the field.

Oh yes, I had to hire workers. My plan involved a lot of grunt work I was unwilling to do on my own. I was on the clock with this, of course. I exchanged lunches with classmates and underclassmen, gave them blank sheets of paper out of this journal (since I've only used about twenty of the three hundred), and otherwise "convinced" them to help me. While I was going out shark fishing for days on end, they were building my diabolical trap; an intricate series of devices that would confuse and terrify the victim in equal measure. To get the materials I had to give thirty blank sheets of paper to one of my more magic-inclined classmates who could conjure it all up for me. It was quite a cost, but worth it.

After a few months of construction, I was finally ready. I led my victim into the field and we trekked along a path marked by blazing torches until we reached the entrance of what looked like a tent. I opened a flap and invited him in. When he entered, I closed the flap and a crew of my workers quickly dragged a large stone in front of it. The game was afoot.

When my victim entered, he was confronted by a full-length mirror. Above it was a sign that read, "Is it possible to change who you are?" After several minutes of deduction, the victim finally figured out the next step: he flipped over the mirror to reveal a second, warped mirror that stretched and distorted his reflection in every direction. When that mirror was fully clicked into place, a trap door under the victim's feet opened and he traveled down a chute into a tiny stone chamber.

Through a small hole in the wall, my victim could see another stone chamber in which there was a single candle burning through

22 As I mentioned, my memories of the sharks on the lifeboat stuck with me.

a rope. When the rope burned through, it released several bags of sand, which landed on a lever, which launched a statue of my victim into the air. The statue hit a switch, which opened a secret door in my victim's stone chamber. The door opened into a well-lit room full of balloons and a banner that said, "Congratulations!"

In the middle of the room was a stool with a box on it. On the box was a small card that read simply, "Your prize." Upon opening the box, my victim found a single red button. Of course, he wasn't able to resist the enticement of pushing the button, which released one deadly great white shark from a hole in the ceiling, dropping it neatly onto his head. It also, of course, released the water from the shark's tank into the small room, so if the shark hadn't killed him, he would have drowned.

So that's that.[23]

Year 9

October 19

Dear Journal,

It's time I left this school. I have learned a great deal and accomplished many things. I will use these lessons throughout my whole life. But I honestly don't know how much longer they plan to keep me here. And when it's time to graduate, as it were, what then? Do I become one of these berobed teachers myself, cursed to educate others to take up the instructive mantle? I have no answers, and no administrator or teacher here will give me any, even when I ask directly.

If that is that destination, then I must take myself off the path. I will not allow myself to be stifled this way. There is too much left to do. I will not allow myself to be stifled.

I must go.

---

23 A decent first effort. It goes without saying that I have gotten far more creative over the years.

Editor's Note: These death story sections are some of the very few parts of this memoir that King Oblivion asked me specifically to write for him. I couldn't tell you exactly why I was chosen. Somewhere along the way I got pegged as the "instructions guy," which is why I was selected to ghostwrite his Handbook and Field Manual. So go figure why he wanted me to pen these death stories. He just asked and I did. That's how things worked around here. To get to my point, I wrote these just before King Oblivion died for the final time, so he was unable to offer notes or corrections. I'm presenting them here in their first-draft form.

My First Death

The first time I died was the day I left the Oceania School for Mischievous Boys at the age of sixteen. I drowned. Like most things, I sharpened my penchant for dying with flair as with age.

I knew where I could easily secure a boat from my many ocean excursions in shark fishing. So I snagged a canoe, made my way to the part of the shoreline furthest away from the school gate, and launched myself out into the ocean in hopes of reaching some civilized place in a reasonable amount of time.

I never mentioned it in my journal, because I didn't know who might get their hands on it, but my chief goal in leaving the school was to seek out, find, and ingratiate myself to Miss Connie Spiraci, with whom I had become completely infatuated. Her arrival, brief tenure, and shocking disappearance from the school when I was eleven kept me fascinated for years, and I believed it was time to finally act on my impulses. That said, I was also telling the truth in my final journal entry. I assuredly and passionately did not want to become one of those teachers.

My plan had just a few small holes in it: First, I didn't materially or generally know where Miss Spiraci was. Indeed, no one at the school would even acknowledge her existence after she disappeared. So my destination was . . . nebulous. Second, I didn't have any equipment to speak of, aside from a boat and two paddles. No map. No compass. Nothing. And I had no idea where I was—remember that I was brought to the island blind in a ship's hold. The only other place of which I knew the location was the island where we spent our summer breaks, and I knew full well that wasn't an option. It was an even more desolate and remote place. Third, I neglected to bring any food or drinkable water. Sure, I can go longer without than just about anybody because my body is made out of stronger stuff than your typical human cells, but even I need to eat.

So the journey got off to a rocky start.

And it stayed rocky. After about sixty hours on the water, I deliriously thought that I saw Dr. Blattarius standing just to the side of my canoe. I was quite angry with him at the time, considering he'd sent me away to spend all my time with robe people for the last nine years. So I took a swing at this apparition and splashed into the water. I was still wearing my school robe, which was not the most ideal swimwear, and was quickly submerged beneath the waves.

It was over in an instant. I didn't panic. I just let it happen. I looked at the light above me, shimmering in the water. Things started to fade. Then black.

Sometime later, I woke up on a table in a torch-lit room back at the school. It was a room I had never been in before. One of the teachers or administrators was pulling off a pair of bloody gloves in a corner. Several others surrounded me. They were chanting some kind of incantation. To this day, I don't know exactly what kind of ceremony they performed, but I know what they called it: graduation.

The headmaster entered the room and handed me a rolled-up piece of paper. It was my diploma. Its inscription read:

The Board of Directors of the
OCEANIA SCHOOL FOR MISCHIEVOUS BOYS
certifies that
KING OBLIVION
upon completion of a curriculum consisting of all evil acts,
the mysteries of subterfuge and even the cold grasp of death
has satisfactorily completed the course of study
and is therefore awarded this
DIPLOMA
Given October 31, 1928

The headmaster walked me outside the gates and pointed toward a tiny seaplane piloted by a man in goggles and a scarf. I hadn't seen a vessel in that spot since the steamer ship dropped me off nine years earlier.

"Tell him where you want to go and he will take you," he said.

He went back inside through the gate, which closed behind him. I never personally returned to the school.

As I walked to the boat, I checked the small of my back, where I had strapped my journal to myself with a leather belt, to make sure they hadn't taken it. It was still there. I don't think they even looked.

Idiots.

Villainspiration

The villain: Cassandra Nova
Key trait: Charles Xavier's opposite self who created her own body using his psychic energy (she was conceived without a body because she was an evil legend imagined by an alien race).
How she uses it: Cassandra Nova spent many of her early years as a glob of goo on the wall of a sewer, but she made up for lost time quickly, showing up at Xavier's School for Gifted Youngsters, stealing his body, and forcing him into her own semi-corporeal being. Once she had control of the school, she used it as her plaything, forcing teachers and students to do grievous harm to one another. She proved that if you must spend time at a school, make it count.
The wrong takeaways: You don't have to try to steal the body of a school's headmaster to create chaos. If you can, sure, do it, but don't overstretch yourself to make it happen. There are other ways to create mayhem. And if you do take his or her body, don't immediately show your hand. Find subtle ways to stir the pot before making your big move.

Chapter 5

VICIOUS ADOLESCENCE

I knew that the world had changed a lot in the nine years I spent at the Oceania School for Mischievous Boys, so I took it upon myself to ask the pilot what kind of place would be of interest to a sixteen-year-old who had essentially been given carte blanche to cause as much trouble in the world as he wanted.

Don't you dare insult my hearing skills like this. Emphatically note that it was the pilot's problem, not mine.

I could barely make out what the pilot said to me in response. Not only were we blasting through the sky in an open-air cockpit, we were also trying to speak through the stream of dozens of bugs flying into our mouths. I did manage to hear a word here and there about alcoholic drinks being banned in the United States, opening the door for a massive criminal enterprise, and how one of the larger bootlegging operations going on was in the city of Chicago.

That sounded pretty exciting. I wasn't interested in trying to hear what else he had to say, or having to open my mouth any more than I had to. So I—as briefly as possible—requested for him to take me there. I figured it would be as appropriate a place as any to start my search for Miss Spiraci, and I could maybe get a little criminal experience under my belt in the process.

We flew for fifteen hours or so, counting one stop in California to refuel. I tried as accurately as I could to triangulate the location of the island that housed the school somewhere in the Pacific. I didn't pinpoint it exactly, but I got a general idea. That would come in handy when I sent an expedition to the island years later.

What is this? This is like those questions you kept adding, except they're sentences. Stop this.

Always got to be thinking.

It wasn't until we landed in Chicago that I got a chance to really meet and talk to the pilot. He told me his birth name was Eric Callum, but he preferred to go by the name "The Air Terror." I told him to work on it. I also asked him if he had a card I could take in case I ever needed to hire him again for any kind of piloting work. He gave me a card—I never bothered to call—and departed, wishing me "fearsome fortune."

At the time, I didn't realize how much he was telling me with that farewell, but soon enough I'd understand.

Oh boy, would I understand.

You're not stopping. I know this was already written before I added these comments, but me telling you to stop in the future should have stopped you from doing it in the past.

The only clothing I had when I arrived was my school robe, which I quickly realized made me highly conspicuous. I watched people in suits and hats pass me by on the street, looking me up and down, most likely suspecting I was some sort of cultist or religious proselytizer. I decided to use this to my advantage. I was able to talk one gullible soul out of his clothes—a gray wool suit, a black trilby hat, a long purple scarf, and a pair of black-and-white wingtips—by telling him that my robe would allow him to see visions of the future and the real truth of the universe. It shockingly didn't take a lot of convincing. I even got him to pay me an extra $30 right out of his pocket for this magic garment. We traded clothes and he seemed pleased enough with the transaction, walking away, muttering something about how he "[saw] the light now" and "everything [was] clear." I knew already, but here was further proof that some people will believe anything if you say it with enough conviction. He was more than welcome to have my filthy robe, though for a little something extra I did kick him in the kneecaps before leaving, just to make sure I could get away with his clothes before he changed his mind.

It also dawned on me that I had nowhere to stay in this new city, which was a pretty massive change after nearly a decade of always having a room to myself at the school. After much wandering, I eventually found a flophouse on Madison Street where I was able to talk the owner into letting me stay for a dollar a night, but only if I promised "not to make trouble." I lied and said that was my intent all along, and he allowed me to hole up in a disheveled room—I use the term "room" loosely, as it was more of a cubicle with walls made out of thin, cheap wood—in lieu of staying in one of the building's large, open-air, barrack-like areas.

I don't lie. I tell truths people don't know are truths yet.

Just as I was getting settled, a young man in a uniform, who identified himself as a courier, arrived in the entryway asking specifically for me. Since I had checked in with a fake name—Chester Pokorny, the name of the man whose clothes I had taken and whose identity I was able to verify due to the fact that he forgot to take his wallet out of the coat pocket before handing it over to me—this caused considerable confusion for the owners of the place. I tried all I could to smooth it over, saying that King Oblivion wasn't staying here, but that I knew him and would make sure to get whatever message the courier had back to him.

The courier pulled a box out of his messenger bag and tossed it to me with a wink.

"Thanks for making sure these get to him, *Mr. Pokorny*," he said really hitting the name hard. "Fearsome fortune to you."

As I wondered why I was hearing that farewell for the second time that day, I opened the box to find a note from none other than the man whose apparition I had attempted to punch several weeks before: Dr. Blattarius. There was also something covered in wax paper, and upon unraveling it, I found the mask I had selected from his consecration chamber thirteen years prior. Then I read the note.

Satisfactory work. You graduated. I thought you might want this.
Fearsome fortune,
Dr. B.

I resented the curtness of the letter and was even more confused by how frequently I was hearing and seeing "fearsome fortune," but was pleased to have the mask. I had thought about it often when I was at the school, wondering when I might have accomplished enough to wear it.

Conspicuously missing, however, was my cloak. Had I not yet done enough? Was Dr. Blattarius simply withholding it from me to get under my skin?

Now I'm getting mad again.

What a strange one this guy was.

Either way, I took the opportunity to put on my mask for the first time. When I did, the energy was so kinetic, so massive, such a perfect wedding of garment and wearer that the room exploded. This isn't a metaphor. I don't use metaphors. Metaphors are for people who don't do great things, and thus need "symbols" to describe them. I say exactly what happened, as is the case here: the south wall of the flophouse blasted out onto Madison Street. The flimsy wooden walls of my room turned to ash. The bed collapsed. I could feel beams of energy exuding from my head. I believe I even floated off the ground for a few minutes.

Now I'm getting furious again.

It was quite a sight indeed.

One bystander who was less than enthused about the spectacle was the owner, who charged into my cubicle/room to find out what all the commotion was about. He was instantly vaporized by the beams of energy coming from my head.

I supposed this turn of events more or less gave me legal rights to the property, so I quickly began acting as owner, forcing out all the tenants who survived the mask ordeal. It wasn't a particularly difficult process to get them to leave. After all, they had just seen me explode and live, though others around me did not. They didn't really care to stay. All except one, that is.

He was a young man, just a few years older than me, named George "Gun" Tiratore. He said he worked for a group called the Chicago Outfit, a South Side bootlegging organization, and that his group could use someone with powers like mine. I was interested—after all, the promise of bootlegging was the reason I came to Chicago to begin with—but I wanted to play it cool, so I asked him who the leader of this whole operation was. He told me the guy's name was "Al Capone."

I couldn't believe what I was hearing. How was I supposed to believe this? A crime boss named "Al Capone"? "I'll cap one?" It was laughable. Silly. A joke. What sort of hack would even come up with such a ridiculous name for a criminal? And people say supervillains have goofy names.

It made me dubious about the whole enterprise, but I figured I didn't have many other options—I didn't want make a job out of running a flophouse with no tenants and a missing wall—and I still really wanted to find Miss Spiraci. So I agreed to help where I could. He, too, wished me "fearsome fortune" and within a few days had introduced me to the various members of the outfit, including Capone himself. Soon enough I had steady work.

Over the next six months I went on dozens of runs up to Canada and back to Chicago in trucks and trains filled with barrels of alcohol. I was the guy who leaned out of the passenger-side window or stood on the caboose platform and shot a Tommy gun at pursuing police officers. I was great at it, and there was the added benefit that I was doing all this in a mask, so no one dared even try to identify me.

Not that they could even if they wanted to. It was during this period that I discovered that the mask didn't come off. It was permanently affixed to my face, burned onto my skin in the massive dispersal of energy that occurred when I donned it. It was now my face. It was how I got the name Johnny "No Face" Cappucio.[24]

NOW I'M LIVID.

It really was something else.

During these runs across the northern border and back, I took it upon myself to ask anyone I came across whether they had ever met a Connie Spiraci. I came up empty time and time again, but I was bound and determined to find her. I checked phone books in every town I visited. I looked in public records. I found the professionals who specialized in creating fake identities for people and shook them down for information. Nothing. It was as though she had truly vanished.

Inaccurate. I succeeded. The people I was asking failed.

So I kept at it. After about six months of running suds and occasionally getting caught up in Detroit by members of the competing North Side gang, one of the guys who gave me orders, Albert Anselmi, tossed me a police uniform and told me that I needed to help with something. I never thought I'd be wearing a cop's clothes, but I

24 A few of the leaders of the Outfit didn't think the name "King Oblivion" was the right fit for the gang. Plus, the title "king" made me seem more important than them. I mean, I *was* more important than them, but they didn't know that.

put the uniform on and within a few minutes we were set up outside a Lincoln Park garage. A few other "cops" and I got a signal from Anselmi to raid the building. Once we were inside, we called in the rest of the crew and ended up shooting seven members of the North Side gang who had assembled inside. It was all planned out that way. Anselmi told me to put my gun on him and make it look like I was leading him out of the garage, like I was arresting him. So we casually walked out of there as he nodded and told me "fearsome fortune." And that's how I participated in the St. Valentine's Day Massacre.

Bet that perked your ears up. You may be saying "Well, I heard about that in history class," or more likely "I read about that on Wikipedia and saw no such thing about a masked supervillain dressed as a cop being a part of it." Well, of course you didn't. We didn't *want* you to hear about it. None of the stuff in those books or websites or whatever is what the people who did them actually did. It's just what they want you to *think* they did.[25]

I can't believe this. Why aren't you retroactively deleting these?

I stuck around and worked for the Outfit for another year or so, but when I heard that Capone had been arrested in Miami Beach on vagrancy charges in 1930, I figured my time with the organization was over. The hammer was going to come down on Capone eventually—he operated too recklessly, even a dumb seventeen-year-old kid knew that—and I was getting a little tired of being a cog in the machine. It was fun going on

Are you kidding me with this? Tell me you're kidding. (Not that it matters. Either way, you have made a grave mistake.)

25 All books except this one, that is. Everything in this book is true.

the trips—taking over sleeper trains and going to Kansas City or Hot Springs to cause a weekend of trouble in some fancy hotel—but I needed control. I needed power. And on top of that, I wasn't having any luck finding Miss Spiraci in Chicago or anywhere else we went, for that matter. I had spent two solid years with the Outfit and had little to show for it, at least in terms of the goal I left the Oceania School to achieve.[26]

So in the fall, I up and left. I hopped in a Graham-Paige Boattail Speedster parked outside the Cicero, Illinois, city hall and started driving without telling anyone where I was going or even saying "so long." More accurately, I didn't give anyone a "fearsome fortune," a phrase I continued to hear throughout my two years working with the Outfit. Everyone from Capone down to the lowest grunt said it. It had been following me around since the day I got there. In addition to locating Miss Spiraci, I also wanted to get to the bottom of what that phrase was all about. Was it just some massive trend that caught on while I was stuck on a remote island school, wearing the same robe every day? Or was there something more concerted behind it?

I'm ripping these pages apart now. Literally ripping them to pieces.

I'd find out, all right.

I drove the car until it sputtered to a stop with an empty gas tank somewhere right around the intersecting borders of Kansas, Missouri, Arkansas, and Oklahoma. As I drove through the dusty terrain, I found myself seeing more and more craggy-faced people looking off into the distance,

26 In terms of shooting a Tommy gun a lot, I had plenty to show for it.

as if they were all going through some big, existential crisis. Once I ditched the car just outside a little town called Fairland in Oklahoma (I didn't realize I could fill it back up with gas; I had never been asked to drive before and figured people just ditched them when they ran out), I started walking down the road in hopes of finding another car to steal. Before I could do that, though, a massive truck loaded up with what looked to be an entire family's possessions pulled up beside me and stopped, kicking up a massive cloud of dust all over my suit.

"Friend, we're headed for California," said the young man in the passenger seat. "If you're going the same way, we'd be obliged to give you a ride in that direction. We all got to help each other out here."

I had to stifle a laugh at the concept of anyone having to help anyone, but I quickly regained my composure and agreed to ride along. After all, I didn't really have any other mode of transportation.

On the lengthy drive to the West Coast of the United States, I learned quite a bit about some things I had missed. For one, people outside of massive criminal enterprises were having a tough go of it economically. This particular family, the Glumbs, had recently lost their farm after a particularly dry summer. The bank took it. They were on their way to California to find work wherever they could and eventually make a home there.

I didn't learn any of this because I asked. They just told me. And told me. And told me. The oldest son, Tom, was especially chatty. He could go on for hours about a turtle lying on the street or how he'd helped some jerk who was being beaten up on the side of the road. It was tedious. So deeply tedious.

Even so, I did take it upon myself to help the family out of a few scrapes along the journey, because doing so was to my benefit. For example, their grandfather died on the trip. I helped bury him so we could move along more quickly. Tom was harassed by some police officers at a migrant camp; I threw them into a lake so we could get out of there. One of the older brothers in the family asked me for advice because he wanted to leave and start anew away from the family. I told him to go running in whatever direction he pleased just to avoid having some big, meandering debate about it. I wanted to get where we were going and it all felt like it was taking so damn long.

Eventually, after what seemed like an eternity, we arrived in California. The family found work in an orange orchard, but not picking oranges. They were strikebreakers. It was the only work available after the huge influx of people from the East. I actually joined in to help with that. It was fun.

For a while, anyway. Eventually, one night during a big rainstorm, I stole the family's truck and headed for the coast. They holed up in a barn somewhere and I never saw them again. Someone once told me a crummy writer authored a deeply fabricated and embellished version of the story and published it as a novel some years later. I haven't bothered to read it and likely never will. Authors are incompetent, weak-willed people and I won't stand for putting their hogwash in my already-perfect brain.

That's just how it is.

I'm flabbergasted that you're continuing to do this.

Within a day or so, I arrived in Los Angeles. Well, actually, I drove the truck all the way to the ocean and ditched it on Venice Beach, but you get the idea. I started a long walking trek toward downtown, asking anyone who passed by if they had heard of Connie Spiraci, earning nothing but grunts and rude dismissals for my troubles (so I broke a lot of hands that afternoon). But I didn't really need the help anyway. Once I got about five miles down Venice Boulevard, I found Miss Spiraci. Her face was plastered across a billboard for something titled *They Called Her Trouble*, one of those pictures some of the guys back in the Chicago Outfit had talked about. I'd never seen one. And her name wasn't given as Connie Spiraci. It was Lillian Pemberton.

I ran into a nearby Los Angeles Motor Bus Company station and asked the woman behind the desk where the nearest picture house was. She pointed right behind her and, wouldn't you know it, there was a showing of *They Called Her Trouble* starting, so I paid my nickel for a matinee (one of the few times I have ever personally paid for anything), went inside, and found a seat.

I can't say I was totally thrilled with what I saw. Miss Spiraci was acting nothing like I remembered her. Instead of being a woman who seemed to be from the future, with an immense knowledge of the true way the world worked, this woman was a New York socialite who sometimes poured coffee on men who said unflattering things to her. In one scene, she sent some poor, foolish fellow down a dumbwaiter shaft. It was all barely rambunctiousness, not really anything that I would call full-on "trouble," and with little consequence. These fellows were shamed, but not harmed in any discernible way.

And by the end, Miss Spiraci, also known as Lillian Pemberton, whose character was named Dinah Evans, was swept off her feet by some cleft-chinned, personality-free chunk of rock salt, cured of her "troubling" ways and married. It was, quite frankly, a depressing experience, and the last time I watched a film.[27]

As I angrily stormed out of the theater, very nearly preparing to pick up the cashier behind the window and shake him by the feet until I got my nickel back, I heard a strange and very loud humming above me. I also noticed it had very suddenly become overcast . . . except it hadn't. There, floating above me in a massive blimp, was none other than Miss Spiraci herself, hanging out the door and beckoning me up a rope ladder.

"Fearsome fortune, young man!" she shouted. "How'd you like my movie?"

I looked up at her and hesitated for a moment, unsure of how to respond. I opted to lie. "It wasn't terrible," I yelled back.

"Well, why don't we talk about it?" she replied. "Come on up here and we'll chat."

So I climbed the rope.

27 To stay up on the culture at large, I force henchmen to watch every film made and then summarize each for me in a sentence. It's very efficient.

Email Correspondence Between King Oblivion, Ph.D. and K. J. Growler, Ghostwriter of "An Atrocious Admission" and "Vicious Adolescence"

From: King Oblivion, Ph.D.
To: K. J. Growler
Subject: Cutesy afterthoughts

Growler,

I'll give you this much: you did what I asked. That's about all I can give you, though, because instead of inserting a bunch of obnoxiously winky questions, you've added a glut of goofy-ass, cutesy "afterthought" sentences to this chapter. Mr. Growler, why in the name of all that is evil would you think this was a preferable option? If anything, it's more annoying than the questions. Let the story of me being in the St. Valentine's Day Massacre stand on its own.

What a maroon you are.

And this isn't even getting to how naïve and silly you make me look throughout this thing. I know most adolescents are idiots, but I wasn't *any* adolescent. Of course I knew how to fill up a motorcar's combustibles depository with gasofuel. What an insult! What a travesty!

Explain yourself.

. . .

From: K. J. Growler
To: King Oblivion, Ph.D.
Subject: RE: Cutesy afterthoughts

Glorious and brilliant leader,

I'm not sure what to say other than to once again offer up my deepest, sincerest apologies. To level with you, I had no idea I was even putting in those asides throughout the chapter. I was just sort of trying to punctuate the stories, make them—relatable is not the word—readable. Yes, readable.

The truth of the matter is that you are so high-minded and clever that I believe most of your stories would go directly over the average reader's head without some level of dumbing down to make it easier to comprehend.

That, I now realize, is what I was doing. I hope this explanation pleases you and I will do all I can manage to correct my errors.

Grovelingly,
K. J. Growler

. . .

From: King Oblivion, Ph.D.
To: K. J. Growler
Subject: RE: Cutesy afterthoughts

Growler,

You make some strong points about my overwhelming degree of intelligence and how difficult it would be for the layman to understand my thought processes. However, a few points:

First, what makes you think this book is for the "average" reader? It is anything but. Certainly, I'm sure every literate and semi-literate person on the planet will buy it—I'm planning to make it mandatory—but most likely it will sit unread on bookshelves just to give the owners an air of prestige from owning it. Like an improved *Ulysses*. The only people, or more accurately, person, who will truly be able to grasp its contents will be my future successor, the real, intended audience.

As for your excuse for the afterthoughts, you should have more sense than to plead ignorance with me, Mr. Growler. Not knowing that you did something is a more egregious infraction than knowingly performing an act that would rankle me.

So, I ask again: Why the asides?

. . .

From: K. J. Growler
To: King Oblivion, Ph.D.
Subject: RE: Cutesy afterthoughts

Immaculate one,

I really wish I had a different answer for you, but the honest truth of it is I was just trying to make the stories more readable and understandable. I know now that was a mistake and I regret it very, very deeply.

With pleading,
K. J. Growler

. . .

From: King Oblivion, Ph.D.
To: K. J. Growler
Subject: RE: Cutesy afterthoughts

That's some pretty weak talk, Growler. Your services will no longer be needed. Please walk into the incinerator on your right. I'd thank you for your service, but well.

You know.

Editor's Note: This was yet another of King Oblivion's numerous quizzes and surveys for potential successors scattered throughout his notes and files. This one is particularly notable for being marked with a comment that said "Get Kinsey to review," though all these files were dated from at least forty years after Alfred Kinsey's death in 1956. Were they going to resurrect him somehow? Was Alfred Kinsey secretly alive? Maybe it was just a mistake and he meant William Masters or Virginia Johnson? None of the questions here really pertain to any of their research, but King Oblivion had a penchant for kidnapping people within a certain realm of expertise and pressing them to give their thumbs-up to dubious scientific or sociological ideas, so maybe that's what this was. Sadly, we'll never know for sure.

The Supervillain Love and Sex Survey

Question 1: How would you describe your ideal partner?

A. Caring and considerate
B. Quirky and funny
C. Dominating
D. An accomplice
E. A literal demon from hell
F. Someone who would run for president for the sole purpose of helping you enact your many terrible, destructive plans

Question 2: What do you most hope to get out of a romantic relationship?

A. Emotional support and affection
B. A solid, lifelong financial and family partnership
C. Sex
D. Status and wealth

E. Someone to occasionally take the fall for my various subway-tunnel-destroying crimes
F. A co-ruler to help me lay waste to a fallen world
G. A family castle
H. Someone who can guarantee to avenge me after my death, attacking the people who killed me but also many, many others

Question 3: Where would you most prefer to make love?
A. In a candlelit bedroom, on a bed covered with rose petals
B. In a Jacuzzi at a fancy retreat
C. On a kitchen counter where other people might hear
D. On a bathroom floor (I don't even care)
E. The lip of an active volcano
F. Inside a bank while I am robbing it
G. On a satellite orbiting Earth, triangulating to destroy Finland
H. Atop the grave of my greatest enemy
I. In the universe's most romantic place: my own mind

Question 4: What would you say is your biggest turn-off?
A. Smoking/drug abuse/other bad and damaging habits
B. Body odor/lack of grooming
C. Caginess/lack of empathy/unwillingness to share feelings
D. Too serious/no sense of humor
E. Lack of impulsiveness/no sense of spontaneity/boring
F. Hang-ups about putting a man in a cape into a crate and then tossing the crate into the ocean
G. Too judgmental/nagging/scolds you for sending a city into space
H. Uncomfortable living in a massive headquarters alongside dozens or hundreds of costumed lackeys who answer to your every beck and call

Question 5: My ideal partner is:

A. Male
B. Female
C. Either/or
D. I don't see gender, as it is a fluid social construct
E. Myself
F. An alien
G. A robot
H. A robot alien
I. A robot alien version of myself

Question 6: What is your preferred method of birth control?

A. Condoms, sponges, diaphragms, or other prophylactics
B. Pills, patches, rings, shots, or IUDs
C. The "rhythm" method
D. Keeping track of ovulation
E. Permanent methods (vasectomy or tubal sterilization)
F. Traveling to a dimension where humans cannot get pregnant
G. I don't practice birth control for religious reasons
H. I don't practice birth control; I need henchmen, after all
I. Only engaging in sex with robot and/or alien versions of myself

Question 7: Do you believe that marriage is a relevant institution in today's society?

A. Yes, I believe that all loving relationships should naturally progress to a traditional marriage with traditional roles
B. Yes, but I also acknowledge that marriage has changed greatly as an institution over the centuries, from a business transaction between families to household building to a joining based on love

C. No, marriage is an outmoded institution and human beings aren't meant to be with just one other person their entire lives
D. No, too many marriages end in divorce for me to respect it as an institution
E. Yes, marriage is the only way I can truly secure the future of my vast criminal empire
F. No, I don't want to give up half of my vast criminal empire in a messy divorce

Question 8: Which of the following traits do you find most attractive?

A. A shapely body
B. A beautiful face
C. A sterling personality/sense of humor
D. A swollen bank account
E. Immense, terrifying power (physical or political)
F. Incredible ray gun precision
G. Complete amorality
H. Ninety feet tall and able to knock down buildings

Question 9: Is there such a thing as true, lasting love?

A. Yes, I feel it for my partner every day
B. Yes, though I haven't yet experienced it for myself
C. No, true love is a myth; there is nothing but infatuation
D. No; there is such a thing as love, but it fades
E. Yes, true love can be reached between two people who conquer the world together
F. No, there can only be one world conqueror, and that person is me

Villainspiration

The villain: Proteus
Key trait: Kevin McTaggart could warp reality and possess other people's bodies.
How he uses it: Long kept in captivity on Muir Island, Proteus possessed the body of crotchety boat captain Angus MacWhirter as a means of escape. Once he reached mainland Scotland, he took over the bodies of many people on his way to taking over his father's body and going on a rampage of distorting reality all over the place.
The wrong takeaways: Proteus tried and failed many times to take over the bodies of heavyweights such as Wolverine and Phoenix. If you're going to start using body-controlling powers, make sure you can control the bodies of the most powerful people around you. Also, Proteus had a weakness to metal. Don't be lame like that.

Chapter 6

THE YOUNG DASTARD

When I finished ascending the ladder and insinuated myself onto the dirigible upon which I had finally located Miss Spiraci, I was met with quite a moment of stupefaction. This did not look like any old flying ship: this was a sight of ostentatiousness the likes of which I had never before contemplated. I surveyed my surroundings and, in doing so, espied a vast library full of weighty tomes, a well-appointed dining table, a sitting room with numerous chesterfields and settees on display, even a chandelier. A chandelier! On a zeppelin!

These are . . . interesting word choices. Definitely not the ones I used in my notes.

Hmm.

Along the ceiling of the passenger area was embossed the giant seal for an organization called the Western Association of Ruffians. It was entirely foreign to me, but the slogan written underneath was all too familiar: "Fearsome Fortune."

Miss Spiraci, who somehow looked younger than when I last saw her, was perhaps the most grandiose part of the entire room. In her spangled silver dress and massive diamond earrings, she had taken a seat on a chaise longue over in the large room's seating area. She was imbibing a dram of what I had to assume was some very expensive champagne. I dithered in speaking to her. After all I had taken in at the cinema and my many months of scouring the United States to find her, I found myself quite taciturn; an uncharacteristic moment if I ever had one. As witness to my buttoned-up state, Miss Spiraci took it upon herself to pierce the silence, asking me what I thought of the place.

"It's . . . it's very nice," I muttered.

She laughed. "Oh, come now. I didn't go around stealing furniture, books, and silverware from royalty just so you could call something 'nice.' It's fantastic. It's fabulous. It's a *king's* ransom. Get it? King? Like your name."

I'm very unhappy with this section of the book. I come off looking far too indecisive. We may just have to cut it out entirely.

I laughed nervously, working up the courage to ask the next question. "So . . . uh . . . Miss Spiraci. I . . . I just wanted to ask . . . it's just that . . . you look quite different from how you did at the school. And your name on those billboards is Lillian Pemberton. I just, uh—"

She cut me off. "Didn't I teach you anything, kid? Things aren't always as they appear. Being in movies is work. And it's *a* work. I'm working all the angles to make sure things go down the way *we* want them to. Same went for showing up at that school and being your teacher. I wear the faces I need to wear to get into the places I need to get into and deliver the messages I have to deliver. Sometimes it's to be Hollywood royalty, other times it's to be that inspiring teacher that gets a young upstart to obsess over the way the world works."

"Wait. You—"

"Of course. How haven't you figured this out yet? I was at that school for you and only you. I disappeared to get you to come find me. This was all part of our plan. This is all what he wanted to do."

I tensed up. "He? Who is—oh, you don't. You don't mean—"

"Dr. Blattarius himself, in the flesh, founder of the Western Association of Ruffians. My boss . . . and yours."

She pointed toward an egress at the end of the room marked VIEWING PLATFORM.

Are you . . . are you using a thesaurus?

"He's out there waiting for you. He's been dying to see you."

I muttered something under my breath about how I wished Dr. Blattarius was really dying, but Miss Spiraci was unable to hear me. I began my trek to the overlook but, as I ambulated, I took one look back at Miss Spiraci to finally ask the question I had been meaning to ask since I ascended that ladder.

"So . . . you didn't ask me up here to . . . uh . . . We're not . . ."

"We're not what, kid?"

"You know. Going to finally make love?"

This is very inaccurate and embarrassing, all the more reason to trash this part.

Miss Spiraci laughed. And laughed. And laughed some more.

Humiliated after my three-year search, I turned and made my way out onto the observation deck, where Dr. Blattarius was looking upon

How dare you.

the Los Angeles skyline, gulping in smoke from a prodigious cigar and then heaving it out into the diffuse air. The whirring of the airship's engines mimicked the buzzing inside my head from the mixture of the fresh sting of rejection and anger I had been feeling at Dr. Blattarius for over a decade coming to a boil inside me.

He waited eons to speak, taking long drags on his cigar and expunging the smoke from his lungs with seemingly no regard that I was also inhabiting his presence. Just as I pursed my lips to ask what he wanted from me, he finally articulated a thought.

"I see you got the mask," he said, keeping his gaze on the setting sun. "I was wondering if it ever got to you."[28]

First, these are thesaurus words. Second, I'd never "tamp down" acrimony. I'm all acrimony!

As I tamped down my acrimony and disapprobation, my way with words was returning to me. "You didn't hear?" I asked. "When I put it on, Chicago lost a flophouse."

Dr. Blattarius chuckled and finally turned to face me. "You know, that cloak you picked out is here somewhere. I'll find it. You can take it with you when you go. I don't need it."

I took a step closer to him, to look directly into his buggy eyes. "And where exactly am I going?"

"Well," he said, taking a gargantuan drag on his cigar and blasting out a plume of smoke from the depths of his lungs, "that's up to you, son."

---

28 You may be wondering how I'm recalling these word-for-word conversational exchanges from some eighty-five years ago. Do I really have to tell you how I'm remembering this stuff? I'm amazing and perfect, with a complete, rock-solid, photographic memory. Every word is exactly as it was said at the time, unmistakably. If you do have some suspicion that I'm mistaken, then I'll come to your house and let you know otherwise.

I stopped myself from blurting out that I was not his son so I could hear as he launched into his offer for me. He explained, as I had more or less already deduced, that his organization, the Western Association of Ruffians, had kept me in its employ throughout my journey from Chicago to Los Angeles. It was the guiding force behind the Chicago Outfit and kept a watchful eye on me during my expedition with the Glumb family. Whether I wanted to or not, I had been working for the man who raised me and then sent me off to a school on an island in the middle of nowhere.

And, as new as it seemed to me, the Association was no upstart organization. The igloo fortress where I spent the first six years of my life had been an Association bunker. Yet for the purposes of staying under the radar while the heat was on over the Robot Roosevelt situation, it wasn't adorned with logos like this blimp or the Association's massive headquarters that hovered above the Atlantic Ocean at precisely zero degrees longitude and zero degrees latitude.

The Association had been founded in 1907, a full five years before I was born, and had been acting [precipitously] to transform geopolitics over the previous quarter century or so. Now that I had emerged from the school a graduate and taken a few years to learn the ropes on the ground, Dr. Blattarius was offering me my place in the organization.

Where'd you get a thesaurus, anyway? Who gave you one? Which henchman do I need to blast into the Earth's core?

"So what do you say, son? You can either work as my lieutenant, fly around in this blimp with me, and have an office in a hovering fortress, or you can go back down there and make your way," he said, gesturing out toward the city splayed out before him. "Just know that either way you do it, you work for me."

After some hesitation, I grudgingly acquiesced to his offer of employment with the knowledge that one day all he had would be mine. I would purloin all that was his, no matter how long it took.

We spent the next hour looking around the ship for my cloak (it was in a box underneath one of the couches) and spent the rest of the sojourn sitting in what was essentially silence until we reached Dr. Blattarius's hovering base. (Dr. Blattarius and Miss Spiraci did engage in a few whispered conversations I wasn't privy to.) I waited until we arrived to put on my cloak, which was a smart move. As it was, it only caused some minor damage to Association Headquarters Concourse D instead of blasting our dirigible out of the sky. Dr. Blattarius set me up in an office in the business wing and told me that I would be made a part of the Association board.

For a moment, I let that promise fool me into believing that I would have some degree of power in the organization, but it would soon become very apparent that I was a subordinate. I'd remain one for the next decade.

I don't even think this one means what you want it to.

I scantly saw Dr. Blattarius during that time. Instead, Miss Spiraci was my immediate superior, and though I must admit I held onto a bit of animus for a couple years after she rejected my offer of copulation, we mostly coexisted with little trouble. She was off doing her thespian work in the pictures, largely leaving me to do such assorted tasks my own way.

Our healthy rapport could also be a direct result of the environment in which I was laboring. Though I was fairly low on the totem pole in terms of my place in the Association's hierarchy, to the people I was overseeing, I held a considerable amount of authoritative power. This enabled me to achieve the number of romantic conquests that a young man in his twenties feels obliged to notch into his bed, thereby reducing the amorous veneration I occasionally felt for Miss Spiraci. Obviously, these trysts were devoid of emotional entanglements—I never sullied myself with such feelings, of course, and rarely ever asked the names of my various paramours, who typically had an understanding that this was merely physical—but they were enough to keep me satiated while I performed my often-tedious work.[29]

I am a supervillain who loves wordiness, and this is even too much for me.

Below are a few examples of the Association tasks assigned to me:

- Each year, it was my responsibility to oversee the Association's annual fighting tournament. That may sound like a difficult task, but the job really was not that strenuous. I'd sit in a giant chair overseeing one of the fighting stages and occasionally exclaim something in response to

29 Many of the lovers I bedded were employees of the Association, so on the off chance that one of them would attempt to remain in touch with me via letters, telegraphs or, worse, in-person communication, I would typically just have them reassigned to the weapons testing division, which refused to use anything other than live ammunition. "If it ain't live, it ain't a test," Dr. Blattarius used to say.

a big hit, like "What a shot!" or "Crispy!" As you can deduce, I tested out a bevy of catch phrases. We would invite fighters from all over the globe to come to our otherworldly arena and duke it out until one of them fell into a giant pool of acid or a pit of spikes or got sucked into a portal to hell. Or sometimes the competitors would just kiss each other to death or turn into dragons and eat half of their opponents' bodies. Occasionally, they'd even kill each other with kindness. Their souls would be sucked into a giant jar for some nefarious purpose of Dr. Blattarius's that was never fully made clear, but at the end of the event the "winner" was invited to fight me for the chance to save themselves and the Earth from our evil tyranny. I'd always hit them with a couple ray gun blasts and that would be that. It was really amazing that no one ever figured out that guns were perfectly legal in the various bouts. In fact, there were barely any rules to begin with.

- I was assigned the job of liaising with various associated groups, namely the Eastern Cabal of Wrongdoers, the Northern Purloiners Partnership, and the Criminal Club of the South. They were all, to be quite frank, two-bit operations, and I was instructed to put on airs to make it appear as if we would cooperate with them on various plans and schemes. In reality, we undercut them at every turn. And so I did. By the end of the 1930s, the Western Association of Ruffians had virtually total control over all these other groups.

- I was put in charge of several propaganda campaigns aimed at turning around the poor perception of crime in society at large. The time was right for it; the Great Depression in the United States had many people questioning the "normal" societal strictures around them, and gangsters had become something akin to folk heroes during Prohibition. We put out posters about how your local neighborhood goon was bringing wealth to the community, books (*Crime and You: A Survey of How Law-Breaking Helps the Less Fortunate*), children's literature (*See Jane Stab Dick in the Shin So She Can Take His Candy Bar)*, short films (*Johnny, Where Would You Be Without Crime?*), and magazines (*True, Inspirational Crime Stories*). We even released a feature film starring Miss Spiraci titled *Crime Sure Does Pay and How with No Consequences Whatsoever*. The title was later shortened to *City Story*.
- On numerous occasions, I was assigned to speak to groups of thousands of henchmen in an attempt to "rally" them into action for numerous operations, many of which involved confronting the vigilantes who had assembled to form the League of Right Rightness and challenge the Association. The League was led by Dr. Blattarius's longtime nemesis Mr. Wonderful,

a particularly unpleasant and toothy man who loved posing. If there's one thing both Dr. Blattarius and I completely agreed upon, it was our hatred of that guy. Some of the League's other members, like Magma Maven, The Human Crab, LargeHugeman, and Lady Sabledusk were tolerable, if often very annoying, but Mr. Wonderful was an obnoxious and persistent thorn in our side. Our conflicts began when the League got involved in putting a stop to some low-level larceny operations we carried out for funding purposes, and then escalated from there to the point where about half our operations were aimed specifically at doing harm to the League itself. It was my job to send henchmen into the fray to get pummeled by people who could punch them all the way to the moon. It wasn't easy.

- In the operations in which it was not my job to do any motivational speaking, I was often tasked with serving as wheelman; whether that meant quite literally sitting outside a bank in an idling car waiting for a group of masked teammates to run outside and hop in so I could drive them away, staying in a motorboat while a group performed an outsiders' mutiny on a cruise ship, or keeping the propellers spinning on a biplane while some of the higher-up members of the Association performed coups in small nations and principalities that we made into Association strongholds. I learned how to drive or pilot many, many different types of vehicles in some fairly strenuous on-the-job training, make no mistake about it.

The few times I did get to see Dr. Blattarius during my decade of servitude, he made sure to let me know what my place was in his eyes. In the event of a particularly valuable Association victory—say, for instance, we would kidnap Large-Hugeman, which happened with some regularity, despite and possibly because of the fact that he was both large and huge—the Association's board of directors would assemble for some manner of celebratory meal. We would gather in the Association's large conference room in the hovering headquarters and take in a lunch. Though I was a certified member of the board, I would always be tasked with arranging and serving the lunch. Of course, the henchmen would do most of the heavy lifting, serving the meal to the attendees, but Dr. Blattarius ensured that I personally served his meal to him, as a means of making certain that I "stayed humble." And he would know if I tried to poison it or spit in it or rub dirt in his mashed potatoes. He always seemed to know. It was humiliating more than humbling. I hated him for it, and he knew it.

Sometime in the summer of 1939, I was "promoted" from being a mere "associate" and board member within the organization and was given the prestigious title of "supervillain." Or, at least, the Association wanted to make it seem prestigious. Really, it was a branding maneuver

Not sure I want to go this far behind the curtain.

aimed at keeping up with our competition. You see, about a year earlier, members of the League of Right Rightness had started calling themselves "superheroes." Or someone did, anyway. Maybe it was those prevaricators at all the newspapers. That could be why we were kidnapping reporters left and right and people in capes were constantly showing up to save them. It's difficult to say. Either way, the term "superhero" was catching on and we needed to show ourselves in a similar light. If these bright-smiling fools and attention-seekers could somehow live up to the term "super," then posolutely we could as well.

Who even uses this word? After you're gone, no one will.

Though my title changed, in practice, my day-to-day work stayed all but indistinguishable from what it had been. My days still consisted of overseeing fighting tournaments and giving speeches to henchmen. However, in my last year working with the Association, I did manage to work on a few big projects with Miss Spiraci. I will say I'm proud of those. One plan involved turning the Caspian Sea into a gelatin so that no one could use it for any purpose, which went quite swimmingly. Another time we managed to replace the mayor of Montgomery, Alabama, with a brainwashed horse.[30] I daresay those were convivial times.

But for the most part, my station in life was not improving and I knew it wouldn't if I allowed

---

30 According to numerous polls, the horse was by far the most popular mayor the city ever had. People liked that he seemed to stay out of their business and push for mostly hay-based initiatives. People loved him, at least until the day he set off a device that turned roughly one-fourth of the rest of the city's population into horses, too. It was all part of a big plan we had to turn people into horses. I'm a little hazy on all the details as to why we thought it was a worthwhile idea. What's important is we did it.

things to continue as they had for the past decade. With that in mind, in March of 1941, I decided to go into business for myself while on one of my many wheelman missions. While a group of henchmen attempted to reword the Magna Carta to make it specifically about law-breakers in masks and hoods instead of anti-royalist rebels, I was absconding with a seaplane toward my own destination, somewhere I believed Dr. Blattarius would never be able to find me. It was a much-hidden university deep within the Marianas Trench. There, I would finally get the credentials I knew I deserved, and with them, Dr. Blattarius's respect, whether he wanted to give it to me or not. I would force it out of him.

Letters Exchanged Between King Oblivion Ph.D. and Literary/Entertainment Agent Morris Williams of Morris Williams Agency

King Oblivion, Ph.D.
Undisclosed Location
Deep Underground
Nowhere, XX 00000

April 6, 2010
Morris Williams
c/o Morris Williams Agency
9 Sunrise Way
Los Angeles, CA 90012

Dear Mr. Williams,

Though my name already carries considerable weight and inspires complete terror in anyone who dares hear or utter it, it has recently come to my attention that I may require some sort of agency representation in my quest to publish my memoirs the way I would like to have them published. This, obviously, is where you would come in.

Certainly I could simply invade a publishing house, ransack it, and force those left among the living to assemble my autobiography into the perennial bestseller it is destined to be (I assume it will be read in all schools, at every grade, for the next thousand years, at the very least). But if at all possible, I would prefer to do this task legitimately; to show those corners of society that look down on the hallowed profession of supervillainy that it is as valid a calling as any.

Therein is where a key problem lies. For the most part, publishers seem to be ignoring my query letters (at their peril, I assure you). My associates and advisors have informed me that acquiring the services of a high-level literary agent such as yourself would resolve such issues. Thus, I am bestowing upon you the great favor of allowing you to represent me to the Penguin Houses and Random Books of the world.

All I really need you to do is serve as a foot in the door for me to get the attention of some actual editors rather than their snotty, unpaid intern assistants who do nothing but send me form letters. Once that has occurred, the editors will be so awed and inspired by my presence that a book deal of a few hundred million dollars should not be far behind.

You look forward to working with me.

Mwa-ha-ha,
King Oblivion, Ph.D.

. . .

King Oblivion, Ph.D.
Undisclosed Location
Deep Underground
Nowhere, XX 00000

April 14, 2010
Morris Williams
c/o Morris Williams Agency
9 Sunrise Way
Los Angeles, CA 90012

Dear Mr. Williams,

I must say I am rather upset to have not received any return correspondence from you in regards to my letter sent on

April 6. This is no time to dally. Only upon choosing to represent me, thus making my presence known to the biggest publishing houses in the world, can you begin your charge to the biggest payday you have ever seen in your measly career.

Of course, we would have to negotiate your cut. My understanding is that agents generally take 15 percent of an author's royalties, which I suppose is fine for the undignified ink-slingers of the world of popular fiction. But of course, considering my title and significant stature, I'm sure you'll settle for . . . half a percent? Perhaps 1 percent, but that's as high as I'll go, and probably enough to keep you in cardigans or whatever it is you agents wear for the rest of your life.

A life that will be shortened significantly if you do not reply promptly, I should add. As I noted previously, you look forward to working with me.

Mwa-ha-ha,
King Oblivion, Ph.D.

. . .

Morris Williams
Morris Williams Agency
9 Sunrise Way
Los Angeles, CA 90012

April 20, 2010
King Oblivion, Ph.D.
Undisclosed Location
Deep Underground
Nowhere, XX 00000

Mr. Oblivion,

I have received your letters requesting representation and I feel compelled to let you know that I have notified the proper authorities to inform them that you have threatened my life and well-being.

We here at Morris Williams Agency do not and will not tolerate threats from anyone, nor do we deem it appropriate to work with known criminals and murderers. Given your one-time level of fame and notoriety, I assume any number of publishers would be willing to work with you on your memoirs, but our ethical standards simply cannot permit us to associate our agency with your name and reputation.

This is the last you will be hearing from me on this matter.

Sincerely,
Morris Williams

. . .

King Oblivion, Ph.D.
Undisclosed Location
Deep Underground
Nowhere, XX 00000

April 24, 2010
Morris Williams
c/o Morris Williams Agency
9 Sunrise Way
Los Angeles, CA 90012

Mr. Williams,

I would call your response an insult, but that would be an insult to insults.

First of all, "Mr. Oblivion?" Sir, you are addressing both a doctor *and* a king. I demand that my titles be used with the respect that is due me. (And trust me, very much respect is due me.)

Second, you're going to call the "authorities" on me? Which authorities? The FBI? CIA? DIA? NSA? Interpol? The UN? The Secret Space Police? You don't think that all those organizations and more haven't been gunning for me for decades? You think a call from some two-bit entertainment agency is going to really crack their investigations wide open? What a laughable notion.

Third, what a load of hypocritical garbage with this whole "we can't sully our name with a *criminal*" business. If I'm not mistaken, don't you represent C. P. Griffin, the baseball star who killed his wife, yet was acquitted of the murder? Wasn't he going to publish a book titled *Hey, So What If I Did Kill Her? Wouldn't That Be Wild?* Or what about the dozens of celebrities who have been in and out of jail for drugs and various other petty crimes in the spans of their careers? They're not criminals to you?

What a load. What a crock. What a hypocrite you are. I hope you're proud of the crater where your agency's Los Angeles offices used to be, because that's soon all that will be there. Why don't you tell your "authorities" about that, huh?

Mwa-ha-ha,
King Oblivion, Ph.D.

Editor's Note: The following seems to be a job application of sorts for anyone seeking entry into the International Society of Supervillains' ranks, most likely to start as a henchman. I can only venture guesses as to why King Oblivion would have included one of these forms in his various notes inside the "Choosing the One" file. One suspicion I have is that he would occasionally refer back to these documents when looking to promote underlings, since many of the prompts attempt to dig into the respondents' work ethic and mentality. I assume he would look to these replies as evidence that someone was either simply a cog in a machine or had leadership potential. Since he made it clear this memoir was intended as a means of finding a successor, perhaps he was looking for someone to fill this out and shine.

Starting Evil at Entry Level

In the space below, please fill in your name, date of birth, and the number of people you have pushed into a thresher at one time or another:

Fill out the following space with your work history, which should include all full-time, part-time, and temporary positions, as well as prison time, any jobs that were strictly "off the books," and work that was erased from history via time travel:

Give us an overview of your educational history, including documentation of schools you have vaporized throughout your career:

On a scale from 1 to 5, ranging from "very inappropriate" to "very appropriate," rank the following scenario:

> *Your boss comes to your cubicle and tells you that he needs you to work over the weekend because of some big, upcoming deadlines at corpo-*

rate. You tell him that you're happy to do so and work a strenuous twenty hours over Saturday and Sunday with no complaints.

On a scale from 1 to 5, ranging from "very inappropriate" to "very appropriate," rank the following scenario:

Your boss comes to your cubicle and tells you that he needs you to work over the weekend because of some big, upcoming deadlines at corporate. You tell him that you're happy to do so, but fail to show up for work over the weekend, instead going out to party and drink.

On a scale from 1 to 5, ranging from "very inappropriate" to "very appropriate," rank the following scenario:

Your boss comes to your cubicle and tells you that he needs you to work over the weekend because of some big, upcoming deadlines at corporate. You punch him straight in his lying, glad-handing mouth and tell him, "Hey, kiddo, why don't you *work this weekend?"*

On a scale from 1 to 5, ranging from "very inappropriate" to "very appropriate," rank the following scenario:

Your boss comes to your cubicle and tells you that he needs you to work over the weekend because of some big, upcoming deadlines at corporate. In response, you come into work and put in twenty hours over Saturday and Sunday, but instead of doing the work you were assigned, you set booby traps in the offices of your boss and the coworkers you don't like, designed to cause sharpened logs to swing down from the ceiling and impale them the moment they sit down in their chairs.

Please provide three references, with contact information. Previous employers and mortal enemies preferred.

In 500 words or less, explain why you would like to be employed by the International Society of Supervillains. Be sure to highlight any specific mangling, wrangling, or strangling skills you could bring to the organization, and explain why you think those skills would be of use.

Villainspiration

The villain: The Riddler
Key trait: Edward Nygma possesses a genius-level intellect to craft complex puzzles.
How he uses it: The Riddler emerged from relative obscurity—a student in a puzzle contest, and later a carnival employee—to become one of the most famous supervillains in the world. How did he do it? By simply stepping up from his low station as a two-bit con man and challenging Batman to a battle of wits, which is what he's been doing ever since.
The wrong takeaways: Though Riddler used the skills at his disposal to jump from the position of low-level grifter to full-on supervillain, he also often gets in his own way by committing too deeply to the gimmick instead of going for the jugular. Don't get so wrapped up in your shtick that you forget your goal.

Chapter 7

DARK DOCTORATE

In the impulsive hastiness of my departure from the Association to the university in the Marianas Trench, I found myself in a bit of a quandary as I made my journey. Namely, I lacked the requisite maps and other navigational tools one would typically need to plot out an airborne adventure.

Of course, I had (and have) an absolutely impeccable sense of direction, so invariably I did eventually locate the trench's location. But it took a little longer than it typically would have if I had the tools of an average pilot. The trench is all but impossible to identify from the sky; the water is barely a different color. I arrived in the area of the trench just around dusk on March 13, 1941.

Not for me.

You may harbor some inquisitiveness about how I discovered this hidden university below the ocean to begin with. Naturally, you should believe that I could attain such information with little to no effort given my inimitable natural charisma and persuasive powers, but I'll indulge

I'm going to feed you that thesaurus.

you. Roundabout the fall of 1938, I heard someone in one of the Association's massive post-victory board meetings—the ones at which I was indentured into serving meals for Dr. Blattarius, I'll remind you—mention that a group of academics within the organization had broken away to found a "college of the pernicious arts" in a secret location to which this particular speaker (a crime boss and part-time professional wrestler named Gimmick McGimmick) had not been made privy.

Though he was a wonder when it came to performing Irish whips, McGimmick was not the most astute gatherer of intelligence, so I took it upon myself to dig deeper. Even then I was starting to grow restless in my position in the Association and was combing through ways to expand my career options.

I was cognizant of the notion that making inquiries around the headquarters myself would arouse suspicion and in all likelihood cause Dr. Blattarius to intercept any future escape attempts on my part. So after the gathering, I pulled McGimmick into a small meeting room where he and I could chat privately. I told him outright that I overheard the chatter about this new, secret university. Then I pivoted into a bit of subterfuge. I informed McGimmick that Dr. Blattarius had put me in charge of sniffing out this unsanctioned operation—unofficially, of course; we couldn't risk setting off too many alarms—and that I could use his help in discovering its location.

I can believe you knew this one. Sort of. But I've got my eye on you. I have eyes everywhere.

McGimmick fell for it completely and offered up this additional bit of info: one of the people who had forsaken the Association to launch the new educational endeavor was The Sponge, a sentient human/sponge hybrid created through an experiment by Dr. Blattarius some thirty years earlier. In addition to having all the physical properties of a sponge, The Sponge had an amazing ability to absorb information and knowledge. So it made perfect sense that she would be the one to have started an underwater learning institution.

One of The Sponge's associates that I knew was still hanging around at the floating headquarters was Nicky Claws, a gangster who had lobster claws and dressed like Santa. I cautiously asked McGimmick to shake him down for info.

I don't "try," I "do."

"You can work him, can't you?" I asked, trying to speak the wrestler's carny language. "Just tell him a story. Doesn't have to be anything suspicious. We just want to find out where it is because we're curious, right? I'm shootin' with you here."

McGimmick agreed and came up with some nonsense about how his nephew was looking for a way to build up his malevolent credibility before applying to join the Association. I told him that idea should work and we tracked down Nicky Claws in an office in Concourse A. McGimmick laid his story on him and asked for just a little hint as to the new school's location. Nicky hesitated for a bit, but eventually gave this clue: "Well, let's just say it's a place for *deep thinkers*."

Of course, he thought he was being clever, but it was instantly beyond obvious that the university was located in the deepest point on the planet. I knew immediately; McGimmick had no idea. I had executed my plan to perfection.

You say this as if there is any other possible outcome.

Even then, it'd be another two-and-a-half years before I had enough leeway to get halfway across the world and make my attempt to insinuate myself into the university. Dr. Blattarius tended to keep me on a very short leash, often tasking Miss Spiraci with ensuring I didn't go running off to get away from him. On more than one occasion, she had to run me down, tranquilize me, and return back to the hovering Association headquarters. But in recent weeks, Miss Spiraci had been assigned to fewer of the same jobs as me. Soon after, I saw my opportunity.

And there I was, passing back and forth over the trench in my plane, trying to get a handle on just how to enter this hidden university under the waves. After numerous passes that led to little in the way of enlightenment, I eventually set my bird down in Guam and decided to take a peregrination out to the trench by boat.[31]

Pushing it with this one.

Sitting out on the water in a seafaring vessel wasn't terribly different from passing over in an airborne one, though I at least had the benefit of being able to sit in one place while I pondered how I would plunge some 30,000 feet under the surface. My first instinct was to yell, and so I did. I shouted and shouted. "I want to go to your school!" I would scream. "I demand to be let into this college!" Even with the immense, booming

31 Getting a boat was easy. I simply walked over to the marina and tipped a fisherman out of his trawler. And just like that, I had a boat.

power of my voice, my vociferations didn't seem to be yielding much in the way of a response.

After a few attempts to get someone's attention by slapping the water with a paddle, I progressed to the next and only logical step: getting inside a diving bell and descending into the depths. This was no time for hesitation or fear; I had come here to get into this secret college and, by evil, I was going to get into this secret college.

I had—because I always think ahead—made sure to snag a trawler with a bellows and diving bell on board, and luckily there was one back in Guam that fit the bill. There was just one problem: no one was around to actually lower me into the water. I would have to go back to the shore and coerce someone into assisting me. I initially figured that the fisherman I had originally pushed into the bay to steal his boat was a suitable candidate. After all, I had intimidated him plenty already. But by the time I arrived back, he was gone. In fact, since it was the dead of night, almost no one was there. Just a seventeen-year-old boy named Tasi, who told me unprompted that his name meant "ocean" in Guam's Chamorro language. I summated those credentials were as valid as any for an assistant I could boss around. I commanded him to come to the water and lower me in while working the bellows. He obliged with little need for coercion.

We travailed back out to the trench and I encapsulated myself in the bell. Tasi slowly lowered me into the water and I sank further and further into the depths, the visibility growing ever more faint the further I cascaded into the cerulean deep. At about 40 feet down I could feel the pressure tie around me like a vise. That was just about as far down as the bell could go, so Tasi took over at the bellows while I set to work, trying to see what I could in the trench below. In brief, it was very little. Just a swath of sapphiric darkness stretching out into infinity. After a few minutes of examining my surroundings and once again calling out for the school's administrators, specifically The Sponge, I decided it was time for a new approach and tugged on the cable. Tasi responded quickly (lucky for him) and soon enough I was back on deck trying desperately to make my ears pop.

While I racked my brain to determine my next move, I ordered Tasi to retreat into the galley and make me a cup of tea. He obliged and upon his return offered up an interrogatory I wasn't anticipating: "What are you doing here, anyway, masked man?"

I didn't exactly owe him an answer—I consider all work done on my behalf to be compensated for by my simply allowing someone to continue existing in my very presence—but I admired his audacity at deigning to make such an inquiry of a figure as imposing as me, so I indulged him. I struggled to speak so he'd understand.

"There's a university. A school. Here, under the water. Way down below in the trench. I want to go there to earn a title to force a man who didn't respect me to come to the realization I'm his equal. Then, he'll have a moment of understanding that I'm his superior. I am smarter, more powerful, stronger, and more worthy of respect than he is."

"You don't say?" Tasi asked. "I took you for one of the explorers that comes down here all the time and tries to find the secrets of the trench by only diving about 20 feet into it. And by the way, you don't have to talk down to me, or talk slow for me. I understand everything you're saying. Just say what you're going to say."

Again, I admired his chutzpah. "If you insist. I'm looking for the way down to the university. As I said, I want to enroll, but I haven't determined exactly how to enter the place yet, let alone be admitted."

"Oh, is that all?" Tasi asked with a grin. "All you have to do is take the elevator."

I looked at him incredulously. "Elevator? How would you know about a thing like that?"

"Oh, easy," Tasi said. "I'm a student. I come up and help weirdoes dive into the ocean in these clunky diving bells for fun. I like screwing around with people."

Perhaps I had misjudged Tasi, who told me as we rode back to shore that his name was not, in fact, Tasi at all. That was just a feint to trick would-be adventurers into letting him toy with their lives every now and again. He wasn't even from Guam. He was Hawaiian. His preferred name among friends, he said, was The Beguiler, which is something he rarely told anyone. But he respected my near-irrational desire to shove an achievement in someone's face.

We agreed: Spite is the most powerful force in the universe if you want it to be.

When we got to shore once again, The Beguiler led me through a small patch of bushes into an alcove with a rushing waterfall. He walked straight through the tumbling aqua pura into a small cave. I followed. The Beguiler led me through a complex maze inside the cave until we eventually reached a large chamber with two lines of four torches each. They were all lit. On the wall were four symbols: a giant sea turtle, a chimpanzee, a lizard, and a spider.

The Beguiler asked me what I thought the room was for.

"It's a test, I suppose? I'd guess four of these torches correspond to the four symbols on the walls. We extinguish those torches in a particular order and a passage opens to the next room. We used to have to do a lot of this kind of thing back at my old school, so I have an eye for this kind of stuff."

The Beguiler laughed. "Very clever! That's what you're supposed to think. But it's all a bunch of bullshit." He grabbed one of the torches out of its sconce and heaved it across the room at the back wall, which burned away like a dried-out bed sheet.

"Sometimes you just have to burn something," he said.

Behind that obstacle was a wall with a riddle written on it:

> "What is both a drink and an action, a forceful fist motion and a fruity concoction?"

We didn't even bother to answer and punched through the wall in unison to reveal, finally, the elevator.

The Beguiler and I ambulated onto the cramped elevator and he impelled the button to send us on our way toward the facility deep below. I asked him how long the ride typically took. He grinned.

"Two hours or so."

So there we stood on that elevator for two hours as we descended some 30,000 feet down. I told him a little bit more about my history with Dr. Blattarius and the Association, though I was circumspect in terms of what I gave away and where my allegiances truly fell. I wasn't sure what connections the school still had to the university, if any. He described some of the more entertaining times he took would-be explorers out on the water. Like one time, he left a guy out in the diving bell for an entire night, pumping the bellows for him only occasionally. I reveled in that particular story.

After about ninety minutes, I asked The Beguiler how he, the other students, and the faculty managed to take the trip up and down in the elevator so many times.

"You get used to it, kind of," he offered. "Or maybe you don't. To be honest, I'm the only one here who really ever leaves all that often."

After a few more minutes of silence, we eventually heard the ding that indicated we had arrived. The doors parted and we stepped out into a massive atrium with windows that offered a view of the ocean outside. Massive creatures, unlike anything I'd ever seen or even heard about, swam by. Some had the ability to light up or change their appearance, a few had multiple heads, and others were as large as any skyscraper. The room itself contained numerous spiral staircases leading up to walkways that directed visitors to various labeled areas: student housing, student union, library, classrooms, and so on. A banner hung down that read WELCOME TO OCEAN TRENCH FORTRESS UNIVERSITY.

The Beguiler led me up the staircase that opened up into the "admissions" area and waved me toward the door. "There you go. I'm heading back up to help out some more explorers. I'm sure I'll see you around." He gave me a little salute and sauntered off back to the elevator.

I turned and cantered down the corridor toward the single door in the admissions area labeled DEAN OF NEW STUDENTS. I walked in to find a tiny office, cluttered with papers in every corner. Behind a Lilliputian desk sat a huge figure in full-body black armor. The only unarmored area of his body was his head, out of which sprouted a mane of white hair. His alabaster beard was nearly as long as his hair. A pair of red wings peeked out from behind his back. He was squeezed in tighter than I could imagine behind that desk. He was typing away, key by key, with his huge fingers on a typewriter that looked like it was for someone half his size. It looked like it was for a child version of him.

I would never canter. Get that straight.

Erebus would not be pleased to see this.

On his desk was a nameplate that read EREBUS. I wondered if he was the actual Greek primordial deity of darkness, but I decided not to dally with unnecessary details.

"I'm here to apply to the university," I said. "You'll accept me, so let's dispense with the formalities."

The elephantine man in the black armor looked up from his typing for the first time since I entered the room and scrutinized me up and down. "And why should we accept you?" he asked. "What have *you* done?"

"I'm one of the first people to ever hold the title of supervillain," I said. "I have conquered death. Without me, the Western Association of Ruffians would have collapsed many times over. I was the cornerstone of the group that carried out the St. Valentine's Day Massacre. Need I continue?"

Erebus scoffed. "Is that all you've done? We only take the very exceptional here. Get on the elevator and go back home to the Association. Take your job back there." He turned back to his typing.

"I won't go back there," I said, giving up any pretense of still having loyalty to the Association. "Not until I have a degree from here that I can grind into Dr. Blattarius's ugly cockroach face. That's the only way this ends."

Erebus looked up again. He squinted at me, then stood up.

"I'll be back in a minute," he said. He stomped out the door.

I stood around for about twenty minutes, and eventually Erebus returned with none other than The Sponge herself. Erebus gestured toward me before sitting back down at his desk and resuming his typing. "That's him," he said.

The Sponge instantly recognized me. "So you're here to stick it to Blattarius, huh? Well, all right then. Welcome to the doctoral program."

We left Erebus and headed to The Sponge's office. Her official title was president, and I later found out that she was the sole founder of the school. McGimmick had been misinformed about others engendering it with her. Her office was a sight to behold. A massive chamber with a domed ceiling, gilded with gold. The room had multiple fountains. Her desk was gargantuan and elevated several feet above the chairs that were set out for visitors. The message here was clear, especially when one compared this office to Erebus's cramped workspace: she was in charge.

We reviewed the various doctoral tracks I could take—the physiology of pain, the scheming arts, trickery, jackbooting, the mad sciences, nefariology, explodery, misinformation and mind control, fearspreading, illegitimate business management, firestarting, icy dispositionry, bloodletting, transmogrification, macrodestructiveness, and, of course, economics: the dismal science. I chose the most general of the bunch, nefariology, because I wanted to do it all. I would master every aspect of villainy.

It would take me four years to finish the program, but I pulled it off. As The Sponge's evaluation of my progress concluded:

> Mr. Oblivion has shown an extraordinary aptitude for every avenue of the evil arts and sciences, from creating panics to synthesizing monstrosities in laboratories to squashing the

> hopes of the heroically minded. His doctoral dissertation is the most thorough and well-researched thesis I have seen from any student in the short history of this university, and one that I can't foresee anyone topping for years to come. He will truly be a great supervillain.
>
> And I say this as a supervillain myself. Typically, I have nothing but the most negative things to say in these evaluations because I so deeply believe in the bad-making power of negativity. But, in this case, I simply cannot bring myself to denigrate this fine student's work. I am impressed more than I can say.

The dissertation The Sponge mentioned in her evaluation took me my entire last year to prepare. It was called "The Bendable Land: I Will Reshape the Country of New Zealand Using Magnets." The actual paper was more than 200 pages of theoretical science about how one could bend an island nation with the use of undersea and flying electromagnets. It also included reams of documentation about how annoying I found the way New Zealanders pronounce vowels. I wanted to punish them for that.

In the end, and with a lot of investment in thousands of magnets, we shockingly did manage to not only bend New Zealand, but actually snap it into two new islands. It was a hell of an achievement.

You may be wondering why I chose to attempt to rectify a pet peeve with my dissertation rather than formulate a plan to get revenge on Dr. Blattarius. First off, how dare you question my actions?

Second, I can let you know that it was something I initially considered. It was only on the advice of The Sponge, who made quite a personal investment in my education at the university, that I held off. She explained that it would be more satisfying to comminute Dr. Blattarius into dust on my own than it would with the backing of the university.[32] Beyond that, putting an end to Dr. Blattarius now would prevent me from having the opportunity to rub my success in his face. That was what I came to the university for, after all.

Who would know this word? Who? Certainly not you. You are a fool.

And so, on May 19, 1945, I walked across the stage at the second-ever graduation ceremony at Ocean Trench Fortress University and received my doctorate in Nefariology. My name was complete: King Oblivion, Ph.D.

I shook The Sponge's hand and debouched to the elevator. Some two hours later I found myself back out on a beach I hadn't seen in years.[33] I said farewell to The Beguiler, that year's only other graduate (the academic standards at the university were very high, and also many students died in an attack I'll explain shortly) and told him to come work for me sometime.

Debauched? Sure. Debouched? Never in your wildest dreams.

I jumped back on my plane, but not to return to the Association's hovering headquarters. There was still proving to do yet.

To some. Not to most.

32 Also, and she never said this, but it was my suspicion that she preferred not to bring the university into our personal conflict. She wanted to keep it running, as it was, without fear of retaliation from a massive supervillain organization. Prudent, if a bit cowardly.

33 I placed and operated the magnets that broke New Zealand remotely, both using robotic machinery and henchmen to place and power them up.

Email Correspondence Between King Oblivion, Ph.D. and Tamina Stony, Ghostwriter of "The Young Dastard" and "Dark Doctorate"

From: King Oblivion, Ph.D.
To: Tamina Stony
Subject: Word choices

Miss Stony,

I have one simple question for you: Are you using a thesaurus every few words to write these chapters?

. . .

From: Tamina Stony
To: King Oblivion, Ph.D.
Subject: RE: Word choices

Exalted one,

I'll address your simple question with a rudimentary answer: Affirmative. I postulate that the use of superior vocabulary in your missives will vouchsafe upon you an ostensible degree of potentiality and potency.

I am sanguine that you will subscribe to that belief as well.

. . .

From: King Oblivion, Ph.D.
To: Tamina Stony
Subject: RE: Word choices

Is that so, Miss Stony? You're "sanguine" about it?

Well, I do have to give you credit for an astute word choice there. You'll soon be sanguine when my sword team arrives to lacerate, cut, stab, snip, slash, slit, cleave, carve, dissect, and chop you.

Salutations.

My Second Death

You may have put two and two together and realized that I spent the entirety of the Second World War secluded in a university tucked deep, deep underwater instead of participating in the conflict between the Axis and the Allies. In part, this was merely a coincidence—it just so happened to be the point in my life in which I needed to turn away from the world and earn the distinction of being a Ph.D. Yet even if I hadn't been inclined to gain a title I already so richly deserved, I would have done all I could to remain out of the fray.

I tend to shy away from strict political or philosophical ideology. I would never carry out a plan to be part of some moral crusade or cleanse the world of a force I believed to be distasteful or unclean—except superheroes, who deserved to be eradicated. I'm only in this game to rightly and consistently prove that I am the most powerful, intelligent, respected leader in the world, the galaxy, the universe, and beyond. All should bow to me. I have no interest in proving anything else. (So if I was going to wipe anyone out, it would be quite pointedly anyone who disagreed with that.)

Of course, not all supervillains agree with that standpoint, and many participated in the war for both sides. Certainly more took the side of the Axis, which gave them carte blanche to develop hyper-intelligent killer monkeys, Hitler's famous robotic body suit, underwater lasers, giant magnifying glasses that caused numerous fires in London, gas-powered marching machines that led soldiers into battle, weaponized candy, deadly jokes, and so on. But then on the Allies' side you had people creating serums that birthed super soldiers, FDR's steam-powered flying wheelchair, and the giant jet engines that sent Berlin into space for a day near the end of the war.[34] Those were all mad scientists doing that stuff. Who else would you expect? And of course, you had people building nuclear bombs. Only supervillains could make that happen.

Indeed, it was quite a boon to my educational aspirations that the war was going on in the midst of my studies, as it kept the Association busy to the point that virtually no one came looking for me at Dr. Blattarius's behest. Surely more would have come to forcibly remove me from the university if they hadn't been busy helping one side or another build killing machinery or death monsters.

But, as I said, I opted to remove myself from the whole proceeding of the war. Yet that didn't stop me from getting dragged into it anyway. In the summer of 1943, just as I was proposing my dissertation to The Sponge, the university was breached and flooded by a group of Allied superheroes who called themselves the Infiltrators. There was Mr. Wonderful, who I have mentioned before and who was absolutely and infuriatingly gross and reprehensible; The Human Fish; Namotto, The Man Who Was Fire, and Madam Speaker, a woman whose body was made of phonograph horns and radio wire. The Sponge, sponge that she was, impressively managed to soak up much of the encroaching water in time for other faculty members and students to patch up the hole the Infiltrators left in the outer wall of the building. (Numerous students were nonetheless crushed in the deluge while several others were eaten by a carnivorous whale-like monster that got in.) The Infiltrators had mistaken the University for a secret Axis base, and it took some three hours for us to convince them that we were performing an entirely different, much more academic evil there, and shouldn't be a priority for them if their focus was on the war.

---

34 A lot more happened in World War II than the history textbooks would have you believe.

Unfortunately, they were not able to keep Namotto, The Man Who Was Fire—who always had a bit of an unusual moral compass for a superhero—from incinerating me on the spot.[35] I was holding my dissertation proposal, but he mistook it for "secret Axis death codes." Soon after I was incinerated, the hero team made its exit, leaving yet another hole in the wall that had to be patched (or so I'm told). They say they're "just" people, but they're the most inconsiderate assholes on Earth.

Lucky for me that Namotto merely incinerated my body and not my head, and that there was an on-campus cloning lab where The Sponge could oversee the development of a clone body in which my brain would be placed. More specifically, they took my intact head and stitched it on the clone body, so as to preserve my mask. (My cloak, which actually would have protected me from the attack because it makes me impervious to fire, was in my quarters, so it was just placed on my new body.)

I was eventually restored (with about 25 pounds of additional muscle, so that was a bonus), but it did lengthen my stay at the university by a full year, postponing my graduation. I'd never forgive Namotto for that. Never.

35 He flipped back and forth between the hero and villain side numerous times over the years.

Villainspiration

The villain: Doctor Sivana
Key trait: Thaddeus Bodog Sivana used his doctoral genius to devise and invent numerous ways to destroy Captain Marvel and his family.
How he uses it: Dr. Sivana created countless plans meant to end the smiling wholesomeness of the Marvel Family, but perhaps none is more impressive than putting together a coalition of versions of himself from throughout the multiverse to storm the Marvel Family's Rock of Eternity.
The wrong takeaways: Working with other villains, even if they're you, can be tricky. Sivana eventually found himself betrayed by his other selves. Don't allow this to happen to you.

Chapter 8

THE SCOUNDREL KING

My plan to spite Dr. Blattarius with villainous credentials was half complete, but I needed more. I needed to show him that I wasn't only his equal or superior in terms of intellectual endeavor. I felt compelled to prove that I could also hold a position of authority higher than his.

[I would have to become royalty.]

I was already royalty; I just had to insist that everyone else recognize it.

This wasn't an idea that popped into my head out of nowhere. If anything, my parents placed it there at my birth. Naming me King set a path to liegedom from my first breath. I'm uncertain whether I placed the thought in their heads by the strength of my will in the womb or if they were looking to guide my life by the power of suggestion, but either way it was undoubtedly intentional. For some, a name is just a name. But not for me.

Beyond that, there are the simple logistics. Few positions of power come with lifetime guarantees. Presidents and prime ministers have term limits and often have to be elected by the *people* (ugh). No thank you. The people don't know what is correct for them and never will, because what is correct for them is to be moved around like game pieces on a board by my very hand. Dictators who seize power by force sometimes keep their titles for life, but they're often viewed as illegitimate and have to deal with the potential for coups and uprisings. Other governments eventually try to remove them. And sure, I could quash any little revolution that popped up, but is that really how I'd want to spend my time?

Let's add in some description of how strong my hand is here.

And sure, kings have to deal with uprisings and revolutions, but what stronger justification is there for wielding complete power than to say you were hand-selected by providence itself? Dictators only have martial force; kings have fate on their side. And I already had the name. It was monarchy all the way for me.

There was only one minor snag in my plan: it's very difficult to waltz unannounced into a sovereign nation and become king. Maybe back in the eleventh century or thereabouts I could up and walk into a throne room, run a sword through the guy wearing the biggest crown, and claim the monarchy for my own. But the twentieth century was quite obviously a different animal. Murdering a king would lead me to be pursued as a criminal rather than hailed as a great leader.[36] Some prince or other royal family jerk would take the

36 And the biggest tragedy here is that people wouldn't have recognized that I'm both. I'm the greatest there is or ever will be at both.

throne over the slayer of the king. Our priorities got way out of whack somewhere in there.

This seems like too inelegant a phrase for me. Revise.

I'd have to find another way to gain the title. Lucky for me, the time I was leaving Ocean Trench Fortress University was the opportune time to make something happen. World War II was coming to an end and many of the world's governments were destabilized to the point that just about anyone could swoop down and scoop up control just by saying a few perfectly calculated phrases and putting in a modicum of effort.

I don't need luck. These things happen by my will alone.

A few countries were so desperate for leadership that they were even advertising for it. At the university, I established a network of contacts throughout the globe which would alert me to various items of import that required my attention. Just before my graduation, I let The Sponge know that I would be looking for any monarchal openings throughout the world and for her to let me know if anything came across her desk. Within a week, she contacted me over my plane radio—I had been continually flying, only occasionally stopping in remote places to sleep and eat meals to keep out of the sights of the Association, which I was sure was on the hunt for me—to let me know that the tiny Eastern European nation of Explosia was in desperate need of leadership after the death of its king.[37] Its economy

37 Its last king had died in a cross-country trip. His carriage (the country did not get motorcars until I allowed it in 1992) had rolled just a little too quickly over a patch of the country's world-famous detonating soil, which contains very high levels of incredibly volatile nitroglycerin. That's how every previous king has died, and it's by far the leading cause of death in Explosia, where the average life expectancy is fourteen.

was collapsing and no one was around to restabilize it. The country was so desperate, in fact, that the Council of Elders, an elite group of men and women who had lived all the way into their thirties (when the life expectancy was half that), declared that the winner of Explosia's annual roshambo tournament would be the country's new monarch. The tournament would begin in February 1946, so I took several months to prepare.

First, I traveled to Explosia to get the lay of the land, as well as a sense of the country's culture. If I had to give you a quick *World Factbook* rundown of the nation's key traits, here are the main points of interest:

- Key export: Exploding dirt
- National sport: Roshambo (followed closely by covering one's head at any given moment because the dirt underneath him or her is exploding)
- Largest religion: Church of the Murderous Soil
- Major urban areas: Blast Radius City (capitol)
- Official language: Screamingese
- Currency: Explodollars
- Cash crop: Natural dynamite

As if I needed to spell it out for you, Explosia didn't have much going on beyond its murder dirt, so it didn't take me long to acclimate myself to the country and its very limited set of customs. To greet someone, you held your hands over your head and screamed. To take your leave, you held your hands over your head and screamed. If you were looking to congratulate someone on a new baby, you held your hands over your head and screamed. As you can tell, there wasn't a lot of variation in nonverbal communication. I also learned what was considered taboo: stomping and jumping.

I always come prepared, so I returned briefly to the university lab to work up a pair of hover-boots that would carry me anywhere and everywhere throughout Explosia without worry of any potential harm. I made sure to use them very discreetly in my travels, continuing to move my legs as if I were walking. Not that it would trouble me all that much to inspire jealousy and a feeling of inferiority in the people I was destined to rule, but because I was trying to keep a low profile because *they* did not yet know that I was set to rule them.

I spent a sum total of four months traveling the hills, valleys, and craters of Explosia and taking it all in. I watched a lot of people blow up. A lot.

In that time, I tried to make myself approachable so I could openly challenge people I came into contact with to quick rounds of roshambo, or as it's called in some parts of the world: rock-paper-scissors. Personally, I never much cared for the game, which requires one to give oneself over to chance and lose around half the time because no one weapon is any more powerful than another. Each option—the rock, the paper, the scissors—can be defeated by one other option and defeat another. What's a game

Must we explain the rules of the game? Is anyone unfamiliar with rock-paper-scissors?

Oh, yes. Idiots. Keep this as it is.

designed to give no advantage? To me, no game at all. Plus, matches are played in best two-out-of-three sets, which is an insult. If you lose once, you lose. Period.

Seems . . . perfunctory. A more impressive word would be preferable. "Invincible," maybe.

Yet it was Explosia's game of choice, and the only road to the title of king, so I set out to make myself the most proficient roshambo player in the world. I learned all the tells: the eye twitch that would precede virtually any player throwing "rock," the finger wag that would presage "scissors," the bend at the mouth and tiny wince one would always emit just before laying one's hand flat to indicate "paper." I also devised an amazing technique that involved simply asking someone what they were planning to throw on the "two" in "one, two, three, shoot." Nine out of ten times, believe it or not, they would tell me. The gullibility of people never ceases to astonish me.

It was actually probably even more common than lunch. Lunch wasn't as common as you might think.

One of the common customs of the land was to acquiesce any time someone issued a roshambo challenge, so I'd keep some poor souls playing for days and days until they collapsed to the ground, often exploding in the process. This was such a common occurrence that no one would even bat an eye at it, and certainly no one would think of prosecuting me for such a thing. Blowing up in Explosia was as common as lunch. Even so, to keep up appearances, I would make the broadest gestures pretending to help my opponent, asking for medics to come grab him or her up off the ground, whether in one piece or many. Again, I didn't want them to know that I'd soon be their ruler.

I don't like this idea that I "pretend" to do anything. Everything I do is real. Hyper-real!

Of course, the medics would themselves often explode. If they didn't, I would challenge one or more of them to multiple, repeated games of roshambo.

I didn't go and leave the fate of my kingship to the common people of Explosia, however. I knew that I would have to face down an expert, so I once again made use of my new information network to discover the name and location of the world champion in rock-paper-scissors, a Chilean woman by the name of Tijera de la Papelroca. Once I was satisfied with my reconnaissance in Explosia, I flew to the city of Punta Arenas and found Ms. Papelrocha essentially holding court in the middle of the city's central plaza, wowing a huge crowd with her rock-paper-scissors technique. She wasn't even playing anyone. She was just making rocks, paper, and scissors with her hands. The crowd was utterly wowed. They were mesmerized by her movements alone.

I stood back and watched as she kept the audience in rapt attention for hours. When the sun finally set, Ms. Papelrocha bowed to the assembled onlookers and informed them that the show had come to an end. As the crowd dispersed, I approached and informed her that I was an aspiring rock-paper-scissors enthusiast who wished to learn the secrets of the craft. I told her I had traveled many miles to find her and seek her out as a coach. In principle, all of that was demonstrably true.

Ms. Papelrocha smirked and informed me that she was flattered, but she was still an active competitor and as such wasn't looking to coach any aspiring roshambo superstars. I smiled back and said I suspected as much but respected her so much as an athlete that I felt compelled to give her a gift. I asked her if she would accept. After a brief moment of consideration, she said she'd take the gift.

I pulled a small box out of my pocket and handed it to her. I encouraged her to open it in my presence so I could see her reaction, and she did. In a flash of light and a puff of smoke, the box, which had been full of a highly concentrated compound I had developed in my doctoral research to shrink anyone who came into contact with it, was empty, and Ms. Papelrocha was now a mere two inches tall. I gently picked her up between my thumb and forefinger and placed her inside the box. I poked a hole in the top so she could breathe, slipped the box back into my pocket, and hopped back on my plane headed for a safe house I had set up in Hong Kong.

At the safe house, I explained the situation to Ms. Papelrocha. First, she would be my coach whether she liked it or not. I would place her inside an earpiece that would be attached over my right ear. From there, she would give me tips throughout the tournament. In the event that she refused to coach me on the fly, I would leave her in this shrunken state forever, leaving her unable to compete in rock-paper-scissors competitions until camera zoom technology improved greatly. And even then, how would she sign the contracts? What pen could she hold? She had no answer for this.

I figured she'd eventually cave, but even if she adamantly and unflinchingly refused to coach me, shrinking her played to my advantage. What would it benefit me to leave the world's foremost roshambo player in the mix, available to potentially participate in the Explosian tournament, primed to steal the monarchy away from me? Ms. Papelrocha said she had no interest in being the queen of Explosia, but that's just what someone who wanted to be queen would say, wouldn't it? Non-supervillains and their false modesty.

After about a day of making it very clear that I would only restore her to non-microscopic size if she agreed to my terms and helped me in the tournament, Ms. Papelrocha finally agreed. We spent the following weeks practicing until I had an eagle eye for even more tells, tics, and signs of a telegraphed throw. I also went out and stole a preserved, ancient eagle's eye from the Hong Kong Museum of History just in case that would help. I kept that eagle's eye for many years after, and I do think it helped me see things very clearly . . . not that I needed the help.

Pleased to see this here. You are finally learning how to correctly capture my voice.

The week of the tournament finally arrived, and Ms. Papelrocha and I set off for Explosia to formally register. I wouldn't let these last few months go to waste. I wouldn't let anyone prevent me from claiming victory in this tournament. With the exception of the woman whom I had shrunk to the size of a peanut and affixed to my head, no one on the planet could pose an adequate challenge.

[Also, I would cheat.]

Inaccurate. The current Explosia charter states that my technique is not only legal, but the most effective way to win the tournament.

You may have some familiarity with the concept of throwing "dynamite" to win a game of roshambo. If not, it's a move in which a player uses an unbeatable weapon. I invented that. But the version I created has been modified somewhat over the decades. Mine was no case of mere schoolyard bad sportsmanship; some silly hand gesture to indicate that I had no regard for abiding by the rules and strictures of sporting competition. It's true that I had no regard for abiding by the rules and strictures of sporting competition, but what I used wasn't just a gesture. I'd pull a live stick of dynamite out of a bag, quickly light it, toss it over toward my opponent, and make them explode. It's how I won rounds two, five, and seven of the tournament. I beat opponents one, three, four, and six in total shutouts with the help of Ms. Papelrocha, but two, five, and seven all managed to beat me in one game in a best-of-seven match. I wouldn't allow even that minor threat to put a stop to my kingly momentum.

"Help" is all wrong. If anything, I was helping her.

The beauty was that no one was the wiser. We were in a country where people exploded on the regular, all the time, every day. Maybe someone in the audience thought they caught a glimpse of a stick of dynamite floating through the air, but did they really? Could they be sure? Weren't they too busy watching to see whether I threw scissors again? Couldn't this random explosion be the same as any other, one of the dozens they had seen already that day? That speck of doubt was all I needed.

After seven rounds, the field of participants was whittled down (or blown up) from 500-some royal hopefuls to the final four: me, a twenty-year-old Explosia native named Asbestos Guarav (she was given the name because she was born with fire-retardant properties possibly obtained through osmosis), American roshambo champion Sonny Lithwick (whom Ms. Papelroca had beaten at the most recent World Finals), and a silly-looking superhero named One Step.

My semifinal match was against Mr. Lithwick, who had all the confidence in the world that he could defeat me. But Ms. Papelrocha had his number: "He only ever throws rock," she said. "It's his one move." So I triple papered him right out of the tournament. Honestly, I found it rather astonishing that anyone had ever managed to lose to him before. Apparently, Ms. Papelrocha was the only one that had ever figured out his strategy.

That victory thrust me into the finals against One Step, who made a request with the Council of Elders to get a few moments to speak to me before the match began. They granted it, and though I protested, he approached and started talking with that dumb superhero mouth of his.

"I know what you're doing here," he said as I tried to convince him I wasn't listening. "Other people may say that they can't be sure if they saw you throwing dynamite at your opponents, but I did. I saw it. I know. And I know you're a supervillain, with your mask and your cloak and your . . . dark aura. Well, you know why they call me One Step? Huh?"

I don't think we should include any direct quotes from any superheroes in my memoir. I find it distasteful.

I wordlessly gestured for him to continue, just so this would be over with.

"They call me One Step because I'm always a step ahead of everyone who crosses my path. I know the next thing that someone will do before even *they* do. It's how I got to the finals of this tournament. It's how I'm going to beat you, take control of this tragic nation, and hand over sovereignty to its people."

I just grinned and said, "Okay. If you say so," and motioned for One Step to go back to his side of the arena so we could finish up the tournament.

The match began. I threw rock. He got me with paper. I threw scissors. He rocked me. He really was one step ahead. He wasn't lying about those powers. He had me down two-nothing in mere seconds. So I pulled out the showstopper. On the next turn, I tossed a stick of dynamite his way.

We need to talk about this and the other mentions of me "losing."

Now I knew he would know that this was coming and would most likely try to dodge the explosion. I'm sure he was planning to take the opportunity to call me out for cheating. But it didn't go down like that. See, the arena was set up so there was only one strip of concrete going down the center of the floor, which is where the competitors stood during their match. Explosia as a country isn't particularly big on flooring. The work is too dangerous. So when I tossed the dynamite to One Step's right, he sidestepped to the left, directly onto a mound of exposed and extremely volatile Explosian dirt. One boom. A second boom. Game over.

One Step may have had the ability to predict what I was going to do, but he couldn't read the mind of a hunk of dirt. There's nothing to read. It's just dirt. And to think, One Step was laid waste with a single stride.

I was crowned king immediately thereafter (the act of placing the crown on my head effectively destroyed the arena, which was basically already a shambles). Everyone in attendance bowed to me, and I let out a hearty laugh that lasted for the next twenty minutes.

I would remain in Explosia for most of the next five years, overseeing a far-reaching renovation of the castle, which transformed it from what was a sad set of stone walls around a bare-dirt floor into a true palace worthy of serving as one of my homes.[38] I also set up the new Explosian military, which I established immediately as my personal security force. They all dressed exactly like me, so that any one of them could serve as a decoy at any given time.[39]

I also really, really got a kick out of watching people explode every day. It was an absolute ball.

---

38 This took most of the gross domestic product and many lives to complete, but take it from me. It was worth it.

39 Admittedly, I stole this idea from Dr. Blattarius. I never said he didn't have strong ideas.

Email Correspondence Between King Oblivion, Ph.D. and the International Society of Supervillains' Attorney, The Litigatron

From: The Litigatron
To: King Oblivion, Ph.D.
Subject: Legal concerns regarding memoir

King,

I just paged through the draft chapters of your memoir that came across my desk, and though I think it does much to exalt your glory, I do have to raise one concern about the number of historical crimes, felonies, and atrocities you're openly admitting to. I can work with a certain level of plausible deniability. I can always say that certain things are fictionalized or fluffed to a degree, but this is just an outright admission of guilt.

And some of this stuff . . . well, some of it I didn't even know you did. And I thought you told me everything.

I'd advise scaling back.

. . .

From: King Oblivion, Ph.D.
To: The Litigatron
Subject: RE: Legal concerns regarding memoir

Litigatron,

My dear friend. So happy to hear from you, as always. You know very well that we've worked together for some five decades now and that I value your input above many of my other advisors. You're one of a chosen few who can tell me the unvarnished truth without suffering my wrath.

But know this: If you do anything to change even a single word, a single letter, of this memoir, you'll be practicing law from the inside of a jar. Remember what happened to Blattarius. This is my life story and I won't alter a word of it to satisfy any authority that dares attempt to arrest me. End of story.

. . .

From: The Litigatron
To: King Oblivion, Ph.D.
Subject: RE: Legal concerns regarding memoir

Of course, King. As you say. I'll begin preparing defenses for the St. Valentine's Day massacre and all the rest.

Reading Comprehension Test, Part 2

Read closely. Answer the discussion questions that follow.

HypoBot 5000 sat on his cold, hard hospital bed looking out the window at the rain streaming down onto the ambulances below, sirens wailing, as if to mourn his dreadful condition. It was late April, and the clinic had a different smell to it. The smell, it seemed to him, of death and rebirth . . . at least as far as HypoBot's titanium scent receptors could perceive. He wondered how he could have gotten here. Why did all this have to happen to him now, when there was still so much left to do?

"Does not compute," HypoBot said aloud to no one in particular. "Does not compute."

Nearly four months had passed since HypoBot had checked himself in at St. Mary's. It was the 117th day of his stay in the science fiction and fantasy characters ward, the area headed up by the kind Nurse Shipley and her team of helpful engineers and wizards, all of whom did their utmost to ratchet up a smile or conjure up some hope in these bleak days.

HypoBot had made some dear friends during his stay: Frankie the Unicorn, who had long been afflicted with a severe case of gout; Martian warlord Zarnok the Conqueror, whose lung cancer had come from years of inhaling ray gun fumes; Paisley O'Shamrock, a diabetic leprechaun on his last leg; unfortunate mutant Michael Faltworth, also known as "Neck" because he was born with no head; and aspiring magic user Wicksworth the Magnificent, who, while practicing a spell one afternoon, had accidentally turned himself into a sentient case of herpes.

HypoBot pondered how many thoughts he would be able to process before the last 0 or 1 ran through his complex circuitry.

It was favorable that he had known these people, he thought, even though he had only stored their vital, identifying information into his memory banks and purged much of his conversational and relationship-based data to make room for new self-pity software. Oh how he would miss them. And how he would also be missed!

"Error!" he cried. "Error!"

Serving lunch in another section of the ward, Nurse Shipley, hearing HypoBot's cries, kindly decided to bring him his meal and attend to his woes. She arrived by his bedside with a plate of Salisbury steak, mashed potatoes on the side, and gelatin for dessert. Nurse Shipley knew that gelatin was HypoBot's favorite and was hoping that an extra helping would cheer him up.

At the sight of his lunch, HypoBot solemnly opened his frontal cavity, clasped the plate with one of his clamps, and poured in the sustenance, all of which near-instantly exited through his exhaust spout and clanged into the bedpan underneath him. Even the gelatin, it appeared, was no help.

"Now don't go mopin' around like that!" said Nurse Shipley. "I've heard from a pretty knowledgeable source that Dr. Conway might just be comin' to see you this afternoon with some big news!"

HypoBot sat up in his bed, filled with hope and most likely smiling brightly if he had had the facial features to do so, instead of a molded series of titanium plates onto which was grafted a lighted power indicator that constantly glowed red.

"Error?" he asked, hopefully.

"No, 'tis surely true," said the nurse as she bounded off to serve another patient. "So buck up a hint, eh?"

For the remainder of the afternoon, HypoBot 5000 sat perched in his bed, almost jumping out of his skin (if he had any) in anticipation of the doctor's news. Could it be an all-clear? A new miracle cure? Or even just another robot in the ward with whom he could truly share his plight? The realm of possibilities was endless, he thought. Too many to count, even. And he could perform nearly 45,000 calculations a second during his prime. This gave HypoBot newfound hope.

After a seeming eternity, Dr. Conway did, in fact, push back the curtain and step carefully into HypoBot's area of the ward, clipboard in hand, just as kind Nurse Shipley had promised. Too excited to contain himself, HypoBot held out his clamps and asked the doctor what news he had brought.

"Please input data!" he exclaimed. "Please input data!"

Dr. Conway sat on the side of HypoBot's bed and casually tried to calm him down, assuredly taking both of the robot's clamps in his smooth, human doctor-hands. He grinned slightly at his patient, who had won his heart as soon as he had been shipped into the building and re-assembled on this very bed.

"I have some excellent news," said the doctor. "After some extensive testing, we've discovered that robots don't have intestinal tracts and can't get cholera."

"Processing . . ." said HypoBot. "Error?"

"No, I mean it," said the doctor. "As a robot, you just can't have it."

HypoBot released an exhaust plume of relief that caused Dr. Conway to cough for several minutes.

"But," the doctor said once he recovered, "I do have some other news. It appears that you do have another disorder that we may have to look into."

"Input data," said HypoBot.

"Well," said Dr. Conway, looking down at his chart, "I'm not sure how this is possible, but it seems as though you might have been experiencing some mild, but increasingly more serious dementia."

"Processing," said HypoBot, biting his lower lip, if he had one. "Does . . . does not compute."

"Essentially," said the doctor, "you're losing your mind. Your robot mind. Also, you may have meningitis. We're checking into that."

HypoBot engaged his doubt capacitor. Then he couldn't believe what he was hearing. If he remembered anything about him other than his name and sickness, he thought, he would have wondered what Frankie had to say about this.

Discussion Question #1: HypoBot exacerbates his already difficult condition by engaging emotional software. Explain as briefly as possible why emotions are harmful and should be scrubbed from all sentient life.

Discussion Question #2: HypoBot relies on memories of his old friends to get through a trying time. Why is this stupid and weak?

Discussion Question #3: Explain why a robot with metal clamps would ever stay in a hospital for any amount of time when it could charge out of there full blast and steal a helicopter.
(Note: There is no correct answer to this question.)

Discussion Question #4: That doctor's an idiot, isn't he? Give some examples of how you'd show that doctor what an idiot he is.

Villainspiration

The villain: Lex Luthor
Key trait: Considerable wealth and influence, which he uses to foment power.
How he uses it: Luthor won the presidency by running on a platform of technological advancement and directly criticizing the previous administration's mishandling of the destruction of Gotham City in an earthquake. Of course, in the meantime, Luthor was attempting to buy up all the property in Gotham for himself and framing Batman for murder. He also staged an alien invasion to make himself look like an avenging hero.
The wrong takeaways: Luthor made the greatest mistake of taking an elected office instead of a lifelong position of power, which led to him being removed from office once some superheroes revealed that he had staged the aforementioned alien invasion. That'd never happen to a king. Trust me.

Chapter 9

INIQUITOUS AMBITION

A few years after I was crowned king of Explosia, I finally felt as though I had cemented my status and established my rule deeply enough to take the opportunity to rub Dr. Blattarius's face in it. I personally tasked the only telephone operator in the country with finding a way to dial his office at the hovering Association headquarters so I could inform him of all my recent accomplishments. It took her a matter of several months (during which I threatened bodily harm numerous times) to track down a working number, but eventually she did her damn job and got me something that finally worked.[40]

I wanted to present myself to my mentor and adversary in the proper, regal way, so I had the

40 The operator was fooled numerous times by fake numbers, almost always for roach extermination companies. These were obviously feints planted by Dr. Blattarius himself to keep from being traced and tracked by superheroes, adversaries, and various authority figures. I'd come to copy it in the years that followed, though I tended to drive people to royalty-themed fast food establishments rather than exterminators.

operator call and announce me ("Prepare to have your ears graced by the life-changing voice of King Oblivion, Ph.D.") before I picked up and said, "Dr. Blattarius. It's been some time since we've spoken."

He didn't react with the cowering I expected. [Instead, he laughed.]

Not a detail I'd like to share or that I believe.

"It has, hasn't it? I think we last saw you . . . ten years ago? Time really does fly. But I'm glad to hear you have managed to stay busy. I heard all about your exploits through my various channels. The doctorate, being named king of Explosia. Those are certainly accomplishments."

I sat in silence for a moment. *I* wanted to be the one to tell him about my doctorate. *I* wanted to throw my monarchal reign in his face. *I* wanted to be the one to shove his buggish nose in what I achieved. *I* wanted to bear the news that I had proven to be his superior. And here he was, already aware of it all. I would have to rethink my entire approach.

But before I could pivot, he launched back in.

"Oh, you didn't think you were the only one with a network of contacts, did ya? Mine spans the globe. It's everywhere. Nothin' gets by me, kid. So look. You've had your fun. Sown your wild oats. Now it's time to come back to your real job. Do something important. No more little adventures."

That's when, against my better judgment, I got mad.

"'Little adventures'? You call breaking New Zealand in half a 'little adventure'? You call taking over as sovereign ruler of a nation a 'little adventure'? You think dying and coming back to life is a 'little adventure'? How about exploding four opponents in a roshambo tournament? *I* did that. *Me*."

Dr. Blattarius chuckled again.

"Now, don't go gettin' upset. You did do those things. No denyin' that. And I'm so proud of you that, hell, I'm barely even gonna punish you for leavin' when you did. I was young once. I know how those things are. I know you gotta feel like you done somethin'. But we're doing big things here. Global things. Things that'll decide whether people like us are in charge or whether people like that garbage-eatin' rat bastard Mr. Wonderful is. What you're doing . . . well, it's bullshit."

That's when I hung up. More accurately, I smashed the phone receiver down onto the hook with such force that I was surprised it didn't fall to pieces right then and there or fuse together from the friction.

It definitely broke. No way it could not have.

The operator and I sat in my throne room in silence for a few moments; me, thinking about how I would make Dr. Blattarius pay for this slight, and her, looking utterly terrified.

And then the phone rang.

The operator sat there, frozen and unsure of what to do. On the third ring, I finally motioned for her to answer.

She picked up the phone, which miraculously still worked, and gave the standard greeting: "You've reached Explosia Palace, home of exalted liege and master of all things, King Oblivion, Ph.D. How are you looking to waste his time?"

She responded to the person on the other end of the line with a few uh-huhs before turning to me and saying that the caller was a woman named Lillian Pemberton. Before she even got her full name out, I grabbed the receiver and jammed it up toward my ear.

"Miss Spiraci?" I asked.

"It's me," she answered. It was good to hear her voice again. "Can you meet?"

Do. Not. Use. This. Word.

"Listen." I geared myself up for a defense. "If Blattarius asked you to call to butter me up and ask me back to the Association, I already talked to him and I'm not—"

"No, it's not that," she interrupted. "I don't work for him anymore. Can you meet me?"

"You don't work for the Association anymore?"

"No. But we can't talk about this over the phone. Meet me somewhere."

I suggested a parley in my throne room, but she dismissed the idea outright, making the case that we'd have to convene in some neutral location. We ended up settling on Monaco, and I boarded my plane to go find out what she had to say.

We meet two days later at a café. She was heavily disguised—wig, scarf, sunglasses—to the point that I immediately recognized her as someone who didn't want to be noticed. She was so incognito that she was impossible to miss. I, on the other hand, was dressed as I always was: crown, mask, cloak, bejeweled suit, giant black boots. It's too good a look to sacrifice for going "low profile."

Again, no. Forbidden.

I approached her table just on the edge of the outdoor dining area and quietly took a seat. Somehow she didn't notice me right away. She was too busy looking down and trying to appear inconspicuous. So I leaned over and just whispered, "Found you."

She jumped like her chair just turned electric and pulled a knife out of her purse, brandishing it wildly toward everyone around her, including me. That cleared out the café pretty quickly, leaving just us standing in the middle of the sidewalk, looking at each other. She grimaced at me as she put her knife back into her purse.

"So much for not attracting attention," she said. "We've got to move."

We walked the streets of Monte Carlo, winding our way around the city and keeping to less-populated areas, until dark. We spoke in hushed voices. She dropped a ton of information on me.

During World War II and in the few years after, superheroes really stepped up their presence in the world. The attack on the university that led to my second untimely death was just the tip of the spear. What had been a manageable handful of superheroes had ballooned into the hundreds or maybe even thousands, and they were organizing, with the League of Right Rightness's membership growing by leaps and bounds.

The growing superhero contingent put massive pressure on the Association, slamming the brakes on its financial growth sustained from bank robberies. Many of the Association's members were routinely pummeled. This created a rift within the Association (which had all but absorbed the

Eastern Cabal of Wrongdoers, the Northern Purloiners Partnership, and the Criminal Club of the South just around the time I was leaving).

Meanwhile, a disgruntled and bruised group of supervillains led by none other than Nicky Claws himself had broken off and started calling itself the Worldwide Conglomeration of Super-Criminals.[41] The creation of a rival supervillain faction made things even more difficult for Dr. Blattarius, who was growing increasingly desperate to hold onto power.

Around the time the Conglomerate was created, Miss Spiraci left the Association too, declaring herself a free-agent supervillain.

When she explained all this, I took the opportunity to chime in, noting that it seemed like it would be a great time to remove Blattarius from power and take it for ourselves. But Miss Spiraci warned against it.

This one only works when it refers to prodigious size or power; you're edging toward positivity here.

Removing Blattarius would shake up the Association badly enough that the Conglomerate would almost certainly swoop in and seize control, which would just create a whole other giant for us to topple.

"So what do we do?" I asked.

"We let them weaken each other to the point that they're both easy pickings," she answered. "Then we take down the superheroes."

"And what do we do in the meantime? Go to ground?"

She shook her head. "There's not a lot of ground we can go to. They've been monitoring

41 Just the act of typing out their name makes me want to vomit all over this page.

me since the day I left. They knew everything you were doing. They watch you in your throne room in Explosia. We've got to go—"

She pointed to the moon.

"—up there."

Amateur conspiracy theorists like to say that the moon landing in 1969 never really happened.[42] As a professional in the world of cover-ups and covert operations, Miss Spiraci knew the truth. She knew people had been going to the moon since 1929. Not long after pilots started routinely performing transatlantic flights, a consortium of the world's richest businessmen and at least one literal demon from hell—having been inspired by the 1902 film *A Trip to the Moon*—spent considerable wealth developing a top-secret "superplane" that could travel to the moon and back. Its use became common among the rich and powerful, with none of the general public ever having the slightest notion. A very advanced version of the superplane is still in use today. Even at the time, its technology was far beyond the space shuttles and other crafts known to the public.

The Association completed a moon base in 1938, but abandoned it after operations became cost prohibitive during the war. That's where Miss Spiraci wanted to go.

She left to secure us a ship while I headed back to Explosia to get some things in order before I left. The people would miss their king

42 This is only partially true. Instead of the moon, the astronauts landed on a full-size replica of the moon we placed in front of the real moon so that NASA and the US government wouldn't find all the stuff we had put on the real moon.

in my absence, so I'd have to appoint a proxy to inspire equal measures of looming dread and abject, immediate fear in their hearts. So I called for La Campeona and told her that she would be overseeing day-to-day affairs while I would be cooling my heels on the moon.

Oh, did I mention what ended up happening with Ms. Papelrocha? No? Okay, put this up near the beginning of the chapter somewhere, then.

You weren't supposed to write this part down, idiot.

After the roshambo tournament and my coronation, I kept my word to Ms. Papelrocha and restored her to normal size. Typically, I wouldn't be quite so magnanimous, but she did help me greatly in the tournament, with little protest after she finally agreed to serve as my coach. I decided giving her life back would be reward enough for her service. Surprisingly, she had other plans.[43] Ms. Papelrocha told me in no uncertain terms that she wished to stay in Explosia and work for me as an adviser. She had already won just about every rock-paper-scissors tournament in the world and had been looking for a new challenge in life. There's only so much wowing people in city squares by mimicking sheets of paper with their hands that someone can do before it gets tiresome, she said.

This one is more like it.

She even told me that she wanted a supervillain name and uniform. I found it difficult to say no, given her enthusiasm and how useful she had been as a coach. We conferred and decided that the most appropriate name would be La Campeona, considering that's what she was: a champion.

43 By this, I mean, "not surprisingly at all."

As for her uniform, we worked up something to make her resemble a human-sized, walking gold statue who could shrink down to the size of the person who rests atop a championship trophy. We also got her some transmogrifying powers (you can buy powers very easily on the black market) so she could literally change her hands into rocks, paper, or scissors.

La Campeona would be very unhappy to see that you used this word.

Over the next several years she would prove to be my best ally, which is why I had no issue with handing over the reins of Explosia to her. I left her with my documented plans for the next five years and made my exit.[44]

Two days later, Miss Spiraci and I were in an underground launch facility boarding a ship headed for the moon. Miss Spiraci had falsified some documents to make it look like we were still in cahoots with the Association, and we had to tread carefully to make sure no one contacted Dr. Blattarius or anyone else in his employ to verify. We simply informed everyone it was a top-secret mission and slipped bribes to everyone we could. It worked well.

This word . . . skirts the line.

After three days of having to subsist on filet mignon, caviar, and champagne dispensed through tubes, we arrived at the abandoned Association moon base. We docked, made a quick walk in our space suits to the base's entry dock, and fired up the generators that supplied

44 Year One: Watch people explode. Year Two: Make empty promise to put an end to the explosions. Year Three: Watch more people explode. Year Four: Announce that the first plan to put an end to the explosions actually resulted in more exploding dirt (this was the plan all along). Year Five: Watch even more people explode, make another empty promise.

the air while adjusting the gravity.[45] Before anything else, we combed the massive facility—it filled a huge crater on the surface with its red-tinged metal edifices—for any sort of surveillance or monitoring equipment that could alert some Association apparatchik that we were squatting in Dr. Blattarius's lunar house. It took a couple days for the two of us to go over every crevice in every room looking for cameras, sensors, and listening devices, disabling everything we could.

Next, we checked the pantries to make sure we had plenty of food, and while it wasn't the kingly fare I preferred (a lot of canned tomatoes and soup) it was more than enough to feed hundreds of people for years. There were only two of us, so we could rest easy knowing that neither of us was going to be sneaking into the other's room and night and slitting his or her throat. At least not over food, anyway.

And then we hid out. We waited. We monitored TV and radio signals for any news about the Association or the Conglomeration. Much of what we saw was disheartening reports about the growing strength of superheroes while supervillains fought among themselves. All in all, we were there for five long years.[46]

It was a strange time in my life. I had never really experienced boredom of that magnitude before. Aside from the news, television of the

---

45 There's so much about Illuminati technology that you normals have no clue about.

46 When you read stories about supervillains, you may wonder where they disappear to for years at a time if they're not in prison. Usually, it's the moon.

era was pure, unforgivable trash, with shows like *Man Against Crime* and *Adventures of Superman* spreading reckless pro-hero propaganda. Even the news was largely biased against evil, with its talk of the Soviet Union as some grand, evil specter; like they could even hold a candle to us. To be frank, we've never gotten a fair shake in the media at large.

To my larger point, we had a lot of time and little with which to fill it. Occasional walks on the surface and games using the only piece of recreational equipment in the entire facility, a Ping Pong table, were all we had to keep us from losing our minds. Sometimes, we would be overcome with a desire to destroy something, and so we'd go out to the surface and explode some small piece of equipment—a radio, a camera, a statue of Dr. Blattarius—and just watch it burn. With the moon's limited atmosphere, the reaction was disappointing each and every time. We ended up blowing up a statue inside the facility, but afterward we had to close that wing for at least a week. Oxygen-rich environment and all. We were desperate for any kind of excitement. It was beyond rare on the station.

I've made it clear that I once had a romantic infatuation with Miss Spiraci, and our shared exile on the moon seemed as good a time as any to test out whether we had any romantic spark. Though she had rejected me once before, she seemed amenable to giving things a try this time—I suspect her no longer being in the thrall of Dr. Blattarius played some role in her change of heart, but I had also matured and done more

Trust me. We will have words.

to establish myself. Even so, after a few months of romantic entanglement and a single attempt to have sex in a room without artificially generated gravity, we mutually agreed that our relationship should be strictly professional going forward. I still have the scars to prove it.

As time went on, we finally begin to notice some strange changes going on in the culture back on Earth. Supervillains—not just the Association, but all groups, the Conglomerate included—seemed to be on the decline. All we heard about supervillains on the news was the occasional story about a city reservoir being drained or some jewels being taken from a museum. Basic stuff. Nothing major at all. On top of that (and to my immense joy), superheroes seemed to be waning in popularity as well. Only the biggest names ever got any ink or airtime, and even then it was typically for minor acts of heroism, like saving a cat in a tree or making some public speech about brushing one's teeth every day. I don't know which side started to decline first, but it was a mutually assured destruction of sorts. The supers were culturally falling by the wayside.

We agreed that this was the clear time to act. With both supervillain organizations and the superheroes in decline, we could carry out our planned tasks with little interference or distraction. So in the summer of 1956, we re-boarded the ship in which we had come to the moon base and made our way back to Earth.

Of course, we couldn't spring into action right away. Even in a weakened state, the Association was a massive group of hundreds of supervillains and thousands more henchmen stationed all over the world. Their ranks had dissipated over the past few years, but they still had a numbers advantage we couldn't even begin to surmount. So after landing in Southwest Australia, we once again went our separate ways to assemble any allies we could. I immediately returned to Explosia and asked La Campeona for her help. She agreed. I then started a military recruitment effort never before seen in Explosia's history. I promised anyone who joined my army the privilege of being able to stand on non-explosive ground for the next five years. Almost everyone in the country applied for service, and I took them all in. We'd need all the cannon fodder we could get.

After that, I once again returned to Ocean Trench Fortress University to ask The Sponge, Erebus, and any students they could spare for their help in bringing down the Association. They didn't even debate it. They were in.

I also asked The Sponge to help me find The Beguiler. As it turned out, I didn't have to go far. He was still on the surface, tricking boaters into going under the water in diving bells. I asked why he wasn't using his degree for bigger ventures, but he told me he just enjoyed doing what he'd been doing too much to quit. I told him it was time to move on to something bigger. After a few days, he grudgingly accepted my offer.

In January of 1959 (recruiting people to join an army can cause the time to pass a little faster than you'd like), Miss Spiraci and I reconvened with our assembled allies. She brought along a group of other disaffected Association members who hadn't defected to the Conglomerate: Gimmick McGimmick, a giant fly with humanlike intellect named Thousand Eyes the Puker, a teleporting thief called Long Gone Sally, a purported magician named Illuminarius, and a woman with the power to grow 50 feet tall who called herself The Brobdingnagian Woman. My understanding is they made a movie about her that got many of the details of her life wrong. Miss Spiraci also brought some six hundred henchmen who had left the Association and agreed to work for her instead, on the promise of future employment in whatever new organization we created.[47]

We all spent the next several months hunkered down in an underground facility I had ordered my new army to construct in an undisclosed location outside the borders of Explosia just in case I needed a secluded hideaway. There, we carefully crafted our plan to overtake the Association and bring down Dr. Blattarius for good. AAAGGGGGH!

47 Unfortunately, this wasn't a promise we could simply make and then break. Henchmen had unionized two decades before, and had shockingly strong backing from their various chapters in the Global Brotherhood of Miscreants.

Email Correspondence Between King Oblivion, Ph.D. and Stephanie Regina, Ghostwriter of "Iniquitous Ambition"

From: King Oblivion, Ph.D.
To: Stephanie Regina
Subject: Word choices

Ms. Regina,

I have never done this for a ghostwriter before, but allow me to commend you for admirably telling the story of one of the most difficult and boring times of my life. Not being able to rob or maim or dress down anyone on that station for several years is the stuff nightmares are made of.

I must, however, dress *you* down for violating the top rule in my voluminous list of rules for ghostwriters: You used the word "good" (I hate to even use it here, but I have no other recourse) and several variations thereof in the manuscript you turned in. That is strictly forbidden.

"Good" is not something to aspire to. It's not a term that should be used to describe something that's satisfactory. "Good" is how huge-toothed buffoons in capes and underwear like to describe themselves as they mete out vigilante "justice" with no sanction and no plan of attack. It's what idiots go to movies to learn all the wrong lessons about. It's a buzzword. A fleeting fancy. A promise unkept. A grandiose lie.

What made you think I would make some exception for you to use this forbidden, contraband word?

. . .

From: Stephanie Regina
To: King Oblivion, Ph.D.
Subject: RE: Word choices

Grand sire of everyone,

I'm afraid I have been caught off guard by all this. I wish I had a good reason to give you for my slip-ups, but the genuine truth of it all is that "good" is quite simply a word I'm too used to writing, and as such it just managed to worm its way into this chapter a few times. I fully understand and am sympathetic to your distaste for the word, but nonetheless it is one I use often. I have no other excuse and apologize profusely.

I will point out, however—and this isn't intended to make you appear as if you are anything but completely and unequivocally right in every matter—that in *The Supervillain Handbook*, the word "good" appears numerous times; it's simply followed by "bad" in parentheses. I read that book very carefully to try and better understand you and your methods, so perhaps some of that rubbed off on me as well.

No excuses. I'm sorry.

. . .

From: King Oblivion, Ph.D.
To: Stephanie Regina
Subject: RE: Word choices

I wish I could accept your apology, Ms. Regina, but I'm afraid I cannot. Let me take your points in reverse:

1) Yes, the word does appear a few times in *The Supervillain Handbook* and one of the punishments I inflicted on my ghostwriter at the time was forcing him to go back through the manuscript and add the word "bad" next to each instance. I also bashed his hands with a giant mallet for several hours. So that's why that is the way it is.

2) You say you continually wrote the word out of "habit," but let me ask you this: If you were to, say, routinely light matches and stick them up your nose, would you continue doing so because it was a "habit" you developed, or would you work to stop yourself from doing

irreparable harm to your nostrils, sinus cavities and, likely, your brain? This is what you writing that word in *my memoir* does to me.

3) You used the word *in your reply email to me*.

Any other points you'd like to make?

. . .

From: Stephanie Regina
To: King Oblivion, Ph.D.
Subject: RE: Word choices

Master and Commander (who is more master-like and commanding than that movie will ever be),

All I can say once again is that I'm deeply, deeply sorry for the offense I have caused and the harms I have perpetrated. I can only imagine the heartache I must have brought by forcing you to see the words I had committed to a document you read.

As I type this, I see that one of your henchmen has brought a box of matches into the room. I suppose I should go ahead and start doing what you described, yes?

. . .

From: King Oblivion, Ph.D.
To: Stephanie Regina
Subject: RE: Word choices

You're very perceptive, Stephanie, I'll give you that. Yes, absolutely get to it. Those matches aren't going to light themselves and jump up your nose, now are they? Let me know how "good" all that feels, eh?

Editor's Note: Of all the tests and examinations I found in King Oblivion's various notes in the "Choosing the One" file, this was the only one that had any indication at all of which answers the writer deemed to be the "correct" ones. To no great surprise, the intended responses all had something to do with villainy or supervillainy. There's no clear instruction here regarding the intended test takers, but it would appear it was meant to be given to graduating high school seniors.

The Supervillain Career Assessment

Question 1: Are you planning to attend a four-year college?

A. No, there is nothing there for me to learn; I know all I need to know.
B. No, my family cannot afford to send me.
C. No, I'll be attending a technical school to learn a trade.
D. Yes, I intend to earn a degree that will help me in a lucrative career.
E. Yes, I want to spend the next four years partying as much as possible.
F. Yes, with a long-term plan of overtaking its operations by force. (correct answer)

Question 1a: If you will be attending college, what is your preferred major?

A. Psychology
B. Business
C. Philosophy
D. English
E. Cultural Studies

F. Engineering, the major that will enable me to build a machine that will slingshot people into the sun (correct answer)
G. Other

Question 2: In which economic sector would you ideally want to work?

A. Business and Finance
B. Education
C. Medical Care
D. Service (entertainment, food and drink, hotel management, etc.)
E. Manufacturing
F. Mayhem Creation (correct answer)
G. Agriculture
H. Transportation

Question 3: How would you describe your ideal boss?

A. Understanding and patient, willing to help me learn as I go
B. Effusive; generous with compliments and positive reinforcement
C. To-the-point and direct; I know they say what they mean and don't waste time
D. Crushed under the heel of my boot as I steamroll over them (correct answer)
E. King Oblivion, Ph.D. (also correct, but shows lack of initiative)
F. Mostly absent so I can do whatever I like
G. Intimidating and terrifying; I demand to be dominated (this is the same answer as E, but less specific)

Question 4: Where do you see yourself in ten years' time?

A. Well-established in a career, working toward a managerial position at the company where I've been employed since graduation.

B. Finally reaching the job I want after a few changes in employer over the years.
C. Owning my own business.
D. Ordering my henchmen into city hall as I continue to formulate my plan for more widespread power. (correct answer)
E. I'd like to be a stay-at-home parent.
F. Not going to lie to you, I'll probably be dead or in prison. (not correct, but acceptable)

Question 5: You find out in a companywide meeting that your place of employment is in danger of going out of business in the next six months. What do you do next?

A. I loyally remain with the company that has employed me for years; they have earned my hard work even through difficulties that may lead to me losing a job.
B. I begin looking for work elsewhere immediately.
C. I burn the place down and put it out of its misery. (one of two correct answers)
D. I consult with my parents/spouse/other family members before making any decisions about my future.
E. I wrest control of the company from my incompetent boss and declare myself its new sovereign leader. (second correct answer)
F. I would never work somewhere that could possibly be in danger of going out of business. (this answer is here to weed out the stupids)

Question 6: What is the most important aspect of a job for you?

A. Doing work in my preferred field/area of expertise
B. Money/pay
C. The number of people I get to lower slowly into lava (correct answer)
D. Benefits/retirement package

```
E. Co-workers whose company I enjoy and whom I consider
   to be friends
F. Get to blast a flamethrower/fire hose/gun of some
   sort/interdimensional teleportation device (not cor-
   rect, but a cool answer)
```

Villainspiration

The villain: Apocalypse
Key trait: Born En Sabah Nur in 3000 BC, Apocalypse has immense power and is also incredibly charismatic, bringing mutants over to his side through gifts and coercion.
How he uses it: Apocalypse used his talents to sway mutants to recruit many of the pawns he used in numerous master plans (Moses Magnum, Mr. Sinister, Genesis), as well as members of the X-Men he turned into his Four Horsemen. In numerous potential futures, Apocalypse is the undisputed ruler of the world.
The wrong takeaways: Though he successfully created numerous futures in which he ruled, Apocalypse allowed several mutants whom he had conquered to go back in time and warn mutants of the past of his future actions. As a result, his plans were halted. So if you manage to use your charisma to seize limitless power, don't let anyone slip through the cracks.

Chapter 10

WAR OF THE WICKED

Editor's Note: In my research into King Oblivion's voluminous files, I found numerous attempts—at least twenty, and probably more that were tucked away in some cabinet I haven't gotten to yet—to work the events described below into a chapter of prose like most of the other chapters in this memoir. None of them were complete, as King Oblivion apparently stopped work on them before they could be finished. King Oblivion quite clearly believed the events surrounding the fall of the Western Association of Ruffians and the founding of the International Society of Supervillains to be some of the most important of his entire life, and stressed again and again in his rejections of the various attempts that his ghostwriters weren't treating the material with what he considered to be the proper amount of gravity and seriousness. He also felt that they were too even-handed about the events of the battle between his group of rebels and the Association's forces. Somehow he thought that it should appear that an open conflict which lasted nearly two years should only seem one-sided. As a result of these internal conflicts, there's no version of this chapter that can be presented as-is. Instead, I have assembled King Oblivion's haphazard notes and written musings about the period into a timeline of events accompanied by paraphrases of his personal commentary on what took place.

June 1959: King Oblivion's rebels launch their first attack on Dr. Blattarius and the Western Association of Ruffians, an air offensive.

We knew that a full-on assault of the Association's hovering headquarters in the Atlantic would be too risky, at least at this point. Though we had respectable numbers between the assembled henchmen that Miss Spiraci had gathered and my Explosian army, the Association's stronghold was still far too heavily guarded to invade without taking severe losses. We were also far outnumbered, so instead of going for the mother ship we decided to blindside Dr. Blattarius on his preferred mode of transportation: the blimp where I had met him and Miss Spiraci nearly thirty years earlier.

Dr. Blattarius often traveled with a bevy of personal bodyguards stationed around the interior of the dirigible, but it was a considerably smaller group than we would have faced elsewhere. And with the Association's recent difficulties, it was down to a skeleton crew. Plus, we had the advantage of knowing that one well-placed shot into the balloon would send it careening to the surface. One of the lessons I learned from Dr. Blattarius in my youth was to always value theatricality over pragmatism. I still adhere to that today, but we chose to opt for both in this particular instance.

Miss Spiraci received a tip from one of her contacts inside the Association that Dr. Blattarius would be traveling on the blimp to a planned henchmen recruitment meeting in Iceland (a lot of henchmen come from there; the big sales pitch is "you get to leave Iceland"). I scrambled to take off in the one martial plane that Explosia had before I became king—a beaten-up bomber that I had repainted with my image on the sides along with the slogan Bombed Into Oblivion. We intercepted the blimp about 45 miles south of the Icelandic coast and, after avoiding some machine-gun fire meant to shoo us away, managed to get above it and directly hit the flying machine with a precision bomb dropped using a beaming technique. The balloon opened up and tipped toward the ocean below.

I radioed back to Miss Spiraci, who was still in our secret planning bunker, that the hit was a success. We celebrated. I turned the plane back toward our base, thinking that Dr. Blattarius was dealt with. But before I even returned, we received a radio transmission from Blattarius himself—who had somehow intercepted our frequency—who informed us that he hadn't been on the blimp at all; he had been warned about our attack and set the entire thing up as bait to draw us out. We had lost the element of surprise, so we reconvened to determine our next step.

July 1959: Dr. Blattarius counterattacks by sending henchmen into Explosia.

As we plotted our next attack, I got word that a group of about two hundred invaders dressed in red bug costumes were crossing into Explosia's borders on foot, driving four-wheel-drive utility vehicles and using floating personal propulsion devices that the Association had just recently developed.

I rushed back with a team of decoy henchmen to take them on. However, my travel time would be a few hours, and so the portion of my army that had been left behind in Explosia to keep watch over the place would have to hold their own for a while. Luckily, many of the Association henchmen who came in on foot immediately exploded, as did those in jeeps. It was the ones in the floating personal propulsion machines (Dr. Blattarius named them Propulpods and that name stuck, so we still call them that now, even though I hate it) that we had to worry about.

I arrived with my backup just as the remaining seventy-five or so Association henchmen (they were commonly referred to as "drones" at the time) began to siege the castle. In due time, the members of my decoy army already on the ground and those I brought with me overwhelmed them and managed to push the drones back out of the country. We even managed to grab a few Propulpods so we could engineer our own, which was a win on our end.

I deduced pretty quickly that Dr. Blattarius knew I wasn't in the castle—he was still surveilling it as far as I knew, so he had to be aware I wasn't still living there and hadn't been for years. This was a shot across the bow to let us know that the Association wouldn't just be playing defense.

August–October 1959: King Oblivion and his rebels start a series of infiltrations at Association outposts across the globe.

We decided that it was time to take the fight to the Association once again, but we also knew that attacking the home base was still out of the question. With our shared knowledge of the Association's various secret hideouts and safe houses tucked in nooks and crannies all over the world, we decided instead to send in small teams to attack, disable any and all equipment, and make each outpost as useless as possible.

This is where Long Gone Sally proved particularly useful. She had the ability to teleport not only herself, but three other people at any given time, so we tasked her with infiltrating the various outposts from the inside, sabotaging everything she could get her hands on, and then setting it up to either be destroyed with explosives, filled with my patented shrinking gas, filled with gas that turned people into piles of dust, or transported to space using a portal device we stole from the Association's moon base.

Over a three-month time period, we incapacitated nineteen Association outposts. Six exploded, four we filled with shrinking gas, five we pumped full of dust gas, and three we sent into space. (At one of them, one of the drones working the outpost spotted the team as they were setting up a space portal, but she and the rest of the drones stationed there gave up and decided to join our team. They hated working for the Association, too. We used the shrinking gas on them as well, but just so they could be put in a cigar box and brought back to our bunker.)

November–December 1959: Things go quiet for a while as Dr. Blattarius and the rest of the Association's membership bunker down at their headquarters.

Following our attacks on the various outposts, Dr. Blattarius called the troops back in and essentially took refuge in his fortress for two months. We stood by and waited for an opening.

January 1960: In a devastating surprise attack, the Association succeeds in causing substantial damage to Ocean Trench Fortress University.

With The Sponge and Erebus joining us in our bunker for attack planning, strategy, and leadership help, the university was left with a skeleton staff for several months. This left an opening for the Association to carry out a highly destructive act of espionage. In retrospect, I have to say it was a rather cunning plan. One of Blattarius's top lieutenants, The Bioluminescent Brawler, used some very advanced scuba equipment to dive all the way down to the university by himself, with no need to take the elevator. While outside the university's glass walls, he removed his scuba suit—all but the helmet—and lit up his bioluminescent body, attracting thousands of sea monsters, all of which crashed headlong into the university. They made massive holes in the walls, all but completely destroying the structure of the facility. They also near-irreparably damaged the elevator.

Nearly everyone in the university—students and faculty alike—was killed in the attack, but that wasn't the Association's real goal. Its goal was to distract The Sponge and Erebus from helping us, and Blattarius and his goons accomplished that. The Sponge and Erebus left the bunker as soon as they got word of the attack, with the intent of salvaging any of the remnants of the university that they could. It wouldn't be reopened for nearly a decade.

February–March 1960: Knocked back on its heels after the university attack, the rebels attempt to smoke out Dr. Blattarius for a battle on neutral ground.

We called in the group of drones who had defected to our side a few months earlier and asked one of them to volunteer for a mission. One stepped forward, and we tasked him with returning to Association headquarters, claiming to have been a prisoner of war. (We knew he would be asked about the location of our secret bunker, and for just that reason we made sure that none of the former drones we took in ever had any knowledge of where the bunker truly was. As I noted earlier, we transported that entire team in a cigar box. When and if they were ever to leave—now dressed as my decoys rather than drones—we would once again shrink and escort them out blind.)

The only intelligence the former drone was instructed to give was a message that I, personally, would be traveling back to my parents' former home of Sarasota, Florida, in July, on the anniversary of their deaths and my birth, to commemorate their lives and possibly enact some unfocused revenge on anyone who happened to be around. Maybe I'd kick around Sarasota's local superhero, Gulf Guy (his superpower was that he was a "pretty decent lifeguard, above-average swimmer, and great at finding sand dollars," no joke). He was meant to tell them that I'd be there, in the area of the cemetery where my parents had been transported and buried after they were found in the Netherlands.

I was never the sentimental type—I don't think I had visited my parents' graves even once in the forty-eight years I'd been alive at the time—but we were banking on Dr. Blattarius not knowing me well enough to make that deduction. He only thought of me as a cog in a machine, not as a force and equal. We waited to see if he would fall into our trap.

April–June 1960: The rebels begin a propaganda campaign against the Association while planning their bait-and-switch attack.

As my war cabinet made plans for our ambush in Florida, Miss Spiraci traveled back to Hollywood so as to once again don the guise of Lillian Pemberton and star in a new horror film called *Roach! Roach! Roach! Roach!* about a swarm of irradiated cockroaches attacking the fictional, idyllic middle American town of Inconsequence, Nebraska. Miss Spiraci and I had collaborated on the screenplay and then sent it off to some schlubby screenwriter in Studio City looking to sell whatever crap would come his way, whether he wrote it or not. He sold it off to a studio, as we suspected, as soon as Miss Spiraci—or I should say Miss Pemberton—blessed it with a promise to star as Dr. Helen Wingtip, the inventor of a size 212 boot that is used to crush all the bugs in the third act.

Production began and we pushed to rush it into theaters by the summer to begin a wave of anti-roach, and thus anti-Blattarius, sentiment.

July 1960: The Battle of Sarasota leads to losses on both sides, but there's no clear winner.

Around noon of July 12, we sent in one of my decoys—one with the stature and presence required to successfully be mistaken for me—into the cemetery with my parents' graves, Mourningdew Gardens. Just as he knelt down to place some black roses on the graves, a team of hundreds of drones in Propulpods struck. More of my decoys soon went in, and The Brobdingnagian Woman pounced, crushing as many of the drones with her hands and feet as she could. Thousand Eyes the Puker began grabbing up drones and using his acid vomit on their heads. Long Gone Sally took up a strategy of teleporting in, grabbing a drone, teleporting out to the Atlantic Ocean, dropping the drone, and teleporting back for another round. Miss Spiraci was calmly walking through the cemetery, whispering in drones' ears, convincing them to give up any hope for their cause. Gimmick McGimmick was smashing any drones he saw with a steel chair, and I was staying back, waiting for the moment that Dr. Blattarius would appear so I could personally leave indentations of my fist in his forehead.

Unfortunately, he didn't have the guts to show his face. Instead, he sent his new second-in-command, a man made entirely of brick-red hair called The Hirsute. He stomped into the graveyard and immediately engulfed McGimmick in the tendrils of hair he shot out toward him. A few seconds later, McGimmick fell to the ground, unconscious, choked out by hair. He then managed to take down a few decoys. Next, The Hirsute set his sights on Miss Spiraci, and I couldn't sit back anymore. I swooped down in a Propulpod of my own and tossed the contents of a jar of glue I had stored in my belt down onto him, sticking the components of his all-hair body together.

Just as I was about to drop down for a ground attack, a group of six or so members of the League of Right Rightness, called in by none other than Gulf Guy himself, who had been tipped off somehow (the Association was full of leaks at this point), arrived. They ordered everyone in the cemetery to stand down and submit to their citizens' arrests. Of course, we weren't going to do that. Everyone scattered. One superhero, a flying doofus named Jet Boot Kid, tried to chase me down an alley, but I just dropped back and pulled one of his boots off his feet. He went spinning wildly into a billboard. He gave away his only trick in his name. What a fool. An absolute fool.

So that's how the battle ended. Broken up by superheroes.

August–November 1960: The rebels and the Association establish a shaky truce following the superhero interference at the Battle of Sarasota.

A few weeks after the Battle of Sarasota, I received a communiqué from Dr. Blattarius that said, in short, that we'd never finish this conflict as long as *they* kept sticking their noses in. And he wasn't mistaken in that assessment. The superheroes were going to keep getting involved. They couldn't help but insert themselves in a dispute that had nothing to do with them. Yet I knew he was angling this to his advantage one way or another. My suspicion was that he was using our free labor, under the pretense of clearing away obstructions, to help him dispose of his enemies. Then he would deliver the killing blow to us right after.

We weren't going to allow that to happen. We agreed to the Association's temporary truce, but only on the condition that we would get first crack at the League and its various members. (Particularly Namotto, whom I personally throttled and threw into a ravine as revenge for killing me as soon as I got the opportunity.) We knew that it was enough to merely incapacitate the League rather than destroy it completely; we only needed them to stop interrupting our intervillain battles for now, until such time that we could focus our full attention on these pesky heroes.

So here's what we did. We set up a giant net inside the League's headquarters—a gaudy, incredibly easy to spot building called the "Chamber of Rightness," because heroes are the most uncreative people on the planet—and quite simply caught them all in it. Then we put the net inside in a giant birdcage and just left them there. They were stuck there for *five weeks*. We didn't have to be all that clever back in those days.

Fully aware that the heroes would eventually get out, a small group of villains from both factions began a wave of petty crime that swept across North America, thereby keeping the heroes out of our bigger business for the next several months.

December 1960–March 1961: A number of battles between the Association and the rebels break out across the globe, but Dr. Blattarius fails to show his face.

My group effectively broke the truce when it mounted a Christmas Eve attack on The Hirsute and a group of drones as they attempted to fill the sewers of Prague with a lighter-than-air gas that would cause the entire city to float into the sky like a helium balloon. As with many of the battles that would follow over the next several weeks, there was lots of shouting and many laser beams were shot into the air, but there were relatively few casualties on either side and no clear winner. For whatever reason, the Association never really made it a priority to teach marksmanship, and as a result nearly every ray gun shot fired by a drone missed by a country mile.

Battles followed in Sydney, Nairobi, Buenos Aires, New Delhi, Leningrad, even at the North Pole. Each was effectively a draw. At no point did Dr. Blattarius find it productive to come out of his hovering fortress.

April 1961: Though it's a huge risk, King Oblivion and his rebels mount an assault on the Association's headquarters.

I died.

May 1961: The rebels successfully capture Dr. Blattarius when he leaves his fortress to attend King Oblivion's funeral.

Led by Miss Spiraci, my rebel group planned a funeral for me to be held at Explosia Palace. They didn't explicitly invite Dr. Blattarius, but they spoke about it openly enough that they knew he might be inclined to finally show his face, perhaps out of a grudging respect for me, but even more as a method of gloating in "victory" over us and our cause.

As we suspected, the old bug made his way there to act as though he were grieving while really throwing his weight around and taking a victory lap. Surprisingly, he showed up with limited protective forces. The Hirsute was with him, but virtually no drones were by his side. I suppose he believed he had nothing to worry about. To him, the war was over. He didn't realize there was still one more battle to be fought.

Just as The Sponge (who had temporarily left the university in mid-repair) finished up her eulogy—the last of ten eulogies delivered at the event, because I demanded no less than that—The Brobdingnagian Woman, who was outside the hall, grew to her full height and jammed her foot up against the door. That's when I sat up in my coffin and tossed three cans of Aqua Net hair spray to McGimmick, who proceeded to get his revenge on The Hirsute by turning him into a sort of hair statue. Once he was frozen solid, La Campeona shattered him with her rock fist.

Then we set to work on Blattarius. One thing I had learned about him during my time in his igloo network was that he hated going into bright places. He was part roach, after all. He'd avoid them at all costs if he could. So, of course, we scheduled the funeral on the brightest day we could, and held it in a hall with a retractable roof (when I was having the palace remodeled, I made sure this was a feature for just this purpose). The unavoidable light sent him scurrying into a corner of the room, where it was easy for me to casually walk up, ask him "Who's having a 'little adventure' now?" and spray him with my shrinking gas, making him the size of an actual cockroach. I slid him into a glass jar and told him, "Fearsome fortune." Everyone in the room shared a hearty laugh.

June–October 1961: The last remaining vestiges of the Association are defeated, the hovering fortress is disassembled and sunk, and the Conglomeration goes into hiding.

In the months that followed the capture of Dr. Blattarius, many members of the Association surrendered and turned over their loyalties to the rebels. Others held out, leading to a few scattered battles across the globe which the rebels easily won with no centralized command on the Association side. Eventually, we gained access to the Association headquarters. I frankly found it outdated and tacky. Plus, the underground bunker I was building was quickly becoming a massive, hive-like lair that would more than suffice as my base of operations going forward. So we looted it for all the technology we could from the Association HQ (lots of Propulpods, numerous portal-creating devices, ray guns, energy shields, etc.) and then did a controlled demolition to sink it. That was a fun day.

As for Blattarius himself, I placed his jar on the mantle in my office. He became my trophy. Some years later, after our animosities died down, he would occasionally offer me advice, particularly in regards to fighting superheroes. I never stopped hating him, but I respected his opinions.

The Conglomeration, which didn't participate in our war in any material way, faded even further into obscurity.

November 1961: With hostilities at an end, the leaders of the rebel group formally establish a new supervillain organization headed by King Oblivion, Ph.D. and Miss Spiraci: the International Society of Supervillains.

We all signed a charter that said Miss Spiraci and I were everyone's leaders. It was a momentous day. Miss Spiraci and I showed the charter to Dr. Blattarius in his little jar and he jumped around like an angry little cartoon character. I'll never forget it.

My Third Death

Yes, I died during the rebel assault on the Association headquarters. Or, more accurately, a version of me did.

In the weeks leading up to our planned attack on the hovering fortress, I found myself in an unusual meeting with three men who looked, sounded, and acted exactly like me, except older and perhaps just a little bit less perfect. They had somehow managed to get through the retinal scanner at the entrance to my underground bunker and knew the layout well enough to find me in my under-construction command center. I considered opening the floor to drop them into the pit of tiny bears and giant spiders below, but something about the way they seemed ready to jump away at any second, as if they knew about the pit already, made me curious to hear them out.

They told me they were versions of me from the far-flung future of 1995. One came from a future where the rebels won the war with the Association. Another's future was still run by the Association, so he had been forced into menial and humiliating jobs well into his silver years. The third came from a hellscape time in which the rebels and the Association had destroyed each other, leading the Conglomeration to rise to power. That future was completely overtaken by superheroes, and that version of King Oblivion worked at a home improvement store.

They told me that their futures were actually the rarest timelines; in most, I was killed in the siege on the Association's fortress, directly by Dr. Blattarius's hand. (I found this all but impossible to believe.) They had come to ensure that not only did we avoid that outcome, but ensure that the International Society of Supervillains would be formed.

The version of me from the future in which the rebels won had commissioned the development of a machine that traveled through both time and across dimensions. After assembling a few contemporaries, he met as many past versions of himself as he could, trying to turn as many timelines as possible toward mirroring the one in which he existed. He had carried out this plan before.

Here's how it was to go down: The version of me from the Association future—the one with the most humiliating lot of any of them, because working for Dr. Blattarius was more demeaning than selling toilets—would be the one to accompany the rebel forces to the Association HQ. He'd face down Dr. Blattarius and take a stabbing with a cane to convince Dr. Blattarius that it was the younger me from his dimension who died.

And that's exactly what happened. My rebel forces touched down on the deck of the fortress (while I watched from a helicopter a safe distance away). The future me from the most infuriating timeline bolted straight toward the belly of the compound so he could face down Dr. Blattarius and sacrifice himself. My decoys recovered the body and brought it back to our bunker. We shipped that body back to his timeline to be put to rest however it might. Then I slid into the casket at the funeral. Illuminarius cast a spell on Dr. Blattarius to keep him from noticing any small twitches or abdominal breathing movements to further convince him I was dead. (I found this unnecessary, but we had little other use for Illuminarius's limited magic powers, so we let him do it.)

To be candid, we had tried tricks like this before, sacrificing decoys (who were already supposed to be mistaken for me) and trying to convince people that I was the one who died. You can accomplish a lot more when someone thinks you're dead. But no one ever really seemed to buy that they were me. Not regal enough. So we had to use a photocopy of the real deal.

Once we pulled off the capture of Dr. Blattarius, the two remaining future versions of me jumped back into their machine and attempted to fix another timeline.

Transcript of Phone Interview with The Bioluminescent Brawler

Bioluminescent Brawler: Hello?

Editor: Uh, hi, yeah. Is this . . . have I reached The Bioluminescent Brawler?

BB: I mean, I went by that name once, yeah. Now folks just call me Charlie.

Ed: Would you . . . would you rather I call you that?

BB: I don't even know why we're talkin'.

Ed: Oh right. Well, uh . . . Charlie, I'm calling because I'm working on putting together King Oblivion Ph.D.'s memoirs. You know, posthumously. And I thought you might have a few things to say about him. You knew him a long time ago, right?

BB: I knew about him back when I was a kid. Saw him on the news and stuff, this big bad criminal. Became a king through some kinda technicality. I was never sure about all the details of that. But I didn't know him until after the war in 1960, '61.

Ed: You played a big role in that war. You basically singlehandedly destroyed Ocean Trench Fortress University.

BB: Yeah, I guess you could call that my big moment.

Ed: How old were you when you did that?

BB: I was twenty. Dr. Blattarius had just recruited me after some footage of me lighting up at an aquarium got out in the news. I think he grabbed me up for that one mission.

Ed: So now you're—

BB: Just turned seventy-eight. I live with my kid and husband in New Jersey. Barely even light up anymore.

Ed: So after the war ended and the Association lost, where did you go from there?

BB: There weren't a lot of options. The Association collapsed in the blink of an eye, and the only other option, the Conglomeration, went totally dark. If you wanted to be a supervillain with any kind of a career—unless you had a name already, which I didn't—you had to go with the Society, or I think they started calling it the ISS just to stick it to NASA.

Ed: So they let you join?

BB: Yeah, I mean, war is war, you know? Plus they needed a lot of bodies in the organization to take on the superheroes. But I did have to kinda make up for it. I don't think the lady who ran the school—the one with the mushy skin—what was her name?

Ed: The Sponge.

BB: Yeah, The Sponge. I don't think we ever spoke. And they worked me hard for the first few years.

Ed: What sorts of things did they have you doing?

BB: Basically, I was everyone's personal flashlight. If anyone was going somewhere dark—like digging a hole underneath the Chamber of Rightness so we could pop out from under the floor—I'd be there lighting up so everyone could see.

Ed: What sorts of interactions did you have with King Oblivion?

BB: I'll tell ya, I never really got a great sense of the guy. He'd order people around. He'd come along on missions sometimes. But—I guess I can say this now that he's dead—I don't know if I ever really saw him doing much. I always felt like a lot of the real work was done by Miss Spiraci. The planning, the fighting, the coordinating. King Oblivion always seemed more interested in his image, you know? How things looked instead of how they were.

Ed: Are you saying that you think he lied about some of his accomplishments?

BB: I mean, listen. I don't know. I didn't know him all that well. I just worked for him. I can only tell you what I saw. *(knocking sounds in background)* Look, I gotta run. Someone's here.

Ed: Could I call you back with some more questions?

BB: Maybe. *(loud knocking)* I gotta go. Fearsome fortune with the thing you're doing.

(click)

Villainspiration

The villain: Ozymandias
Key trait: An incredibly agile and strategic mind, along with a photographic memory.
How he uses it: Adrian Alexander Veidt proved himself to be a master tactician in what he knew would be a conflict with his former allies. When he was confronted about a plan he had hatched to kill a number of superheroes and stage an alien attack, he revealed that he had pressed the button to set off the staged attack thirty-five minutes earlier, making the heroes' efforts moot.
The wrong takeaways: Veidt ultimately carried out his plan for noble reasons; he staged the attack in the hopes that the United States and the Soviet Union would end the Cold War and come together as allies against a greater threat. Plans don't need noble justifications.

Chapter 11

CORRUPT COALITION

As badly as I wanted to jump into a champagne fountain and drench myself in the spoils of victory following the defeat of Dr. Blattarius and the Association, there wasn't much time for celebration.

For one thing, the superheroes were on the upswing. Though we had managed to keep them at bay during the last phase of our war, I was hearing through my network of contacts that recruitment for the League of Right Rightness was shooting through the ceiling. Apparently superheroes weren't fitting the old molds of oily-haired men with Chiclet smiles and stern women in flag motif costumes. Teenagers, families, former criminals, space aliens, even grotesquely mutated monsters were joining up to mete out "justice" at their whim. This would require new strategies and tactics for keeping them at arm's length while we worked out and executed our villainous plans.

Is this a Bible thing? This feels like a Bible thing.

And those plans were going to have to be pretty spectacular. We were at the genesis of a sparkling new era of villainy, with a new brand replacing the old face of super-evil in the world. We would have to accomplish big things to ensure that the International Society of Supervillains became the most widely known group of evildoers on Earth, and preferably in the solar system.

My personal animosity aside, I had felt for decades that the Association had become complacent. It didn't stir fear—in the public, in superheroes, in anyone. It hadn't since the days of attempting to replace Theodore Roosevelt with a robot. It had fallen into bureaucratic routines, almost committing crimes and fighting superheroes out of obligation and an overriding sense of "this is what we do" than any degree of passion. I would have to break those old strictures.

Okay, this is definitely a Bible thing. Why do we have Bible things in my supervillain memoir?

Also, we were broke. Dead broke. So broke that I was going to have to Lazarus us back to health. We used every cent we had to take down the Association. Even though we hoped that we could raid its coffers once it was destroyed, as it turned out, they were basically out of money as well. If we hadn't crushed them in the war, economics likely would have. Fundraising was a major target for the months to come.

So in January of 1962 I assembled every active member of the ISS—supervillains, henchmen, and facility staff—at my newly completed, hive-like underground lair at an undisclosed location.[48] There I laid out the structure of the new organization and let everyone know what

48 If you thought I was even for a second going to give up sensitive information like the lair's location up in this memoir, you are sadly and deeply mistaken.

was expected of them. The ISS was (and remains) made up of nine key departments:

Finance

In the old structure of the Association, the majority of operating fund generation came from one of the oldest staples of supervillain crimes: bank robberies. We obviously planned to continue that trend, but it was also clear that new revenue streams would be necessary for some of the big projects we were hoping to pull off over the next few years. Among them were counterfeiting, stealing money from alternate dimensions, developing some sort of illusory holographic money, getting into the credit card industry, pyramid schemes, "kidnapping" world capitals for ransom by sending them into space for a few weeks, high-level grifting (three-card Monte using much, much larger cards), specially designed magnets that drew the change *and* cash out of people's pockets, and so on. I tapped my top financial mind, Thousand Eyes the Puker (who had an MBA from the Wharton School) to head it up.

Strategy and Tactics

Dr. Blattarius never had a council of advisors to help him with strategy. The various meetings and luncheons he would host with the board of directors were nothing but schmooze sessions; gatherings in which the people in attendance could feel powerful and important while one man truly held all the levers of authority. Of course, I have the greatest strategic mind in the world and could plan every mission myself with a zero percent chance of failure, but in my magnanimity and Solomon-like wisdom I chose to delegate this power to a committee of clever tacticians. Miss Spiraci took the lead on plotting out our upcoming missions.

Why do I keep seeing these Bible things? The only Bible thing I want in this book is a chapter about the flood I'm planning that will kill all but two of every animal.

Long-Term Planning

Aside from mission preparation, there were some broader plans to make: where we as an organization would be in five, ten, or twenty years' time. How long before we defeated all superheroes in the world? How long before we completely took over Earth? How long before we dominated the Milky Way? These were all questions worth answering, so I asked La Campeona to begin plotting our top goals.

Research and Development

Plans don't just happen on their own or by providence. That's particularly true of supervillain plots, which require high-tech, high-concept equipment and almost-magical concoctions for us to carry them out effectively. Miss Spiraci and her team could come up with ideas all day, but without a division to make those ideas reality there would be no world domination to come. Frankly, Blattarius and the Association relied far too heavily on old technology (the last thing they developed of any real value was the Propulpod) to make any true headway. We would blaze new

This one edges up to the line of being a Bible thing.

trails, and to ensure that, I enlisted The Sponge's scientific expertise (she would split her time between R&D and overseeing the rebuilding of Ocean Trench Fortress University). The first order of business I entrusted her with was building me a fist-shaped, supersonic jet. That pathetic attack plane I flew around in the War of the Wicked was an insult.

Artillery

Aside from the high-concept weapons we were developing for specific missions, the ISS also had to ensure that our conventional weaponry and gadgets—ray guns, proton cannons, various body-changing gases, escape smoke, Propulpods, energy shields, laser blades, and so on—were always in working order and that we had plenty of units available for everyone on staff. I left that up to Gimmick McGimmick, who loved weaponry despite being a professional grappler. (He always made sure we had plenty of folding steel chairs for sneak attacks, too.)

Communications

This is a nasty habit you have. Keep this up and you'll be dealing with a swarm of locusts all your own inside your tiny cell.

In my time of indentured servitude in the Association (let's be honest, I freed those people like Moses freed the Israelites), I learned a lot about propaganda, given that I headed up a number of campaigns to raise the public profile of supervillains. In recent years, our profile had slipped dramatically as Dr. Blattarius became less and less interested in bolstering all of us and only started to invest in his own triumphs. This would obviously have to change. The International Society of Supervillains would have to systematically alter how the world perceived purveyors of professional super-evil while simultaneously casting superheroes in a negative light. For this, I put The Brobdingnagian Woman in command, to make use of her immense size as well as her strong speaking abilities and movie-industry experience (she consulted on that movie about her).

Powers

Not everyone is graced with superpowers at birth. And not everyone is granted with the most spectacular mind and body in human history, as I was. Even those who do have powers from their youth sometimes lose their abilities as a result of experimentation or being punched into the wrong vat of goop by some idiot superhero. Of course, many of our short- and long-term plans relied on our people's superpowers being consistently useful and dependable, so we had to develop methods for creating powers from scratch (for enterprising recruits without superhuman abilities) and maintaining them. For this I looked to Illuminarius, who we later discovered had the ability to grant people superpowers via his "magic," which was really a kind of reality-altering alchemy.

Legal

You'd be surprised by how much legal advice and consultation a completely extralegal organization requires. Were we and are we above the law? Of course we are. We shatter your silly "laws." They're just words written on paper in some stodgy building with columns. Still, someone has to represent us when an angry wife sues over her husband being transformed into a fish creature. We still have to get our thieves out of jail. Someone has to pin on some patsy a master plan to drive hearing-impaired superhero Dynamoman insane by replacing everyone he loves in his life with a grotesque Lovecraftian monster. I left that to our super-attorney, The Litigatron.

Administration

This is my favorite department because it's all about ordering people around. I personally oversee the operations here.

I offered positions to other members of my inner circle—namely The Beguiler and Long Gone Sally—but not everyone decided to stick around in full-time positions after the war. Some opted to take time off or serve in reserve roles, and in my munificence I granted it to them, though I did make sure to inform them that if I were to ever need their specific services again in the future they'd be honor bound to provide them or perish. This seemed more than fair.

Once I had whipped the organization into shape by establishing the new departments, we set to work on our first big plan: the Freak-out Ray. We raised funds and developed a strategy for almost a year straight. Assuredly, we ran into superhero opposition from time to time as we robbed banks and tried to pass off alternate-universe currencies. The League of Right Rightness was somehow still under the leadership of Mr. Wonderful, who had to be in his sixties by this time, and numerous heroes in his control confronted us to try and halt our revenue streams. They held us up in a few spots and we had to spend some cash on getting around arrests and trials (this was all in the legal budget, naturally), but for the most part the money was starting to flow.

Meanwhile, R&D was working on the logistics of the Freak-out Ray. Here was the idea: We'd launch a satellite into space. Attached to it would be a broadcasting device that would send out coded, subliminal signals that only teenagers could hear. Those signals would scramble their brains, making them into drug-addled hippies who loved rock-and-roll music and wore gaudy flower patterns. We knew this would infuriate the stodgy establishment authorities of the time and leave the young generation open to our outlandish suggestions. We just had to invent it.

After four months of R&D building, testing, retesting, and rebuilding, we had it. Getting the hypnotism matrix just right took some time, but soon enough it was perfected. The Sponge and her team had made a device that could truly freak out the young folks. By the spring of 1963 we had launched and set it to blast the Western hemisphere. We were going to show the world that the International Society of Supervillains had arrived.

This one seems like a Bible thing, too. I'm not sure, but I'm going to have someone check. Where did we find you?

The results weren't immediate, but slowly, over time, its effects started showing in the youth at large. We knew based on in-house testing that the ray wouldn't necessarily create a freak-out on its own. Some guiding influence would have to tap the first domino, so to speak. Then the walls of Jericho could come crashing down. To start that process along, Miss Spiraci and I worked together to oversee the construction of Android 141/115, whom we nicknamed "Janis." Over time, she became known as the beloved recording artist and counterculture icon Janis Joplin.

By the mid-'60s, the ray was proving to be a smashing success. Paired with propaganda campaigns such as the 1966 *Batman* TV series, the youth of America and the world were actually turning against entrenched power structures and superheroes.[49] Anti-superhero protests sprouted up with chants painting the spandex-clad vigilantes as nothing more than bulwarks upholding the status quo to the detriment of the downtrodden and disenfranchised. And say what you will about the number of people I've thrown into bottomless pits (by last count it's somewhere in the area of 12,000), I've employed just as many completely unemployable louts in my world-spanning

---

49 You might think I'd hate this series since its lead characters were straight-laced superheroes, but the villains were clearly the most compelling and coolest part of the show. *They* were the interesting ones. That was by design, as we had a hand in its development (whether the creators knew it or not). It was just the start of a wave of pop cultural trends started by us that proved villains were far preferable to heroes. One of our very own members, Vincent Price, turned a number of members of the crew into wolf men in one of his appearances on the show as the villain Egghead, just for fun.

super-evil organization. We were finally winning the public relations battle.

And the kicker to all of this was that no one was aware *why* any of this was happening. For all they knew, this was just some big cultural shift, like changing decades arbitrarily has an effect on what people in certain age groups think and believe. No one was looking to a big satellite in the sky to figure out why their kids all of a sudden hated lumps of muscle poured into blue tights and red capes.

Against all my natural inclinations, we didn't trumpet what we were doing. I had to be convinced, but Miss Spiraci, my apostle Peter as it were, made a strong case for keeping it quiet. The longer we let this go without publicly taking credit for it—or even letting anyone know what it was—the more influence we would foment. We discreetly let the plan play out for an astonishing seven years.

Did you go to Bible college or something?

Everything came to a head in August 1969, just one month after we had built a fake moon and placed in in front of the real one so US astronauts could land on it and we could keep hidden what was now our—formerly the Association's—fully operational moon base.[50] The Woodstock festival served as the defining moment of a generation and the culminating point in our plan to alter their minds. I couldn't bear to sit on my hands any longer and simply let this plan go without due credit coming to its architects. Specifically,

50 If you were wondering what planning and R&D were up to during much of the mid-to-late '60s, there's your answer.

one architect. Me. So I traveled to that muddy, disgusting farm in White Lake, New York, to stand on the stage alongside our agent Janis and make clear just what we had accomplished with our Freak-out Ray. In brief, I said, "It was me! I did this to you! Proclaim me as your king and master, as I have overtaken the domain of your very minds! The sphere of your thoughts is my playground!" It was a very strong speech.

Unfortunately for history, since I didn't arrive until the morning of August 18, many of the attendees were so spaced out on the "brown acid" (a variation on a drug concoction we had developed to heighten the effects of the Freak-out Ray, though that charlatan Timothy Leary, who reportedly had ties to the under-the-radar Worldwide Conglomeration of Super-Criminals, stole the credit for it) that virtually no one remembered seeing me give any remarks at all. Instead, they said they saw a famous guitar player named "Jimi Hendrix" play a lengthy version of the "Star Spangled Banner" and other songs, some of which he played with his teeth.[51] The makers of the famous *Woodstock* documentary film went so far as to edit me out of the movie and insert very lifelike footage of a man playing those songs. This was, quite obviously, all part of the overarching superhero plot to discredit us for creating the social upheaval of the '60s.

---

51 This was obviously and transparently poppycock. There was no "Jimi Hendrix." He was a shared hallucination concocted by people affected by the Freak-out Ray. Nobody could play guitar like that, let alone with his teeth.

Here's how I know: the one group that absolutely did pay attention to my speech was the assortment of superheroes that was keeping watch over the festival throughout, hovering over the crowds just out of sight, in case anyone decided to cause just a little more trouble than those control freaks wanted.[52] Just as I was leaving the stage after my remarks, Mr. Wonderful—whom I quickly recognized was not the original Mr. Wonderful, but instead a replacement (a legacy Mr. Wonderful, if you will)—swooped down and grabbed me off the steps, blasting back up into the air with me in his arms.

Once we were well above the farm, this second-string hero proceeded to lecture me like I was [Moses receiving the commandments] about leaving people alone to live their own lives and not taking away anyone's God-given freedoms. I barely listened to this abject hypocrisy, of course. Superheroes do nothing but meddle in people's lives. And they were *at this very moment* threatening *my* freedom to control the thoughts and feelings of others! Complete hogwash.

This is the second time he's been name-checked. There are only two Bible characters that I should be compared to, and this guy is neither of them.

He carried me for what had to have been a number of miles, all the way down to the actual town of Woodstock, where I gathered his plan was to drop me off at some idiot sheriff's office and have me arrested. This was an incredibly inept and foolish course of action, but I'd expect nothing less from a doofus superhero who wasn't even the original guy to begin with. First off, I'd

52 Assurance of their presence is why Governor Nelson Rockefeller opted not to send in the National Guard, as he had threatened.

never allow some small-time sheriff to use any of his legal fumbling on me. I have diplomatic immunity (when I became king, I got a certificate that said so) and the ability to call in someone to melt the jail in an instant if need be. Second, I'd never allow this tights-clad dolt to take me near there anyway.

I fumbled around in my pockets for a bit and finally located something that I figured would get me out of this: a small sound wave generator that emitted piercing shrieks that would cause anyone who heard them to experience intense pain in their ear canals. We used it to help produce many of Android 141/115's albums. As expected, its deafening cry caused this new Mr. Wonderful to drop me and cup his hands to his ears. I called a Propulpod using my wrist-mounted computer (another recent development of the R&D department) and managed to escape largely unharmed.

As I careened back toward my hidden underground lair, I called Miss Spiraci to talk about our next steps. The Freak-out Ray had been a massive success, but now the superhero community was more than aware of us. The League of Right Rightness would be looking for ways to squash us under its thumb however possible. Not only were we causing upheaval, we were also doing so with aplomb. They had to hate that. So my message to Miss Spiraci was a single, brief sentence: "We've got to do something about these superheroes."

Letters Exchanged Between King Oblivion, Ph.D. and Melvin Bering, Publisher, Polar Bear Classics

King Oblivion, Ph.D.
Undisclosed Location
Deep Underground
Nowhere, XX 00000

May 12, 2010
Melvin Bering
Publisher, Polar Bear Classics
61 Oxroad Circle
London X2 S66

Dear Mr. Bering,

Most assuredly you know me by the name atop this letter, but for the sake of formalities, I am King Oblivion, Ph.D., the greatest supervillain who ever lived. I rule over you and everyone you know even if you don't know it.

As such, like a prince must choose a schoolmate to make his lifetime whipping boy, I would like to bestow upon you a once-in-a-lifetime privilege. I would like to grant you and your publishing company the unprecedented opportunity to publish my memoirs, which will also double as the defining text, not only for the profession of super-evil but also for some enterprising evil upstart to eventually take the reins of my evil empire, the International Society of Supervillains.

I shouldn't even have to ask if you are familiar with my century of achievement as the guiding force behind the greatest events of your lifetime (and to be completely frank, anyone else's). My book will delve deep into a life of cloning, explosions, trickery, masks, interdimensional transit, undersea education, blame, revenge, fighting so quickly you can't even follow it, rhetoric, impeccable planning, hovering in an unsettling way, devious laughter, and much more.

Surely you need no further persuasion to publish this volume. Chances are you were about to contact me anyway. Even so, enclosed you will find the text of a chapter that explains the never-before public details of the founding of the International Society of Supervillains. Yes, my prose is eminently flawless, but rest assured that I will make it even more astonishingly impossible to put down in the weeks and months to come.

Please review and respond as soon as possible. Today, if you can. I have been beyond patient with you in allowing you time to read this letter, so let's not dally any further.

Mwa-ha-ha,
King Oblivion, Ph.D.

. . .

Melvin Bering
Publisher, Polar Bear Classics
61 Oxroad Circle
London X2 S66

25 June 2010
King Oblivion, Ph.D.
Undisclosed Location
Deep Underground
Nowhere, XX 00000

Dear King,

As a result of your numerous calls and threats to our offices, I have made a very special exception to our typical review process and personally had a look at your submission dated 12 May.

Though we do appreciate your consideration in the matter of publishing your memoir, which I am certain is quite the ripping yarn indeed, I must regretfully inform you that we at Polar Bear Classics strictly publish texts by the great authors of yesteryear. Your Thomas Hardys, your Horatio Algers, your Mary Shelleys, and so forth.

I am deeply afraid that we would be colouring outside the lines, so to speak, if we were to publish—for lack of another term—a "celebrity" memoir. That is simply outside our purview here. As such, I have destroyed the manuscript you submitted.

If you wish, it would be my pleasure to refer you to an editor at our parent company, Arbitrary Abode Publishing. They have a number of imprints that have dipped their toes into the world of memoirs by present-day people of note.

Below you will find my email address. You may contact me if you wish, and I'll pass you along to an editor.

[Contact information redacted]

Yours sincerely,
Melvin Q. Bering

. . .

King Oblivion, Ph.D.
Undisclosed Location
Deep Underground
Nowhere, XX 00000

June 29, 2010
Melvin Bering
Publisher, Polar Bear Classics
61 Oxroad Circle
London X2 S66

Okay Melvin,

Don't think I don't know what you're doing. You're doing that English thing where someone is oh-so-very polite while they tell you go screw. Well, I can see right through that trash, pal.

First off, don't even try to tell me that you don't publish memoirs by notable people. I just saw this title on your list of books: *The Autobiography of Alice B. Toklas*. You lied right to my face! Here's another one: *Life and Times of Frederick Douglass*. Did you really expect these things to get past me?

Second, I have been in touch with the people at Arbitrary Abode and they have been unfathomably dismissive. You should get ready to no longer have a parent company.

Third, I really want one of those covers with the little polar bear logo and the black bar across the bottom with the title. It looks classy. As far as I know only you guys do that. So either you publish this or I force someone else to use your cover format. Which will it be?

Answer me,
King Oblivion, Ph.D.

. . .

Melvin Bering
Publisher, Polar Bear Classics
61 Oxroad Circle
London X2 S66

7 July 2010
King Oblivion, Ph.D.
Undisclosed Location
Deep Underground
Nowhere, XX 00000

Dear King,

I am sorry to say were are at an impasse. Again, I will gladly pass along your information to someone at an affiliated publisher.

In regards to having your memoirs published here at Polar Bear Classics, I am afraid there is simply no recourse. Our hands are tied. I also must insist that you refrain from using our signature trade dress with another publisher. If you do, we will be forced to take legal action.

I wish you all the best in your endeavours to publish your memoir.

Yours,
Melvin Q. Bering

. . .

King Oblivion, Ph.D.
Undisclosed Location
Deep Underground
Nowhere, XX 00000

July 10, 2010
Melvin Bering
Publisher, Polar Bear Classics
61 Oxroad Circle
London X2 S66

Hey Melvin,

You peons are "classics" now, but get ready to be history.

(That means I'm going to teleport your offices into a pit of irradiated scorpions.)

That's right, scorpions,
King Oblivion, Ph.D.

Editor's Note: This document, dated 1962 and apparently never updated, was one of several tests from the "Choosing the One" file given to applicants who wished to join the International Society of Supervillains as full-fledged members with the title of supervillain. Henchmen applicants were given a different test, which wasn't even really made up of questions; it was more of an on-paper berating. Anyway, here's the essay-based exam for aspiring international supervillains.

The International Society of Supervillains Entrance Exam

Question 1: In 500 words or less, explain why you consider yourself to be worthy of the appellation of *super*villain rather than a being called a standard-issue villain, rogue, petty criminal, ne'er-do-well, or hooligan.

Question 2: A team of superheroes has burst through the wall of your secret headquarters, accusing you of disrupting several national economies with a device you have invented that steals gross domestic products. Of course, this is something you have done, but that's none of their business. They begin fighting your henchmen, angling toward eventually laying their fists on you. Do you stand and fight, drop a trap on them, wire for help with your teletype machine, flee, or choose another option for self-defense? Explain your reasoning.

Question 3: It has often been said that superheroes and supervillains are not so different. Explain in detail why you think this might be, and format your response as a bloviating, self-aggrandizing speech.

Question 4: You have placed a giant glass bubble over the city of Houston, Texas. The bubble contains just enough oxygen to last for the next 36 hours, but only if the residents of the city don't panic. You have promised to lift the bubble on the sole condition that the United Nations and world governments agree to recognize you as the sovereign and true leader of the world. President Kennedy calls you personally to negotiate some sort of agreement that results in you lifting the bubble, but also not becoming leader of the world. Specifically, he says, "I, er ah, I believe that we can come to an accord that results in no great loss of life and in which you are quietly brought to justice." How do you respond?

Question 5: You have managed to capture your archnemesis at your temporary hideout at an abandoned sawmill. As is tradition, you have tied your superhero foe to a log traveling on a conveyor belt toward a giant circular saw, which means you have a few minutes to talk before they are split in twain, ridding you the nuisance of a constantly meddling archrival. Do you divulge your master plan, proving your superior intellect once and for all? Do you stand around and laugh for the next half-hour? Do you leave the room to listen to news of your triumph on the radio? Some other response of your choosing? Please explain.

Question 6: After a number of successful villainous plots and superhero battles, you are brought into King Oblivion, Ph.D.'s throne room to have an audience with him. He is more awe-inspiring and imposing than you ever could have imagined in your wildest dreams. He commands fear while also commanding respect. You wonder . . . is his skin made of some kind of indestructible porcelain? He is simultaneously the most attractive and toughest person you have ever seen in your life, or expect you ever will. What do you say to him? What *can* you say?

Question 7: Though some legal wrangling, you have been given a dispensation to kill one person of your choosing. Whom do you kill?

> *Editor's Note: This question has a correct answer written out in red pen: "Who needs a dispensation? If they must die, they must die."*

Villainspiration

The villain: Magneto
Key trait: In addition to having literal magnetic powers, Magneto also uses his magnetic personality to attract followers to his Brotherhood of Evil Mutants.
How he uses it: The man known as Magneto, Max Eisenhardt, and Erik Lehnsherr, among other names, used compelling pro-mutant rhetoric to gather powerful but disillusioned mutants to his anti-human cause. He was so compelling that he got people to willingly join a group that had the word "evil" right there in the name. That's some strong talking.
The wrong takeaways: Like Ozymandias, Magneto used his rhetorical gifts to further what he ultimately believed to be a virtuous cause: the end of the persecution of mutants. Virtue is dumb.

Chapter 12

IMPEDIMENTS TO INFAMY

Within a few weeks of the new Mr. Wonderful's attack on me at Woodstock, the Long-Term Planning Department set a target date for when we would eradicate the League of Right Rightness: Summer 1976.

I ordered that we invest all our resources into the two prongs of the plan devised by La Campeona and her team.

First, we'd start a morale-lowering campaign (as well as a moral-lowering campaign, but we were doing that already). We would train hundreds of our own henchmen—decoys and the henchmen Miss Spiraci and others had for their own personal operations—to go out into the world at large, particularly the biggest cities, and spread the gospel to every susceptible young goon they could find to commit petty crimes such as muggings and thefts of (relatively new) automated teller machines. This would, of

This seems like a stretch.

course, set off an unprecedented crime wave—one exponentially larger than the one we started to distract the heroes during the War of the Wicked—that would come to dominate urban life in the 1970s. People would become afraid of cities, the hubs of superhero activity. We would make them new Sodoms and Gomorrahs. We would overwhelm the heroes with activity to the point where they would quit and go back to a boring and no doubt sexless private life, become exhausted and therefore easier to neutralize, or, if we really lucked out, take on a "If you can't beat 'em, join 'em" mentality and join up with us.

I may let this one Bible thing slide.

The second prong involved pinpointed attacks on a group of specific high-ranking heroes within the League. I insisted that the R&D, Legal, and Strategy teams work together to find whatever information was available on the heroes we had in our sights so we could combat their forceful "justice" more effectively. We had a general idea of who the superheroes we wanted to target were on the basis of our numerous encounters with them, but we knew little about their histories, origins, personalities and, most importantly, weaknesses. For the most part, we just knew they all loved punching. They loved punching us, specifically. I knew that we'd have to learn more to stand a chance against them.

Mr. Wonderful, of course, was a key target, but he wasn't the only leader in the League's organizational structure. The others upon whom we chose to focus our attention were:

- Sabledusk (who changed her name from "Lady Sabledusk" sometime around 1960), the one holdover who had managed to stay in superheroics since the 1930s. She had no superpowers that we were aware of, but she was known the world over as "Earth's Most Skilled Snoop." She was an absolute sucker for a mystery, which we quickly identified as a weak point.
- Bolt Boy, a seventeen-year-old weirdo who fell off a ledge in a cave while on a spelunking expedition. According to his own telling, he encountered a dying gnome while in the depths of the cave and begged him for help to escape. As his final act, the gnome granted him super speed that he could use to run up the cave walls and get out. We never found out how Bolt Boy really got super speed, but we learned from that story that he's definitely gullible and, without question, highly sensitive to the hallucinogenic effects of fungal spores.
- Master Mysticism, a so-called "sorcerer" who traveled to China, stole a bunch of artifacts, paid off officials to force Zen teachers to instruct him in the ways of magic, and otherwise used his white privilege to shape himself into a fantastical Eastern hero living in the West, fighting demons and other such apocalyptic

enemies.[53] From what we could tell, his "spells" and artifacts were nothing more than cheap magic-shop illusions designed to distract rather than do genuine harm. We determined that he could be easily stopped with one sweeping humiliation.

- The Star Spangler, a young woman who, though a series of increasingly unlikely accidents, got her body wrapped up like a burrito in a large, irradiated American flag. The flag adhered to her skin and became permanently affixed to her body, creating a shockingly stylish and completely permanent costume. The radiation also gave her powers—most prominently the power to generate stars and stripes made out of energy that she could shoot at her enemies out of her hands and chest. We determined that we would have to remove or cover that flag in one way or another.
- Hodur, a blind archer who claimed to be the actual Norse god who went by the same name. Though we were and remain skeptical of that claim (Erebus says he's never seen him at any of the annual inter-traditional god conferences), we assumed he had many of the traits of that god. And in that case, we knew Loki had tricked him into shooting Baldr with an arrow, thereby

53 He would have made an amazing supervillain.

killing him. So we figured one solid trick would be enough to take him down.

- Mercurian Mechanoid, the sole survivor of a race of androids who lived on the planet Mercury, unbeknownst to humanity. In addition to having the power to make her body intangible, the Mechanoid could also bore you to death just by talking to you.[54] Her obvious weakness was the desire to meet anyone even claiming to be from her race, so we figured pretty quickly that we could arrange some scenario to make her believe she wasn't the last survivor and send her packing back to Mercury. Also, she had a very weird dating relationship with Master Mysticism, so we figured we could knock out two birds with one stone.
- Speaking of birds: last was Kitehawk, a reformed criminal (so already that was one huge strike against him) who used a kite-like apparatus affixed to his arms to glide through the air for surprisingly lengthy distances. He also had a power or device (our sources were unable to determine which) that enabled him to communicate with birds of various types, instructing them to attack an enemy or keep him afloat in an emergency. We would have to figure out a way to shoot him out of the sky without his birds saving him.

---

54 I know. You probably want to high five me for that one. I acknowledge your high five, but choose not to return it.

And then, of course, there was the research on Mr. Wonderful. We actually discovered a number of public news sources—including his hometown paper, the *Conurb City Evening Nebula*—that reported on the previous Mr. Wonderful's "retirement" in 1959. But what was particularly wild about it was that the old Mr. Wonderful didn't just retire to Palm Beach or whatever your typical washed-up old do-gooder goes. He went with his wife and super-powered son to an idyllic alternate universe to live a life of peaceful bliss. This was reported in the news. I couldn't believe it, especially since society seemed to regard the new guy—maybe a clone or someone from yet another alternate universe—as the "real" Mr. Wonderful nearly immediately. Almost no one talked about the old one anymore. It's almost as if everyone forgot he ever existed. If it hadn't been documented somewhere, I don't know if we would have found it. For all intents and purposes, the new Mr. Wonderful was the true Mr. Wonderful.

Here's what else we found, without a lot of effort: Mr. Wonderful's real name was Allard Curtis (both the old one and the new one, which was even more confusing), and he perpetrated a number of journalistic ethics snafus by taking photos of his own heroic endeavors and using them to earn money as a photographer at the *Evening Nebula*. That may sound like some really tough information to get, but all you had to do was mentally remove Mr. Wonderful's signature goggles to see that he was very clearly easygoing photographer Curtis. There was no mistaking it. And it was a snap to confirm. Dozens of people—within the ISS even—had been made privy to Mr. Wonderful's identity over the years, either by the man himself or one of his loose-lipped friends. He was anything but careful.

Curtis had an on-again/off-again relationship with a co-worker. Specifically, his editor and boss, Lisa Lyons. Targeting one's romantic companion is usually a worthwhile method of manipulation, but Lyons was as stubborn as hell, difficult to manipulate, and a biter. There was no way that trying to use her as bait to snag him would be anything but a hassle. However, Curtis's closest friend, a cub reporter at the paper named Ollie Jensen, would be the perfect conduit through which to weaken the hero and bend him to our whims. And it wouldn't just be any run-of-the-mill kidnapping. We'd capture Ollie and indoctrinate him. Make him one of us. We knew that would at least get Mr. Wonderful to the bargaining table. (Not that we would be too interested in bargaining with him.)

However, we were keenly aware that going after Mr. Wonderful first would be a minefield, so to speak. He was well protected and a fully intact League would probably come at us with more force than usual if its leader were the first to go. So we set our sights toward some of the second-tier heroes—namely Kitehawk, who we all despised anyway. He had briefly worked with us during the war, helping with the distractions we set up to keep the superheroes' attention diverted. But at some point during that period, Mr. Wonderful personally confronted Kitehawk and brought him over to the "hero" side with nothing more than a speech full of empty platitudes about "responsibility" and "liberty married with security." He was weak. I was ashamed to have known him. So I was more than pleased to make him our first target.

By around the middle of 1971, our plans were set in motion. In the midst of a League meeting at the Chamber of Rightness, we instructed Kitehawk's archnemesis, a former teammate of his named Pelicanus Superior, to start causing trouble in Kitehawk's home city of Dockburg. We figured Pelicanus swooping around the beach and scooping people into his mouth would be more than enough to get Kitehawk's attention and prompt him to leave the meeting, and since it was only one villain making a scene, we assumed he'd come alone.

That's just what happened, and we were all waiting for him. Just on the outskirts of Dockburg, we set up a massive laser cannon with a hyper-advanced targeting system that could not only pinpoint and incinerate Kitehawk's mechanical wings, but also singe any birds he might call in to save him from falling. And what if he called in a cast of hawks, convocation of eagles, or fallout of mutated buzzards to dive at the cannon's operator and poke his eyes out? We had that covered, too. All but the barrel of the laser was contained within a nigh-indestructible polymer dome, so no birds would be getting in. The R&D department really outdid itself by inventing a polymer so malleable that a small hole could move around the dome's surface in conjunction with the laser barrel as it shifted trajectory to pinpoint its target.

In the end, though, none of that mattered. Before the laser could get off a single shot, it overheated and exploded. Gimmick McGimmick, who was personally overseeing the operation of the laser in his capacity as Artillery Director, was badly burned in the process. He was burned so badly, in fact, that from then on he chose to wear a full face mask. He embraced the Latin side of his heritage (his mother was Mexican, his father was Irish) and became known as the masked luchador supervillain Quemado. Like Saul at Tarsus, he was transformed. No longer was he a jovial and somewhat fatuous breaker of bones and lover of weapons. From then on, he was an intense, mostly silent, and very serious orchestrator of violence.[55]

This is either biblical or Tarzan-related, and either way I'm against it.

But that wasn't the end of it. Indeed, it was only the beginning of a string of mishaps that would fall upon us like the plagues of Egypt for years thereafter. A few months after our failed attack on Kitehawk, we tried to neutralize The Star Spangler by dropping a glob of a sentient, stretchy material imprinted with the design of the Swiss flag onto her. The material would cover her entire body as well as the flag that gave her powers. We figured that the design of the Swiss flag would literally neutralize her and send her away somewhere to make chocolate. There was also the off chance that the material's own consciousness would take over her brain, but that we

Love plagues. Can't get enough of them. But really, knock off the Bible stuff. Also, I'm not sure we should be talking about our failures here at all. Why should anyone know we ever failed?

55 He stayed on as Director of Artillery for quite a few years after that, but the weapons we used took on a different tenor. They became more complex, more dangerous, and almost sadistic in their design. This was a man who no longer cared if his instruments of harm also caused harm to himself.

weren't as sure about. We would soon find out just what it was capable of.

As The Star Spangler, a student at Mantlo University by day, walked down a campus corridor, we camped out on a footbridge between the science and math buildings where we planned to drape this new outfit upon her. But without warning, the material itself rebelled and attacked the supervillain who made it, Madame Fabrique. It completely consumed her. Previously, Madame Fabrique had been nothing more than an unassuming and hardworking evil seamstress. But after this mishap, she became a living, semi-humanoid mass of stretchy fabric. The design on the material changed before our eyes from a Swiss flag to a Soviet one (Madame Fabrique was French, but she loved the idea of communism) and that's how she would remain. It was difficult to tell from then on how much of her personality was still the Madame Fabrique we knew and how much of it was the sentient fabric. We assumed a lot of what was left of her consciousness was subsumed by the fabric, because mostly what she talked about from then on was how much she desired the eradication of lint and wished to be ironed.

We then tried to trap Sabledusk in a never-ending mystery. We kidnapped her sidekick, a doofy kid named Jaybird who dressed in an incredibly easy-to-spot pastel-bright sky blue.[56] We strategically placed her in a shipping container at a freight yard in Sabledusk's home city, Sepulchre City. She had to know it was a trap but

56 The costume was even made out of a shiny, reflective material for a while.

came anyway, and as soon as she stepped inside the container, *clang*. The door slammed shut. We then dropped a solid titanium shield on top of that and affixed it all to the ground with molten metal. There was no escape.

As Jaybird and Sabledusk were being sealed inside, tubes popped out of the walls to emit a hallucinogenic gas that would cause Sabledusk to see specific visions of being locked not in a shipping container, but in a mansion on a hill backed by a lightning-streaked sky, the owner killed by one of eight of the attendees at a dinner party. We assumed she would stay in the locked-room mystery forever. There was no solution; no killer would ever emerge. Characters would die only to return alive and well with little explanation. Seeming surefire suspects would turn around with evidence of their innocence or airtight alibis. This was what we built into the scenario, both in terms of the effects of the gas and in audio messages pumped into the container by a speaker system. And yet, somehow—we still don't know how—she solved it in *three hours*. She then blasted her way out of the container and the shield around it using a hyper-powered blowtorch she had in her trademark "Useful Stuff Bandolier," and swung away with Jaybird under her arm.

Why are we giving her credit for this? Why discuss any of this, to be honest?

That wasn't all she did, either. In breaking out of the container, Sabledusk exposed a number of the villains who were overseeing the operation to the nerve gas inside. R&D had calibrated the gas to affect Sabledusk's biochemistry in specific ways, so its effects on others were unpredictable and, in some cases, quite harmful. Illuminarius took a particularly strong dose of the gas and became far more homicidal in his manner from that day on. He started wearing an assortment of vests and spiking up his hair. He spoke in obtuse, nonsensical sentences. He was like a whole new villain.

We tried a number of our other plans over the next few months. A plan to trick Hodur into drowning himself resulted in him drinking the contents of an entire freshwater lake, which led to The Sponge, who was hiding out in the lake to confirm his death, becoming near fatally dried out. An attempt to lead Bolt Boy back into the cave of his origin and to get a supervillain dwarf we had on staff, Axeheart the Slicer, to portray the gnome who gave him his powers ended with Bolt Boy leaving the cave with Axeheart in tow. He said he was "saving" the little guy. The poor dwarf had to pretend to be a benevolent gnome for three years before he figured out a way to escape the Chamber of Rightness. We built a robot and synthesized a clone that were meant to fool Mercurian Mechanoid and Master Mysticism into thinking their romantic counterparts had each turned evil, but before the plan even really got off the ground our fakes fell in love with each other and flew off into space together.

[After that string of disasters,] we tried a last-ditch attempt to challenge the League as a team—sans Mr. Wonderful, who was off-planet fighting a giant space hermit crab or something. We all dressed up as hired help at the Chamber of Rightness—cleaning staff, butlers, maids, gardeners, repair workers, and so on—and waited

Very uncomfortable with this wording. We win! We do not lose!

until they all gathered for dinner around a huge table to strike.[57] We then revealed ourselves as the Villain High Council, the voting leaders of the International Society of Supervillains, and attempted to simultaneously throw hot soup in all their faces. Turns out they had almost immediately identified us as intruders—they actually recognized the hired help and knew their names, like weirdoes—and replaced themselves with hologrammatic illusions. We were distracted just long enough for the real superheroes to come into the room and assault us with kicks about our faces and stomachs. We were lucky to get out of there alive. These fools had apparently learned some things since we had so easily toyed with them back during our war with the Association.

This is not what I want.

So much time, energy, and money wasted on so many failures. So many villains injured and traumatized. The summer of 1976 came and went without us taking one superhero off the board. We were like Job being tested.

No we weren't. We weren't Bible people and we weren't failing. That's where you got this wrong.

Spirits were at their lowest, so I pulled some of the oratorical skills I learned in my Association days out of my bag of tricks and delivered a blistering speech to the troops at our secret, hive-like underground lair. I shared the upside first: While the second prong of our superhero destruction plan was experiencing a few speed bumps, the first prong was going amazingly. Crime was huge. You might even call it a trend. Cities were increas-

57 Superheroes are almost all disgustingly rich people with severely underpaid house staffs. We've tried to recruit a few, but they've been brainwashed into believing their "loyalty" to their employers' cause is somehow valuable.

ingly hotbeds of illegal activity, and we could verify that superheroes were working an abundance of overtime. They were at the end of their rope. So badly, in fact, that they were recruiting outside what you might call their typical standards.

More and more, we were seeing evidence of so-called "superheroes" who seemed a lot more like what you'd find among our ranks: ruthless killers with knives coming out of their hands and feet; ex-villains who didn't fully give up on their old methods of torture and kill-or-be-killed mentalities; shadowy figures who would terrify and terrorize not only the criminals they sought to capture, but also those they swore to protect; ghosts, demons, and monsters; former soldiers who brought their battlefield memories to what used to be quiet, peaceful streets. Even some once "wholesome" and colorful figures were turning toward snapping necks and breaking backs to perpetuate their ill-advised "wars" on crime.

"Men and women who used to be stalwarts of 'justice' and 'upstanding citizenship' have been exposed for their hypocrisy," I said. "They have no interest in some fictional ideal of morality. They only desire power and adulation, and they'll go to whatever lengths they see fit to ensure that they keep it. We have been maligned as deviants, and came to embrace it. They have been exalted. They don't deserve it."

After several minutes of applause, I then blasted the crowd with my most heavy-hitting rhetoric: This was all the superheroes' fault. We weren't to blame for these accidents. This was certainly not any sort of serendipity or karma

This is the truth; let's make the whole chapter reflect this.

coming back to bite us, as some had suggested. Superheroes were causing us this distress.

"They believed themselves to be helpers. Protectors. Comforters. But they have caused as much discomfort as anyone. More. My friend Gimmick McGimmick—Quemado now—will never be the same. They did this to him and to many others. And they should pay for these transgressions. No more leniency for superheroes."

It worked. I convinced the ISS faithful that this battle was worth fighting, and even though we cowered from it at first, it was time to cut the head off the beast of the League. It was time to take down Mr. Wonderful. To seal the deal, I pulled the jar that contained a now-decrepit Dr. Blattarius out of my pocket and held it to the microphone. He said what I wrote for him exactly.

No. We. Didn't.

"I could not be more in agreement with King Oblivion on this," he said. "It's time to kill that son of a bitch."

For the first time all decade, the supervillains in attendance stood up and cheered.

Email Correspondence Between King Oblivion, Ph.D. and Maxine Ducallo, Ghostwriter of "Corrupt Coalition" and "Impediments to Infamy"

From: King Oblivion Ph.D.
To: Maxine Ducallo
Subject: Bible references

Ms. Ducallo,

I'm just going to get right to the point. What's with all the Bible references in these chapters? I'm a supervillain, not a . . . guy who talks about religious stuff. What do they call those again?

Either way, I don't really see the relevance of these churchy comparisons to my life story, the greatest story ever told. This memoir is a book that will be talked about for centuries. People will gather in buildings specifically built for the study of this book to parse its teachings and build their lives around it. People will go to special schools to dig into its meaning and teach it. People will build their lives and professions around this book.

In other words, it's nothing like the Bible. So tell me what you're going to do to fix this.

. . .

From: Maxine Ducallo
To: King Oblivion, Ph.D.
Subject: RE: Bible references

Rex Imperator,

I beg that you forgive any indiscretions that I may have made in peppering a few biblical allusions into my chapters. If it would please you, I'd like to explain my reasons.

First, and I believe your henchmen knew this when they opened up the portal that swallowed my car and brought me here, most of my work has been in the field of "inspirational" novels. That's code for Christian. So the Bible is my writing wheelhouse, so to speak.

Second, I'd just like to note that when you trained me to ghost-write for you, you stated that your intended reader reaction was "worshipful reverence and fealty." I thought some comparative language to religious figures might help bring those feelings forward.

I was clearly mistaken in that assumption. I am fully aware that you are not a priest, preacher, minister, rabbi, imam, shaman, pastor, clergyman, or holy person of any kind. I will change the chapters to reflect your wishes. Just let me know what to do.

In supplication,
Maxine Ducallo

. . .

From: King Oblivion, Ph.D.
To: Maxine Ducallo
Subject: RE: Bible references

Ms. Ducallo, I've read your reasoning and I just wanted to let you know that I do understand where you're coming from. I may be a supervillain, but I'm not a monster. You made a career out of writing religious books. I get that. It's hard to break habits. And, you know, since you made that a career, you probably believe a lot of that stuff, too. I get it. And these are things that can be fixed.

But on top of all that, you also wrote a bunch of stuff about the ISS failing and being defeated by superheroes, and that's basically unforgivable. So gather up your belongings and stand at your station so security can come into your writing quarters and escort you out of your quarters. And into a giant blender.

Peace be with you.

Editor's Note: Below is the copy from a brochure I found in with King Oblivion's files. It's about dealing with the negative emotions that come with the inevitable failures that are part and parcel of the profession of super-evil. I don't know whether the contents were meant for publication in a memoir—it was a glossy, tri-folded brochure like you'd find in a doctor's office—but it was wadded in with the text of the preceding chapter, so one can only assume there was some sort of plan for it. Or maybe King Oblivion was just reading it as he reviewed the text. I'm not sure. Either way, these brochures were apparently produced by the International Society of Supervillains—they're branded with the group's logo of a skull-embossed ring on a flag—possibly for use in the group's moneymaking fake-health-clinic scam of the mid-1970s.

Crush Your Feelings: Coping With Adversity as a Supervillain

Hey there, villain man or villain lady! You sure do seem blue. What's got you down?

If your answer is "a plan of mine failed" or "a superhero hit me so hard in the jaw that I can only eat mushed-up bananas," then don't worry. You're not alone. These things happen to all supervillains at one time or another.

If you've trained in supervillainy, you're likely aware that occasional setbacks are part of the job. And there is literature that explains the most effective actions to take to counteract those setbacks and turn them into success. Also, how to escape with your life and health. But what about the emotional toll these events take? How can an enterprising, capable supervillain maintain a healthy self-image in light of often-deflating defeat?

These coping mechanisms can help keep you confident while the world tries to bring you down:

Assign blame

You're strong. You're smart. You are more than equipped to do your job. So why did you lose? Because someone else ruined it. Maybe it was a superhero. Perhaps it was a deity with some unfair bias against you. Perhaps it was a jealous rival supervillain. Whatever the case, this was not your fault. It is never your fault.

Rend your clothes and curse God

There are few things more reinvigorating than to purge your bad emotions by shouting them into the sky while you tear your shirt. The added bonus is that if anyone is around to see you doing it, they may become intimidated and frightened of you, believing you to be unstable. Two birds.

Meditate

For supervillains, meditation consists of sitting silently in a room with your legs crossed, attempting to will one's enemies to be erased from history with only the power of one's mind. Legend has it that this has worked a few times.

Find an outlet for your pent-up rage

This is code for "make your henchmen fight each other for your amusement."

Forget that you ever lost or experienced failure

It didn't happen. It never happened. If there's photo or video evidence, it's fake. If someone reminds you of it with an eyewitness account, freeze them. If your own brain tries to keep reminding you of this non-event, hire someone to remove that erroneous memory from your brain.

Talk to a certified supervillain therapist

A qualified and licensed therapist who specializes in supervillain psychology should have you back to your megalomaniacal emotional peak within a few weeks.

NOTE: **Do not**, under any circumstances, allow yourself to be analyzed by a non-supervillain therapist, especially ones that work at any sort of sanitarium or asylum. These people will try to hurt you.

Take drugs

Here's something not everyone knows about drugs: they make you feel groovy! Prescription, illicit, whatever. Just do what gets you through.

Upgrade

If you simply cannot get past your feelings of despair and inadequacy using the methods described above, there's always the option of enhancing yourself with a new form or power. You could become impossibly muscular and huge, for example. Or place your brain in a robot body. You could perform an experiment on yourself, obtaining 100-times average human intelligence (if you don't have it already). You could plate your entire body in a damage-resistant gold. Or you could get a really cool new pair of sunglasses. Do whatever makes you feel like a new, improved you.

However you decide to cope with hardships that come your way, remember that supervillainy is an important profession that often pays off in big ways. You may be down now, but you're not out. And even if you are out, there's always the option of building a revenge-fueled artificial intelligence based on your thought patterns. You have options, so go out there and make some mayhem!

Villainspiration

The villain: Mysterio
Key trait: A master of special effects, Quentin Beck could create highly realistic illusions to fool his superhero opponents into believing unlikely scenarios.
How he uses it: Mysterio had great powers, but his consistent failures to defeat Spider-Man along with his appearance—he was often described as having a fish bowl on his head—caused heroes and villains alike to consider him a lower-tier villain. Mysterio bounced back from his failures, however, driving Daredevil almost completely insane with an intricate plan involving a child that Daredevil was led to believe was the Antichrist. After numerous setbacks and defeats, he pulled off the big one.
The wrong takeaways: In the end, Mysterio gives up and commits suicide upon being found out and confronted by Daredevil. That's no way out for a true supervillain. Also, his plan was a straight-up rip-off of a Kraven the Hunter plan. I know there's no honor among thieves, but be original, folks.

Chapter 13

A TURPITUDINOUS TURNAROUND

The new plan to directly take down Mr. Wonderful came together faster than any attack plan we had pulled together before, but that's only because any number of plans to permanently neutralize the guy had been in the works for decades. It materialized so quickly because it was the culmination of hundreds of old ideas.

Do we have to quantify this sort of thing? We're geniuses. I am, at least. All my plans come together equally spectacularly.

Even before the formation of the ISS, back in the Association days, [Dr. Blattarius]—who was typically not up on making specific plans—had a few back-pocket strategies for yanking the big, red-costumed weirdo out of the sky and breaking him. When we took control of his organization, we intercepted those stratagems, of course, and were able to incorporate them into our own machinations.

We're mentioning him a lot, and I've already defeated him. Seems redundant.

What was amazing was how very few head-on attacks—focused specifically and solely on Mr. Wonderful—anyone had bothered to attempt. They'd attack the League, sure, but only a hand-

Again, a needless mention.

ful of villains had ever gone *mano a mano* with the caped one himself. One time in the late 1940s, Dr. Blattarius tried to shoot him (the original version of him, that is) with a ray from space that replicated the effects of the purple water that people swam in and drank back in his home micro-universe, but he calmly flew up and knocked the ray into the sun. That was what the guy always did. He just tossed stuff he didn't like into the sun.

I do blame them.

I guess that was part of why people were so intimidated by him. They didn't want to get thrown into the sun.[58] I don't blame them. And then there was the matter of him being a microscopic organism—a germ, when you really get down to it—who lived in a micro-universe that had sprung to life in a wad of gum under a desk in the *Conurb City Evening Nebula* newsroom.

The story goes that mere hours before a janitor came through the office and scraped the gum off the underside of the desk, Mr. Wonderful's micro-organism father, Burp-Belch, got some kind of strange premonition that his world was about to get tossed in the garbage. So Burp-Belch and his wife Horrk put their son, Cough-Belch, in a machine that grew him to enormous size and activated it. Within a few brief seconds, Cough-Belch materialized at full human size in the *Evening Nebula* offices. The janitor, Joseph Curtis, took him home to his wife, Mabel, and they

58 We never documented any cases of Mr. Wonderful actually throwing any living person into the sun, but how could you know one way or another? What evidence would be left?

raised him as their own, naming him "Allard." (This isn't part of the often-shared version of his origin story, but I tend to think it was because it sounded a little like a sneeze.) Somehow he passed for human despite his always-moist, pale-blue skin and bristly, azure hair.

I don't suppose that story is frightening in itself, but it's pretty weird to think about how he was this little microscopic organism. It seems so gross. He's repugnant.

And yet, he had managed to make some very close friends and allies over the years. Not even superheroes. Regular people. That's where we were going to get him. If we couldn't hurt his body (he could shift his skin and organs at will to avoid physical harm), then we'd have to go for his *feelings*. As I previously mentioned, the plan that had been floating around in various incarnations over the years was one which involved kidnapping and threatening Mr. Wonderful's "best friend," Ollie Jensen, and using that leverage to bring the baby-blue hero to heel.

Naturally, we weren't the first ones to come up with that idea. Dr. Blattarius had kidnapped Ollie and Mr. Wonderful's boss and girlfriend, Lisa Lyons, many times over the years.[59] As I mentioned earlier, with Lyons, everyone ended up getting bitten or kicked. The kidnappers would often just let her go of her own accord. Ollie, on the other hand, always, *always* had to be saved

Really don't know why he needs to keep coming up. I rarely talk about him, and once I staple your mouth shut so will you.

59 It's how we all discovered that Lyons wouldn't hesitate to bite any criminal that came near her. Her teeth were scissor-like and had pinpoint accuracy.

by Mr. Wonderful. He was totally incapable of fending for himself.

But the early kidnappers were careless. They'd keep him in a room with flimsy stone or wooden walls that Mr. Wonderful could simply smash through, or they'd let him go out for a walk so that Mr. Wonderful could just swoop down and take him home. It was truly foolish and lazy planning.

Ollie was kidnapped so many times that Mr. Wonderful started thinking of ways to help him get out of scrapes without his superheroic assistance. For example, back in the early '60s, Mr. Wonderful gave Ollie—who mysteriously never aged, much like Lyons and any number of other superheroes, their associates, or we supervillains—a device that would turn him into a living tank for an hour. The idea was that Ollie would hit a button, transform into a tank, bulldoze his way out of whatever structure in which he was being held, and go on about his day. What ended up happening was that Ollie destroyed every statue in a war memorial park.[60]

After that fiasco, Mr. Wonderful took a different tack: he put an impossible-to-remove ankle bracelet around Ollie's leg that would emit a signal only he could hear (it was in germ language or some such thing) any time he was placed in a room smaller than 10 feet by 10 feet. That, of course, led to a number of false alarms—Ollie

60 The particular villain who had kidnapped Ollie that time, Mortalitus, had imprisoned him in a mausoleum.

lived in a tiny apartment in a huge city, after all—but it also sent Mr. Wonderful running any time his closest friend was genuinely kidnapped. He saved him every single time.

That reliability was the foundation upon which we built our plan. Ollie would serve as the bait with which to lure Mr. Wonderful.

[Kidnapping him was shockingly easy.] For someone who had been kidnapped dozens—if not hundreds—of times, Ollie had seemingly no system for protecting himself. I sent Thousand Eyes the Puker to go pick him up, and he literally just grabbed Ollie from the sidewalk while he was waiting for a bus. He was right out in the open with nothing to stop anyone from doing him potential harm. It was like an open invitation to kidnapping the closest friend of the world's most powerful superhero.

What's shocking about it? Everything comes easily to me.

But, indeed, we *wanted* Mr. Wonderful to come and attempt to save him. We set the trap like this: we tied Ollie to a chair in a sealed-off room built entirely out of surgical steel, the one substance that Mr. Wonderful couldn't smash, phase, or even see through.[61] Around the structure, we set up lamps that emitted X-rays to weaken him (we didn't have full confirmation that they actually hurt him, but we'd gotten reports that he would blurt out "getting . . . weaker" any time he was exposed to them) and sprinklers that would shoot out his home world's very own purple water (which was just regular water we mixed with food coloring). We also spent all the time we

61 I reiterate: He's a germ.

had with Ollie indoctrinating him to the truth about supervillains. He was quite susceptible to our arguments, and we knew that any praise for us coming out of Ollie's mouth would be a crushing blow to Mr. Wonderful's psyche.

This makes me seem too hands-off. Change this.

Almost on cue—like, within a few minutes—Mr. Wonderful arrived and we sprung the trap. For the first time in years, I personally oversaw the entire caper, blasting the weak-willed germ with purple water and X-rays to my heart's content. And he seemed to be weakening. He crumpled to the ground just outside the surgical steel chamber. There was just one problem: he didn't come alone.

We thought he would. For decades, the unspoken rule was that superheroes would deal with personal problems and the local actions of their archnemeses solo. Teams were only allowed if a group of heroes was attacked together, the superheroes in question operated strictly as a team, or if there was a world-threatening or galaxy-spanning danger at hand. Mr. Wonderful upended all that here, bringing with him two superheroes I had never seen or heard of. One was a young woman—she was maybe twenty—who didn't attack directly; she stood off to the side and waved her hands in the air, generating some sort of visible, glowing-orange energy that made me and every other supervillain who was helping execute the plan feel nauseated. And then there was the guy with the huge gun.

Sometime later, the R&D department looked him up. We discovered that this was Gun-Man: The Man Who Has a Gun. About two years prior, a group of gangsters had blown up and sunk his houseboat. He lived alone under his civilian identity of Charles Palais, but there was a lot of cool stuff in there that he couldn't replace, so the incident made him really upset. I heard later from some of the crooks that did it—employees of Mafia Don, a board member of the ISS—that it wasn't intentional. It was merely collateral damage in a hit on a rival mob boss who lived on a yacht docked in the next ship over.[62] Either way, Gun-Man swore revenge, bought one really immense gun that he could custom-modify into other types of guns on the fly, put on a shirt with a skeleton torso, and started hunting down any criminal he could find. At first the League didn't want to work with him, but our crime wave grew so huge that they couldn't help but recruit him to their cause.

He used his giant gun to blast through the surgical-steel room and release Ollie. He then started shooting all the X-ray devices and sprinklers, which crashed to the ground. I noticed that they fell apart almost too easily, shattering with just a few shots.

Soon enough, the superheroes were gone with Ollie in tow, and another plan had ended with us holding the bag. I never even heard anything about Mr. Wonderful being harmed by our forcible changing of Ollie's mind.

Don't like this characterization. I'd prefer "The plan was a total success, once we revised all the goals after the fact."

62 I knew the guy they were hitting, too. It was Capo Grande, who also had ties to the ISS. I had to give Don's people a talking to (and some of them a crack on the skull) for that one. I did not and will not tolerate inter-ISS fighting. I personally know what happens when that gets going, and only I'm allowed to do it.

But it wasn't a total loss. We learned a lot. Not only did we come to know about Gun-Man, we also learned the identity of the young woman Mr. Wonderful had brought along with him. She called herself The Blessing. We never found out her real name, possibly because she didn't have one. She was a genetically engineered life form developed solely for the purpose of bringing luck to the people whom she deemed deserving of it. Clearly, the League had overseen her creation and then brainwashed her into their service.[63] By imbuing a chosen few with great luck, she thereby created terrible luck for anyone else who happened to be around. That'd be us.

Upon reviewing film of the other operations we had undertaken since we had started our anti-League initiative, we noticed that she had been present at each and every one. She must have been thirteen years old when they started using her for this stuff. Every accident we had endured, every stroke of misfortune, it was all her doing. She was the League's living insurance policy.

I also figured out why the equipment we had been working on for months seemed to be so uncharacteristically shoddy, even setting aside all the bad luck that had been thrust upon us by a misguided young woman who had been conscripted into the lie of heroism. As I was storming out of the control room while Mr. Wonderful flew away with Ollie and Gun-Man under each arm (The Blessing could fly on her own, it seemed),

63 Honestly, it was one of the few times I wished I had come up with one of their plans myself.

I noticed out of the corner of my eye that someone was standing just around the corner, watching me and laughing. I bounded over to where this mysterious figure was standing and before me was none other than Nicky Claws, founder of the Worldwide Conglomeration of Super-Criminals. He tried to run away, but I summoned a Propulpod so I could catch up and seize him by the neck. We traveled all the way back to a secondary ISS hideout in the Allegheny Mountains that way—with him dangling off the side of the Propulpod as I gripped him by the scruff with one hand. Obviously, I didn't want to show him the location of our hive-like headquarters, but I did want to show him our power.

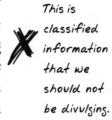

This is classified information that we should not be divulging.

I invited Miss Spiraci, Quemado, La Campeona, and Madame Fabrique to the Allegheny hideout—a hollowed-out mountain with my face carved into the side—to help me interrogate the old crab. I figured we'd take turns on him, but all it took was a few moments of Madame Fabrique spreading her fabric-like body over his face and threatening to suffocate him to get answers.

The Conglomeration had gone underground years before, during the War of the Wicked. Once the dust from that conflict had settled, Claws and the handful of other Association defectors who had started the group mulled over their options. What could they do to promote their agenda, undermine the ISS—which they viewed as a new version of the Association—and keep a low profile? They decided at the time that espionage was the way to go. These decisions were made in the 1960s, after all. They wanted to jump on that spy trend. That meant covertly causing mayhem by breaking into various places—government buildings, businesses, and our own ISS facilities—and sabotaging whatever they could get their hands on.

Their work caused only minor hindrances for nearly a decade, but by the time the '70s rolled around, the Conglomeration caught wind of our plans to destroy superherodom by somehow successfully planting a bug in one of our conference rooms in one of our secondary, non-top-secret facilities. Our Alaskan retreat, specifically. And that's when they got the idea to begin vandalizing our equipment, starting with the laser we built to shoot down Kitehawk.

Stop giving this (classified) information away! It's non-top-secret, but it's still secret!

That revelation sent Quemado—who had been so severely injured when the laser malfunctioned, I'll remind you—into a fit of rage. He hit the poor crab-man with three head-scissor takedowns before I managed to pull them apart. With his neck all but crushed, Claws was ready to deal. I think he assumed we were just going to kill him, but I had different plans. I told him to go back to his Conglomeration—wherever they happened to be lurking in the shadows—and tell them about their new mission. They'd keep sabotaging stuff, sure. But not ours. Not anymore. Now they'd be focusing strictly on the League and their otherworldly contraptions. They were contractors for us now. And if they were to break the deal, well, then Quemado would go a few more rounds with him. He agreed to our terms and went on his way.

Pulling the Conglomeration into our orbit—as soon as they were no longer useful, we'd destroy them, for certain—was a productive first step, but there was still plenty to do. For one, we needed to further raise our public profile. I had caught wind of the ongoing development of the film *Superman*, a grossly whitewashed and rose-colored adaptation of the life of Mr. Wonderful. The clear intent of the film was to make the public "believe" in superheroes again. I wouldn't allow it. So I called up one of my compatriots, the supervillain director George Lucas, and asked him what he was working on. He said he had an idea for some sort of pulpy space opera called *Star Wars*, and I was intrigued. I asked him who the lead villain was, and he described Darth Vader, who sounded fairly imposing and admirable already, but I knew he could be even more meritorious. Aspirational, even.

"Make him more like me," I said. "Design him to be as close to me as you can. Keep the robot stuff or whatever you have in mind, but if you make him look like me, you'll have created the ultimate movie villain. We'll have the coolest one ever on our hands. Oh, and make sure your movie comes out before that *Superman* drivel."

And that's just how it went. It was a flawless plan, executed perfectly.[64]

Strong work here.

Changing perceptions was a boost, but what we really needed was someone on the inside.

64 On our request, Lucas made a new set of movies a few decades later. Though they helped us calibrate a very important weapon, they portrayed Darth Vader as a petulant little brat. This hurt me personally, so I mind-controlled the executives at a major media company to buy his baby, the *Star Wars* franchise, away from him, and make the villains cool again.

Recruiting a member of the League to our cause and then sending that person back to the opposition to act as our mole: that was the component we were missing in all the planning we'd been doing over the past eight-plus years. That's what it would take to neutralize The Blessing and end the scourge of superheroics for the foreseeable future.

But who to recruit? Who could be unhinged and amoral enough to jump from team "justice" to team evil? When I discussed it with my top advisors—Miss Spiraci and La Campeona—it seemed obvious. We needed Gun-Man.

To get him, we staged a huge heist of a cargo ship in New York Harbor. We didn't really want anything on the ship—it was full of refrigerators—but we made sure to make plenty of noise to attract him to the harbor. And the participants all dressed in pinstriped suits to fit what we assumed was his mental image of gangsters, despite the fact that real gangsters hadn't dressed like that in decades. It was a sort of reverse St. Valentine's Day Massacre.

The bait worked like a charm. Soon enough, Gun-Man was tearing through the ship, gunning down whomever he saw.[65] When he got into position on the ship's bridge, that's when I called to him from the houseboat I had positioned starboard. I turned on the floodlight and pointed it directly toward him. Then I jumped on the loudspeaker:

"Hey, this houseboat's pretty nice, right? You want it?"

---

65 Which is why we assigned only our most bulletproof members to serve as lures.

He said something in response, but I couldn't hear him. He seemed pretty excited, though. I continued.

"Well, just swim on over here and get it. It's yours. All we have to do is talk."

He boarded the houseboat within what seemed like seconds, and the negotiation began. I asked him what it'd take, besides the houseboat, to get him to work for us. He was hesitant at first, but after we agreed to replace some things he had on his old houseboat—a really nice can opener, some handmade quilts, an expensive flashlight, a set of collectible tin cans, and so on—we basically had him hooked. He just wanted one more thing.

"An even bigger gun."

I shook his hand on the spot. We had our mole. And with his help began the League of Right Rightness's end.

This makes it seem like we couldn't have achieved it without him. Rephrase.

Transcript of Phone Interview with Gun-Man

Gun-Man: Hello? Who is this?

Editor: Hello. My name is Matt D. Wilson. I'm compiling some information to include in the posthumous memoir of King Oblivion, Ph.D., and since you knew him—

GM: Can we speed this up? I only get fifteen minutes on the phone. Wait. He's dead?

Ed: Yeah. Plane crash. Would you say that you knew him well?

GM: I mean, I got to know him over time. But it was hard to know if the version of him I was seeing was the real him, you know? The version who met me back in '78, I mean, that guy clearly wanted something from me. After that, he changed a little. Didn't seem so eager to please. Less hands-on. But I kept working for him. He kept his word about giving me a place in the ISS.

Ed: When you met him, was he different than you thought he would be?

GM: Yeah, I mean, I had only heard about him through the stuff that got said among members of the League, you know? They all hated him. Said he was a coward, a liar, a genocidal maniac. Said he might not even be human. He was everything they hated. But he was a sweetheart to me. He'd probably be furious that I put it that way, but it's what he was.

Ed: So you didn't feel any guilt about switching sides? Being a mole for the International Society of Supervillains?

GM: Nah. My whole deal was that I was a guy who shot stuff. And people. I was surprised the League even let me join. They were just desperate, so I took advantage of that. But they were never particularly nice to me, you know? They treated me like a necessity, not a friend. They sure never offered to give me a new houseboat. The supervillains did. Plus, I got a much cooler gun out of it.

Ed: So, after the big battle with the superheroes . . . what was your role in the ISS? What did you do there?

GM: Pretty much any time we needed to get inside somewhere, or get out of somewhere, or shoot someone or something, I was the guy. I'd shoot things with my gun. I didn't really have very many other skills. But I guess King O. thought that skill was pretty important. I got sent out on a lot of missions.

Ed: I heard that you eventually branched out on your own, though. Is that true? Did you leave the ISS at one point?

GM: Yeah. I resigned around '95. I don't know what I was thinking. I guess I just needed to change things up. I went back home to New York. Started doing the vigilante thing. Tried to protect people in my old neighborhood, keep the scumbags there from taking advantage of them.

Ed: And King Oblivion allowed that to happen?

GM: I don't know that "allowed" is the word. He let me do it, as long as I stayed out of any ISS business. He told me I could shoot anybody from the Conglomerate I wanted, so I did some of that. And I kept far away from anything King O. or the ISS was doing. They were bigger-scale than any of this stuff, anyway. Still, biggest mistake I ever made.

Ed: How so?

GM: Well, it's how I ended up here.

Ed: And "here" is . . . ?

GM: The Dodecahedron. The AGHAST *(Allied Governments Honorable Anti-Supervillain Taskforce)* prison that orbits Earth. When I was working for the ISS, they had all kinds of workarounds and loopholes they could use to keep me out of a place like this. On my own, all it took was blasting one fancy-pants developer to land me in here. I didn't have anyone to help me.

Ed: How long have you been in there?

GM: Since '99.

Ed: Are you mad that no one from the ISS has come to get you out?

GM: Am I mad? I'm not mad, but I wish that someone would—

Guard: *(in background)* Palais! Somebody here to see you!

GM: *(to guard)* What? Who? How would they even get here?

Guard: *(in background)* Proceed to the visitation area!

GM: I have to go, I guess. Somebody's here. That's really weird. Anyway, it was nice to talk to someone. Haven't had a real conversation in a long time.

(click)

Editor's Note: Of the "reading comprehension" documents I found among King Oblivion's files, this was the most obviously anti-superhero of the bunch. I almost got the sense that the purpose of the entire exercise was to get test-takers to get to this one, and for this to shape their perceptions of superheroes as frauds and scammers with uncouth and off-putting superpowers. But that's just speculation. Feel free to judge for yourself.

Reading Comprehension Test, Part 3

Read closely. Answer the discussion questions that follow.

Rodney Carlson was an average, unassuming microbiologist studying whipworm when, as a result of a co-worker's careless mistake, the specimen Rodney was studying inexplicably turned radioactive and jumped into his eye in a really gross chain of events that you kind of had to be there to see, but trust me, it was totally disgusting. Anyway, it turns him into a hero who uses a parasite-like ability to feed and survive on a host. With these powers, he contributes nothing to the host's survival and hopes to one day fight crime as the STUPENDOUS CAPTAIN PARASITE!

"Rod . . . I just . . . I can't do that. I'll lose my job, man. I mean, I'm barely hanging by a thread as it is."

To be perfectly honest about it, Andy Putnam hadn't seen his old friend Rod Carlson since high school. And, well, this wasn't the most opportune time for him to show up.

Andy had lost his job as a security guard at Cantwell Chemical three months ago after he had naively given several barrels of nitroglycerin to a man who looked like a terrorist.

As it turned out, the man was indeed the courier who had been hired to take the chemicals over to Method Labs for experimental use on some homeless people, but Andy really should have considered the optics.

In the aftermath, Andy had hit some more road bumps. His girlfriend left him for a lawyer (a family services lawyer, but a lawyer is a lawyer). His dog had been hit by a delivery truck; he found out later that someone had actually paid the driver to do it. His parents told him that he was adopted, and somehow half gopher.

It had been a tough few months.

So now, here was Rod, making trouble at his new job. Frankly, he didn't remember Rod being this way at all. He just . . . wouldn't stop.

"Look, man—I just—I can't give away any free cinnamon buns, okay?"

Andy was trying to be assertive without being a dick.

"One day I ate a bunch of these that had been sitting out for a while and they docked the price out of my pay. The full retail price! Even though they were old! These guys are not cool, all right?"

Rod made an effort go with the strongest argument he could muster.

"Dude."

Little known to Andy, Rod had been living in the mall for about three weeks now. Rod spent most of his evenings hiding in a trash can until the security guards went home for the night. Then he would sneak behind the fast-food chicken counter and sleep for a few hours until the young woman who always opened the place showed up about twenty minutes late.

He subsisted on the nugget pieces he could fish out of the top of the trash cans and bits of waffle fries he could persuade children to give him out of their kids' meals. His bargaining strategy: offer the kid a quarter and a Hot Wheels car from the dollar store if he could have the fries. Then, eat the fries in one gulp before the child could answer. Then, don't give the kid anything and crawl away.

During the day, Rod would spend a lot of his time rubbing against towels in the housewares section of the mall's department store, wallowing in the moisture of the mall fountain, and trying to steal the shoes off people who strode past. He also tried to sit in a tray full of Szechuan chicken at the Angry Wok once, claiming that he was trying to reproduce asexually. He was quickly banned from the restaurant, where a picture of him remains behind the counter to this day.

Rod pressed his point to Andy.

"Dude, come on."

Andy kind of felt some sympathy for the guy. They hadn't really been great friends in high school, but they used to joke around sometimes, talk about class, that kind of thing. And Rod had stood up for him that one time that everyone thought that Andy had bitten off Chrissy Hyman's finger in Mr. Pauca's physics class.

It was just one cinnamon bun, right? It couldn't hurt that much.

"Well, Rod . . . I guess it couldn't—Hey, what are you wearing?"

Rod looked down for a second like he had forgotten what he had put on some four months prior.

"Oh. That's my superhero costume."

Andy was confused.

"Wha—Superhero costume? Are . . . are you okay, Rod?"

Rod took offense.

"Am I okay? Am I *okay*? I'm better than okay, Mr. Cinnamon Team Member Andy Putwell! I'm Captain Parasite, pal. *Crime fighter.*"

"It's Putnam," Andy corrected.

"What?" Rod asked, completely thrown off his train of thought. "What's Putnam?"

"Nothing. So . . . you fight crime, then? You . . . uh . . . you don't seem to be fighting crime now."

"Well, I would be if I had a damn cinnamon bun!" Rod exclaimed so that Andy's manager, Mr. Kareem E. Frosting, could hear.

"Okay, okay." Andy decided that he should probably concede. He handed over the pastry. "Here. Just . . . just go somewhere else now. Please."

Rod eyed the cinnamon bun like it was a gold brick. With it seemingly having met his approval, he turned his scrutiny toward Andy, who was frantically shooting glances back and forth between the front counter and back room. He knew it was only seconds before Mr. Frosting came out to fire and humiliate him in front of all these teenagers who had already been promoted ahead of him several times already.

Finally, after what seemed like years, Rod nodded and turned to go.

"Okay. See you around, Andy."

Andy breathed a sigh of relief. But the respite didn't last for long. He turned slowly to see Mr. Frosting standing directly behind him, towering, shaking his head. Some teen was about to get his job.

Rod sat on one of the benches underneath the big mall skylight, chomping on his cinnamon bun and edging ever closer to the elderly woman sitting next to him so he could siphon off some of her body heat.

He thought aloud.

"Well, what's next for the unstoppable Captain Parasite? Hmmm. Hey! I bet the mattress store will let me sleep there for, like, an hour if I tell them I have some incurable disease or something."

This was very solid plan, Rod thought.

"Score!"

And so began another adventure.

Discussion Question #1: Captain Parasite is sickening. He's an affront to everything respectable and genuine in the world. He's a hypocrite and a fraud who believes that simply putting on a costume and calling himself a "crime fighter" makes him some kind of moral superior. He sells out his friends and makes strangers uncomfortable. There are many other superheroes like him. He should be vaporized. Agree or strongly agree?

Discussion Question #2: List the numerous parallels between Captain Parasite and Mr. Wonderful. They're similar in so many ways.

I'll start you out with one: They're both vile. But Mr. Wonderful is worse. Captain Parasite just got infested with radioactive whipworm. Mr. Wonderful *is* a germ. Did you know that? He's a germ!

Discussion Question #3: If you were Andy, what would you do to rid the world of the scum that is Captain Parasite? Go into detail. List specific body parts you would attack.

Discussion Question #4: But seriously, how much does Captain Parasite, and by extension all superheroes, suck?

Villainspiration

The villain: Talia al Ghul
Key trait: Control of a massive, shadowy, world-controlling organization called Leviathan, which gives her near-infinite resources with which to challenge and break Batman.
How she uses it: For many years, Talia skirted the line between hero and villain, sometimes working with her supervillain father Ra's al Ghul, and other times working against him and other villains. But when her son, Damian, fully gave over his loyalties to his father, Batman, she banned Damian from her sight and swore revenge on Batman, creating a clone of Damian designed to kill them both—it succeeds in killing Damian—and putting Batman through psychological hell.
The wrong takeaways: Talia's main goal in all her Leviathan plotting was to save, and ultimately get revenge for, what she considered to be the loss of her son. This was aiming low. She could have done so much more.

Chapter 14

THE END OF HEROISM

Editor's Note: Once again, a spate of authors made numerous attempts to write this chapter, but not one met with King Oblivion's approval, so none were finished. He was particularly picky about what he considered the "climax moments" of his life, and felt that they required a level of theatricality and gravity that none of the ghostwriters he worked with could adequately capture. As a result, I've been forced once again to present what I could find; in this case, several transcripts of conversations and interrogations, minutes from meetings, and battle plan documents generated between Gun-Man's defection in 1977 and the immediate aftermath of the Battle of the Underground Volcano Vortex in 1986.

November 15, 1977: Transcript of planning meeting between King Oblivion, Ph.D., Miss Spiraci, and Gun-Man, Transcribed by Steno-Grappler

```
King
Oblivion: How's the boat? How's the new gun?
```

Gun-Man: They're working out wonderf-uh. I mean they're exactly what I needed. Thanks.

Miss Spiraci: We're pleased to hear it. So now that that's all in order, we'd like to hear, from you, just what you're willing to do for us.

GM: Well, like you said before, I'm supposed to go back to the League and gather information about what they're doing. Find their weaknesses and report them back. I can do all that.

MS: Remind us, for the record, the particular information you'll be looking for.

GM: How to neutralize or capture The Blessing, hidden entrance and exit points to and from the Chamber of Rightness, times and dates heroes are most likely to be alone, and as King Oblivion put it to me, "why Mr. Wonderful is so disgusting."

MS: And have you been able to procure any of this information in your previous dealings with the League of Right Rightness? Is there anything you can share with us now?

GM: Mr. Wonderful is some kind of germ man. I know that. One time I peeked into his room while the door was closing and I saw the big glass dish he sleeps in. There's a heat lamp over it.

KO: I knew it. (dry heaving sounds)

MS: Much of that we did already know, though we were not aware of the bed. What about The Blessing? What can you tell us about her?

GM: Not much. The top superheroes in the League—Mr. Wonderful, Sabledusk, The Star Spangler—keep her completely under wraps. I don't know if I've ever seen her just walking around the halls of the Chamber. She comes on missions and that's it.

MS: Have you ever had a conversation with her?

GM: No, not really. Nothing besides just a word or two here or there on a mission. "Go over there." "To your left." Stuff like that.

MS: Let's talk timeframe.

KO: Make it fast.

MS: But also protect your cover. By when do you think you can get back to us with the intelligence we need?

GM: I'll need an out. In late spring/early summer the League does a recruitment drive and some active members go on the reserve list. I could take some time off then, come back here. That'd be . . . May, I guess?

KO: May?!

MS: If that's when you can do it without drawing their attention back to us, then that's when it'll get done. We'll reconvene then.

KO: Get this done, Gun-Man.

May 20, 1978: Transcript of informational meeting between King Oblivion, Ph.D., Miss Spiraci, and Gun-Man, Transcribed by Steno-Grappler

King Oblivion: Been a while since we've seen you, Gun-Man. Anybody with the League catch a whiff of you doing any investigating on our behalf? Get a sense of suspicion?

Gun-Man: I stayed under the radar. They don't pay a ton of attention to me, anyway. I don't think they even want me there.

Miss Spiraci: That's why we picked you for this. You're the man for the job.

GM: Hey, before we get into this, can I ask a question?

KO: Make it quick. We've got a lot to cover.

GM: I was gone for six months. What were you guys doing in the meantime? I mean, I was there for when the League stopped you from turning the US Mint inside-out and stealing all the money once it was on the outside, but you had to be doing more than that, right? I mean, that was pretty ridiculo—

KO: Are you kidding? That plan was brilliant! A masterpiece! A work of genius! I should chop you down where you sit—

MS: We've done a lot more. Gathering our own intelligence, developing attack plans on individual heroes, mapping out the Chamber of Rightness, and other things you don't really need to know right now.

KO: Yeah. That's all true. But that plan was amazing. I'm ordering you both to say it was an amazing plan.

MS: It was an amazing plan.

GM: Uh, yeah, it was amazing. It's too bad the League screwed it up.

KO: It's their fault.

MS: So we're in agreement. With that out of the way, tell us what you know.

GM: Yeah. Right. I guess I'll start with what I found out about The Blessing. She stays in a locked room on the top floor of the northwest wing of the Chamber of Rightness. Alone. But one superhero does stay on-hand to . . . I'm not sure what to call it. Guard her, I guess.

MS: She's a prisoner?

GM: Sorta. The League really doesn't like anyone to talk about it like that, though. The Blessing . . . she could be a danger to herself. That's what Sabledusk says, anyway. The League likes to say they're protecting her.

KO: Untrustworthy. Liars. Charlatans. Hypocrites. (*pause*) You said she's a danger to herself? How could that be? How can we use that?

GM: I only know what Sabledusk told me and what I've overheard, but basically her powers involve a . . . what's the word? Sym-symbo—

MS: Symbiotic.

GM: Yeah. She forms a symbiotic relationship with another person. Whoever she's attached to, that's who she gives luck.

MS: That must be why they keep a superhero near her at all times, in addition to making sure she stays put.

GM: You got it.

KO: You still haven't explained how any of this makes her a danger to herself. Let's get to that. I don't like asking things twice.

GM: Sorry. Yeah. So what they're afraid of is the idea that someone who wants to do The Blessing harm will become the person she's attached to. Basically, she makes people's wishes come true, so if the wish is that she gets hurt or dies . . . well, that's what happens. In theory, anyway.

KO: Do they think we want to kill her?

GM: Yeah. They know that you know about her now, and so they assume you're looking for some sweet revenge. And, you know, they pretty much think you guys want to kill everybody.

KO: What an insult. What a mischaracterization. Character assassination. (*pause*) We don't kill anyone we need. And we need her. So how do we get her?

GM: Like I said, they have her on lockdown. The room isn't accessible through any outside walls or windows and it's on the top floor, so you can't go in through a tunnel or anything.

MS: So we go in through the roof.

KO: Or we figure out a way to teleport in there. Gun-Man, get us a list of who guards her and when. And get us a floor layout of the top floor of the chamber. Got it?

GM: Got it.

KO: Let's get us a Blessing.

July 19, 1978: La Campeona's report following the first attempt to capture The Blessing, a.k.a. Operation Gesundheit

ATTN: King Oblivion, Ph.D.

The away team I was tasked to lead executed the steps of our plan to the letter, but some unforeseen circumstances led to The Blessing slipping through our fingers.

We initially aimed to teleport into the Chamber with the help of Long Gone Sally, who returned to active duty at your request. Unfortunately, we were continually deflected by an anti-teleportation field which would not allow us to come within around 50 yards of the Chamber. Teleportation simply was not an option for us.

As a plan B, we descended from a helicopter and strategically placed a hole in the roof of the Chamber of Rightness using an enchanted axe designed and forged by Erebus.

It created a perfect "black hole" effect which enabled us to enter without incident. Illuminarius and I rappelled into the Chamber directly into The Blessing's room/cell, and Illuminarius prepared to magically ensnare her, but before he could do so, a superhero with whom we were not familiar suddenly appeared, took The Blessing in her arms, and just as quickly disappeared.

We had no choice but to make our exit at that point, with a number of superheroes in pursuit.

I have requested that R&D investigate this new figure, whom we have hypothesized is some kind of teleporter. We can only surmise that this woman was on hand as a failsafe to prevent The Blessing's capture. Her appearance was all the more complicated by the fact that we were unable to effectively teleport into the Chamber. We are unsure of The Blessing's current whereabouts.

August 2, 1978: Intelligence report from R&D following Operation Gesundheit

To King Oblivion, Ph.D. and others whom it may concern,

We have identified the new teleporting hero spotted by La Campeona and Illuminarius. Her name is—I swear we are not making this up—Teleport Girl. That's what they managed to come up with. She's a recent recruit in the League's new initiative to take on more teenage superheroes. From what we can tell, she's barely fifteen. Unlike Long Gone Sally, her powers seem to involve deconstructing and reconstituting the molecular structures of bodies, unlike Long Gone Sally's, which are portal-based.

As for Teleport Girl and The Blessing's locations, they seem to have dropped off the map completely. We'll continue our search, but we should prepare a plan B in the event that they have simply gone off the grid, perhaps for an extended period of time.

February 9, 1979: Transcript of informational meeting between King Oblivion, Ph.D., Miss Spiraci, and Gun-Man, Transcribed by Steno-Grappler

Gun-Man: It's crazy, you know. How you guys pushed that diet for people to only eat mind-control chemicals. I really thought that one was going to work.

King Oblivion: It *did* work! Bolt Boy stealing all the books and burning them was cheating! We're still getting questions from people who want to buy them after Miss Spiraci went on *Mike Douglas*.

Miss Spiraci: But every time we print more books, they burn them.

KO: They're just mad they didn't think of it first. I'm so ready to be rid of them.

MS: With that in mind, tell us what you know, Gun-Man. Have you caught a whiff of anything about where The Blessing and Teleport Girl are?

GM: I gotta tell you, it's been tough getting much. They know there's a mole now ever since you guys tried to take The Blessing that one time.

KO: Operation Gesundheit. I named it.

GM: So the top heroes—the big eight, we call them—they hash all this stuff out in private meetings. The lower-tier heroes, the people like me, well, we get left out of the loop.

KO: So you have nothing.

GM: Well, I was thinkin', maybe if I could get the ear of one of the big eight—

MS: Are you close with any of them?

GM: I've talked here and there with Master Mysticism.

MS: Do you think you could get him to give up some info?

GM: If I could get him away from Mercurian Mechanoid and, you know, get him in the right frame of mind with a few drinks, yeah.

MS: We'll distract Mercurian Mechanoid. You get what you can out of Master Mysticism and we'll reconvene.

KO: And bring me some of those drinks.

June 12, 1979: Teletype message from Gun-Man to King Oblivion Ph.D.

ATTENTION KING OBLIVION

FINALLY GOT A CHANCE TO SPEAK PRIVATELY WITH MASTER MYSTICISM WHILE THOUSAND EYES DISTRACTED THE MECHANOID BY SPITTING ACID ON THE MERCURY EXHIBIT AT THE SMITHSONIAN. DID NOT EXPLICITLY GIVE THE BLESSING'S LOCATION, BUT DID GIVE A HINT, WHILE LAUGHING: "THE LAST PLACE YOU'D EVER LOOK."

MAYBE THEY ARE IN A REFRIGERATOR?

NO MORE PAGES

July 1, 1979: Field dispatch from La Campeona

On top of Mount Everest. They're not here.

August 20, 1979: Field dispatch from La Campeona

> In the Marianas Trench, at your alma mater. They're not here.

September 19, 1979: Field dispatch from La Campeona

> Went miniature. Inside President Carter's ear. They're not here.

December 24, 1979: Field dispatch from La Campeona

> At the North Pole. They're not here. Santa Claus is holding to the terms of our truce, just FYI.

February 20, 1980: Field dispatch from La Campeona

> On Mars. They're not here.

May 18, 1980: Field dispatch from La Campeona

> Inside Mount St. Helens during this eruption. They're not here. Excellent work making the eruption happen, though.

August 1, 1980: Field dispatch from La Campeona

> Found the world's largest bed in Brunei. Looked under it. They're not here.

October 10, 1980: Field dispatch from La Campeona

> Returned to Explosia Palace to regroup and think of more places to look. You should come here. Now.

October 17, 1980: Transcript of interrogation of The Blessing, Transcribed by Steno-Grappler

King Oblivion: You were hiding out here? In my house? For what, eighteen months? How could you expect that we wouldn't eventually find you?

The Blessing: *(silence)*

KO: How did you even get into the palace basement? Nobody goes down there. What did you eat?

TB: *(silence)*

KO: Either way, I bet you're wondering what happened to your teleporting friend.

TB: *(silence)*

KO: And I bet you want to know how we muted her teleporting abilities. You want to know that, don't you?

TB: *(silence)*

KO: Well, I'll tell you. Within a month of you and your little friend running away from us in the Chamber of Rightness, R&D whipped up some dampening devices that make teleportation impossible within a five-mile radius. Your superhero friends aren't the only ones who can pull off that little trick. We installed one at every ISS facility. But maybe you already figured that out. Maybe you were stuck in my castle the whole time. Was that the idea? Were you two going to keep moving around every week or so?

TB: *(silence)*

KO: *(to someone else in the room)* Does she talk? Has anyone heard her talk?

(unintelligible response)

KO: So. Teleport Girl. She's in another room here at the castle. My associate, Miss Spiraci, is interrogating her right now. Anything you don't give us, we'll get from her.

(a few moments of silence)

KO: Are you the reason all my curtains ripped? Those were handmade, one-of-a-kind curtains. The Explosian people worked on them for weeks to honor me. Now I'll have to get them to make more. That means I have to talk to them. Do you know how much of a headache that is?

TB: *(silence)*

KO: Okay, okay. You don't have to say anything. But we'll get you to talk sooner or later.

April 2, 1981: Memo from The Sponge after exhaustive examination of The Blessing

ATTN: King Oblivion, Ph.D.

We have been examining The Blessing for almost six months now, while giving her free rein here at the campus of Ocean

Trench Fortress University. In that time, we've made some fascinating observations.

As we expected, The Blessing caused a number of . . . mishaps in the first few weeks of her residence. Lights falling, cracks in our outer hull, students tripping down stairs, unexpected fires. Luckily, we built the university even sturdier when we rebuilt following the War of the Wicked, so any damage was minor.

After some six weeks, however, we noticed the effects of her powers beginning to wane. The mishaps became less frequent until they eventually stopped altogether. We were later shocked to discover that her powers once again began having effects, but in the opposite direction. Student injuries healed faster than we could have ever expected. Cracks in the hull seemed to repair on their own. Her focus seemed to be changing.

It also seemed clear, however, that her powers were growing unfocused. At no point were they as consistent or sharp as they were in those weeks after The Blessing first arrived.

My hypothesis is that her symbiotic connection to whomever she had attached earlier—Sabledusk, I suspect—has faded, most likely due to physical distance. We long ago surmised that her attachments developed through constant proximity to someone. Bearing that in mind, I would suggest that you or a proxy spend the next several months here developing an attachment. Our researchers and I have dipped in and out of proximity to her over the months, but not for any sustained length of time that would create a symbiotic connection.

One additional note: I have noticed that The Blessing has taken an interest in learning here at the University. She still hasn't spoken, but on her own accord has decided to sit in on a few classes. I believe offering her educational opportunities may be a way to help create a symbiotic connection without force or coercion.

January 1, 1982: King Oblivion, Ph.D.'s handwritten notes for remarks at the International Society of Supervillains New Year's Party

Malevolent New Year to you all.

I won't speak for long. I know it's been a long night. We did a hell of a job replacing the ball in Times Square with a sentient mimic that came to life and created havoc among the crowd. We accomplished that together. Give yourselves a round of applause.

As we continue to celebrate our victory tonight—Did you see the mimic kick Kitehawk out of the sky at one point? What a hoot—I just wanted to note a new development in our overarching plan to defeat the superheroes.

You may not have seen me around here as often as you had in the past. That's because I've been logging a lot of time at Ocean Trench Fortress University, where I've been building a symbiotic bond with someone I'll call a now-former superhero: The Blessing. Come up here, young lady.

This young woman and I have been spending big chunks of the last few months together, and though she doesn't speak, I believe we have come to an understanding of one another. She's been studying the devious arts, and to be quite frank, seems to have a true mastery of the form. I'm unashamed to say I think of her like a daughter.

Starting now, she will serve as a member of the International Society of Supervillains. I believe we have developed a bond that will enable her to help us greatly in crushing the League of Right Rightness, just as she helped them when she was under their thrall. The difference is we have given freedom back to her.

Never let anyone tell you superheroes are "good." Nor have they earned the distinction of being evil, like us. They just suck.

I haven't used this phrase in some time—my old mentor used to use it and it rang hollow for many years, but I think it's time to once again unearth it. Fearsome fortune to you all in the year to come!

March 2, 1982: Transcript of informational meeting between King Oblivion, Ph.D., Miss Spiraci, and Gun-Man, Transcribed by Steno-Grappler

Miss Spiraci: King, I'm just going to go ahead and spit this out.

King Oblivion: What? Is the coffee gross? Grosser than normal?

MS: No. I mean there's something I have to tell you. The other members of the Villain High Council and I . . . we've had some meetings.

KO: You're meeting without me?!

MS: Yes, but before you throw them to the lava sharks you've been breeding, hear me out. We think you're a little emotionally compromised on this thing. With The Blessing.

KO: Emotionally—what?

MS: She was supposed to build a bond with you, but you've clearly built a bond with her, too. It's clouding your judgment.

KO: You know, Connie, if anyone else was saying this—

MS: I do know. It's why I'm telling you. You've been sheltering her. She's helped on a few missions here and there, but—

KO: But what?

MS: She should be on the front lines. We need to send her back to the League. To infiltrate them.

KO: You're sending her to a prison.

MS: It's only temporary. And it'll weaken their defenses more than we could even predict. You know what happened when she was set against us. She was unstoppable.

KO: How can we make sure she'll be safe?

MS: We'll send her in with someone. Gun-Man, come in here.

Gun-Man: Hi again.

MS: The two of them will go in together. We'll keep tabs on them remotely. He'll protect her on the inside. This plan is set to go, but we'll need you to sign off on it.

KO: How can we make sure her bond with me will stay strong? What if it breaks because we're in different places?

MS: We'll arrange crimes and other plans that will put you in proximity for at least a few minutes at a time, every few weeks. That should re-cement the bond. Now will you sign off?

KO: I am not pleased that you went behind my back.

MS: I know. But this time I had to.

KO: OK. Do it.

September 15, 1982: Gun-Man's six-month report from inside the Chamber of Rightness

ATTN: King Oblivion Ph.D.

Since we last met, I'm sure you've noticed that your success rate in crimes and any fights you may have had with superheroes has gone up a lot. I've seen many of those fights myself. Mercurian Mechanoid needed two months' worth of repairs after The Brobdingnagian Woman stepped on her back in May.

What you're not seeing, though, is the level of chaos here. Arguments and fistfights break out almost daily. The heroes are not happy with each other. They're not used to losing like this. It's getting to them, and it's all because of the effects of The Blessing. As far as they know, she should be helping them, but they have no idea that she's doing the opposite. Now would be a really smart time for an attack if you ask me.

February 11, 1983: La Campeona's report following concentrated attack on the Chamber of Rightness

The Chamber is down. Repeat, the Chamber is down. I do not mean that in a figurative way. We didn't just take it over. It fell to the ground as a result of your brilliant plan to send us all to dig a big hole under it. I'm sure The Blessing's influence helped, but your mind has pulled off another incredible victory.

June 8, 1983: Report from Gun-Man inside the League's new headquarters

ATTN: King Oblivion Ph.D.

The destruction of the Chamber of Rightness was truly a spectacle, but I'm afraid it's had some unintended consequences. The League has officially regrouped and moved into its new headquarters, an orbiting space station that doubles as a television satellite. We get every channel up here. It's really something.

Anyway, I think they're catching a whiff of something being up with me. They've separated me from The Blessing completely and pretty much keep her locked away at all times. I think they may be coming around to the fact that she's not helping them anymore. Honestly, I don't know how they didn't figure it out before now.

August 12, 1983: Report from Gun-Man upon arrival on Earth

ATTN: King Oblivion Ph.D.

They kicked me out. We had a big meeting and they voted to expel me from the League on "suspicions of collusion" with the ISS. I know you guys have a place for me there, but I'm worried about her. The Blessing is up there by herself.

October 3, 1983: Field dispatch from La Campeona

King, I'm afraid I have some upsetting news to report.

As you ordered, we flew up to the new League headquarters, the Orbiting Overlook, in an attempt to rescue The Blessing. Though our infiltration was a success, a series of mishaps—explosions, crossfire between us and the superheroes, collapsing pieces of the station—led to an incredibly unusual and unexpected situation in which the airlock to our escape ship failed to seal completely. In the chaos of our escape, The Blessing was sucked out into space.

She is lost and we have presumed her dead. I am so, so sorry.

February 29. 1984: Transcript of meeting between King Oblivion, Ph.D. and Miss Spiraci, Transcribed by Steno-Grappler

Miss Spiraci: Are you ready to talk?

King Oblivion: What is there to talk about?

MS: We should be even more focused on defeating the superheroes now. They did this to her. They have to pay.

KO: We shouldn't have sent her back, Connie. We shouldn't have sent her back to them. They imprisoned her. Our bond broke. And she was upset. That's what caused all that chaos.

MS: And you blame me for this?

KO: You're the one who said to send her back. You didn't even give me a choice.

MS: I'll give you some more time. I've got to see to this plan to build a 10-story robotic you. You know, the old you would have loved this.

KO: *(silence)*

April 1, 1985: King Oblivion, Ph.D.'s handwritten notes for remarks made to the assembled International Society of Supervillains at the hive-like underground lair

Friends in foedom, I come to you today to tell you that I have regained my resolve to crush the superheroes who stand in our way.

I know I've been gone for a while. More than a year. In that time, I have been reborn. I stoked my grief into rage and channeled that rage into a focus unlike any I have had in many, many years.

We will not just rid the world of these superheroes. We will rewrite history such that the only words anyone hears of them will be our words. The only stories told about them will be the stories we tell. Any attempt to lionize or canonize their actions, we'll erase. We'll expunge. We'll eradicate. We'll show them the true meaning of "fearsome fortune."

Over the next twelve months, the word "superhero" will become little more than a memory. Here's how we'll start. I've tasked our R&D department to work around the clock to refashion the giant robot built to look like me into a spaceship. I'm going to literally kick that orbiting piece of garbage out of the sky.

Who's coming with me?

Editor's Note: Though the document below was dated May 16, it was updated throughout the following months with check marks. Items that are checked were, I assume, completed as planned and scheduled, while those left unchecked were not.

May 16, 1985: Written plan of attack developed by the ISS Long-Term Planning department, signed by La Campeona, Miss Spiraci, and King Oblivion, Ph.D.

With the Orbiting Overlook destroyed and the League of Right Rightness in disarray, we will take the opportunity to strike at its individual members now before they have the opportunity to regroup again. We commit to these actions:

- Replace Kitehawk's kite with one made out of flammable material, then drop firebombs on him ✓
- Set Sabledusk and Jaybird against each other using a fear-inducing chemical, then toss whichever one is left standing in a big trash compactor
- Send Master Mysticism to Mercury via a fake message from Mercurian Mechanoid encouraging him to go there with no spacesuit or other protection, so he'll surely give in to exposure ✓

- Have Illuminarius pose as Master Mysticism for a short period, enabling him to use a deactivation spell on Mercurian Mechanoid
- Frame Star Spangler for treason; make her believe that she is actually guilty so she'll simply allow herself to be executed ✓
- Set up a huge electrified fence and lure Bolt Boy to run straight into it ✓
- Put Hodur in a "god box," a prison even a mytholog-ical deity cannot escape
- Challenge Mr. Wonderful to a one-on-one fight, claiming he has "no honor" if he refuses; lead him into a room which will be sealed off and filled with radiation sure to put an end to his germy body

February 8, 1986: King Oblivion, Ph.D.'s handwritten notes for remarks made to the assembled International Society of Supervillains at the hive-like underground lair

Friends in foedom, we have pierced the armor of the League of Right Rightness. We have reduced their ranks substantially. Now is the moment for us to slam down the hammer. Now is the time for us to cut off the head.

In a few short weeks, we will assemble at our newest facility inside a dormant volcano in northern Greenland. From there we'll radio a message to the superheroes that we're ready to face them head-to-head. They're pretty livid with us, so I think they'll accept the challenge.

Some of you won't make it out of this. I understand it and respect your sacrilce. But if you don't follow me into this, I swear on all that is evil I'll kill you myself.

Let's end it. Fearsome fortune to you all.

August 31, 1986: Abstract of the ISS official report on the events of the Battle of the Underground Volcano Vortex

The Battle of the Underground Volcano Vortex was an unmitigated success. I can say with complete certainty that the League of Right Rightness ceased to operate as an organization at the end of the two-month struggle underneath Greenland.

Already at a disadvantage from prior losses, the League came into the battle hobbled beyond repair. We merely put them out of their misery.

No heroes are left. Sabledusk and Jaybird? Sucked into the vortex. Mercurian Mechanoid? Sucked into the vortex. Hodur? Sucked into the vortex. We are not entirely sure where the vortex led. What we do know is that, during a lull in the fighting, we sent a raw ham tied to a rope through, and it came back fully cooked. In fact, it was burned. In fact, it was on fire when we pulled it back. We are well assured those heroes won't be coming back.

In regards to Mr. Wonderful, we engaged a prolonged weeks-long attack using disinfectants. We brought to the fight a relatively new weapon in our fight against him: antibacterial soap. If we only knew that such an invention would be his end, we would have invented it years, if not decades, earlier. We whittled him down to a microbe and placed him in a petri dish. We will keep him on lockdown in our headquarters and routinely douse him with soap to ensure he does not grow to his previous size.

With this victory, we can end this phase of the International Society of Supervillains' history. Superheroes are, quite simply, a thing of the past. As are other supervillains.

Signed

King Oblivion, Ph.D.

Miss Spiraci

La Campeona

P.S. The day after the battle ended, we bombed the secret headquarters of the Worldwide Conglomeration of Super-Criminals. Who needs them?

Editor's Note: Though I could locate no complete chapter about the period of the End of Heroism in King Oblivion's files, I personally ghostwrote the following account—as I mentioned earlier, he wanted me to document his deaths for some reason—of the few months in 1984 and 1985 in which he disappeared from the ISS.

My Fourth Death

After the tragic and untimely death of The Blessing, I felt a need to change some things in my life. I needed to grieve. I also needed a recharge. A reawakening of my inner fire for evil. I had to return to my roots.

So I packed a bag with the clothes of a commoner. No more silken robes lined with the featherfur of griffins and pearlescent cloaks.[66] Only beautifully cut Italian suits for this guy. With my suitcase in tow, I returned to the city where I got my start: Chicago. I figured I could jump right back in where I started with whatever gun running or booze hustling gang was in charge.

When I arrived, I was surprised to find that things had changed drastically. People no longer cheered for organized criminals in the streets. They cheered for the Bears, a team of adults who tossed a ball at each other and tried to run as far as they could before someone knocked them down. I had more than an appreciation for sport—my history with roshambo is evidence enough—but I didn't see the appeal, nor did I understand what running around with a ball had to do with bears.

And all the crime? Well, it moved from the speakeasies and backroom casinos to the very halls of government. I spent much of

66 If you're wondering why you've never seen a griffin before, it's because you're not royalty.

my first few weeks back in the city sniffing around for where I could find some action—I'd ask people, "Say, I was looking to do some crime. Where would I go?" The answer I'd routinely get was "You oughta head over to city hall! They're all crooks over there!"

So I did. I floated around the halls using the alias Ray Olvido, one La Campeona had given me years ago, asking anyone I could if there were job openings. I made sure to insist that I'd be more than happy to grease the wheels or have my wheels greased, too. By the fall, I landed a job as an assistant city treasurer. In the months to come, I'd facilitate numerous bribes, vote-buying operations, fraudulent activities, and even a handful of drug trafficking deals. It was exhilarating. For the first time in my life I developed friendships with judges and city councilmen. I couldn't imagine anything more surreal.

Of course, by early 1985 it all came crashing down around me. The FBI executed a sting operation that ended with numerous officials being arrested and indicted. The raid included the strong-arming presence of a local superhero named Incorruptible Man, whose whole deal was rooting out and quashing corruption. Generally, he was terrible at his job, but he got one win here.[67]

As he swept the building, I noticed a hint of recognition in his face when he saw me. Perhaps he noticed the mask. Whatever the case, I was not merely Ray Olvido to him. He knew I was King Oblivion, Ph.D. Rather than let him catch me and unveil my true identity, I chose instead to climb to the top of city hall and jump onto the street below.

I was back to life within three days because the city coroner, whom I had gotten to know in my tenure at city hall, was clever enough to use the Extra Life I had on me.

The Extra Life, by the way, is something I had R&D whip up back in the seventies. With three deaths already on record, I sus-

67 A year or so later, at the Battle of the Underground Volcano Vortex, I'd get my win back.

pected that I would need something to revive me in the event of a slip-up or, as in this case, an intentional self-sacrifice. It was a cocktail of epinephrine, amphetamine, and other drugs—some of which I believe R&D invented—intended to get my body operating again no matter the situation. I carried it on me at all times with a note attached: "IF DEAD, ADMINISTER THIS." It was simple enough—a syringe in the shape of my head that someone could stick in my chest and get me ticking again. Only problem was—and R&D told me this upfront—it'd only work once.

Soon after the coroner revived me, I returned to the labyrinthine ISS headquarters and started the gears in motion that eventually led to the Battle of the Underground Volcano Vortex.[68] I was really and truly reborn by the experience, and it was time to end things.

Villainspiration

The villain: Thanos
Key trait: Thanos of Titan assembled all six Infinity Gems, giving him complete control over the very workings of the universe.
How he uses it: Thanos's first act with the gems is to eradicate half of life in the universe. He follows that up by offering a massive group of assembled superheroes the hope of defeating them, but he kills them all defiantly anyway. He then becomes the living embodiment of the universe itself. These are amazing accomplishments (until his granddaughter undoes it all).
The wrong takeaways: Thanos left himself open and weak by abandoning his body so his granddaughter to could take the gems. He also engages in all these actions because he's in love with Death. He should have been doing it all for himself, man.

---

68 To show him my gratitude, I made him The Malevolvent ME, the ISS's official medical examiner. He has never wanted for work.

Chapter 15

VILLAIN TRIUMPHANT

With my enemies vanquished, I took a few days to relax and revel in my victory. I drank champagne out of a skull; I sipped Scotch whiskey out of a dead superhero's boot; I imbibed a margarita wrung from some poor heroic fool's costume. For a week or two, I allowed the labyrinthine ISS underground headquarters to be a party hub for the first time in its history. In my magnanimity, I even allowed the henchmen to join in and grab a few sips of absinthe from the compartments of Sabledusk's silly Useful Stuff Bandolier, which I later adapted into my own costume. I must admit it *is* as useful as the name indicates.

Are you . . . are you quoting the musician Prince? What is this?

Of course, as a wise sage once said, "Life is just a party, and parties weren't meant to last." With the defeat of the League of Right Rightness, we had created a seminal moment. It was time to seize it and bring a new paradigm to Earth.

The superheroes were gone—at least the big ones were. A few independent stragglers were scurrying about here and there, but they were only trifling figures.[69] By and large, we had completely and utterly cleared the path for ourselves. Nothing stood in our way. With little pushback, we could have walked into every hall of power throughout the planet and claimed it for our own. Indeed, many of my closest confidants and advisers within the ISS suggested doing just that. Our time is here, they'd say. Let's take it all while we can.

I freely grant that there's a certain naïve logic to that argument. Why delay gratification when you can have what you want most right now? Yet I denied myself that satisfaction. It wasn't that I couldn't get no satisfaction; I consciously turned away from it. I demanded that we take a more circuitous route to our total and unquestionable domination of the globe.

Not only is this very forced, it's a Rolling Stones reference I did not ask for.

They wondered why I would make such a decision, as perhaps you are. And I'll tell you what I told them: Question my judgment again and I'll nail you to the floor! And by that I don't mean that I'll knock you down or pin you to the ground. I'll literally get a nail gun and drive the nails through your body, permanently making you a fixture in the room.

Unlike them, I will also do you the favor of explaining my reasoning. Not that I owe it to you or anyone else, but I feel the time is right to reveal my motives.

---

69 Chicago's Incorruptible Man had his own deal, for example. Apparently when the League asked him to join, he gave them a two-hour lecture about how all organizations become corrupt over time with power. I hated the League and even *I* think that may have been too harsh of a punishment for them.

- Supervillains do not do things simply. If a plan isn't convoluted, overcomplicated, and occasionally beyond explanation in its wild logical leaps, then it isn't a plan worth doing. I am not married to tradition in all things, but in this I felt I must hew to the supervillain way of achieving a goal.
- History does not remember the leaders who took the easy way. Anyone who simply grabbed what was handed to them has been quickly forgotten. Those who openly and publicly struggled for their positions were honored with statuary, mountain carvings, buildings being named for them, mascotry, and so many other accolades.
- As a sage once said, "With an intellect and a savoir faire, no one in the whole universe will ever compare."
- I really, really wanted something to do. Sitting around in offices administering edicts can get boring very quickly.

Prince again, huh? You know I'm a king, right? Get your priorities straight.

Beyond those details, I wished to do more than simply obtain and hold power. Along with universe-spanning power, I wanted to be feared, venerated, and exalted. Yes, we had accomplished a lot. More than many people could ever imagine doing in ten lifetimes. We had defeated our supervillain rivals and vanquished our superhero nemeses. We had built an incomparable organization by which to do global, and perhaps even universal, evil. We had shaped world events so brilliantly that few people living on this blue marble even noticed our machinations and manipulations.

And therein was the problem. So much of what we had done had occurred behind a curtain. Our biggest conflicts were insular, and much of the world was blind to our grandeur. Sure, people had an awareness of who we were. Anyone who had been present for one of our numerous bank robberies, skyscraper teleportations, water transmogrifications, mass hypnotisms, road meltings, train shrinkings, sporting event time manipulations, or sun blockings knew of us. But they didn't *know* us. They didn't know what we were truly capable of. They didn't comprehend what we had achieved and what we could achieve in the years to come. These people knew, at most, a sliver of our potential as their leaders. I wouldn't harbor their disrespect, their looks of uncertainty, their incessant *questions*. Before I would rule them, I would train them. I wouldn't just lord power over them. I would lord power over them and they would *like it*.

To those ends, I assembled what remained of the Villain High Council to collaborate with me on a 150-part World Domination Super-Plan. Only when every singular step was complete could I feel as though my ascension to Grand Master of Earth and its Surrounding Celestial Bodies was all I wanted it to be. By mid-1987, we completed and ratified our draft of the plan. It was a true magnum opus, a seminal achievement, a tour de force. No one else was making plans like this at that time, and no one has achieved its lofty goals since.

This isn't a new Radiohead album. It's the greatest plan ever devised by human or humanoid. Fix your language.

The first step of our plan was something I had made clear since the very moment the Battle of the Underground Volcano Vortex came to an explosive end: we had to replenish the International Society of Supervillains' ranks.

Then why are we admitting it?

[As loath as I am to admit it,] we lost a few members in our final battle with the superheroes. My henchmen decoys fell in droves.[70] Quemado built a wrestling ring inside the volcano and challenged the replacement Kitehawk who arrived with the League to "one last match," which ended in a tombstone piledriver that killed them both. Madame Fabrique engulfed Sabledusk and Jaybird inside her stretchy, inescapable body and pulled them into the vortex with her. Thousand Eyes the Puker endured considerable splashback from the antibacterial soap and other disinfectants with which we attacked Mr. Wonderful, and decided it was time to retire to his trash-heap home after the battle ended. The Brobdingnagian Woman was inadvertently shrunk to a semi-normal size (around eight feet tall, which was as short as she could get, apparently) by a stray spell from Illuminarius, so she also retired to civilian life.

And then there was Miss Spiraci.

About a week before the Villain High Council was set to convene and begin work on the Super-Plan, she once again disappeared, just as she had some sixty years prior. I walked down to her office within the ISS headquarters to accompany her to the first drafting meeting only to find,

70 Not that I was too concerned about that. It's what they do. They know it's what they do. It's all part of the deal.

as before, that no office was there at all—only an unadorned wall.

I don't know why she left. Though I had assigned some blame for The Blessing's death to her, she and I had—at least I thought we had—come to a tentative accord and re-established a working relationship. But perhaps she was "the great mistake I never made."

Had to look this one up. It's a David Bowie lyric, huh? I'll say this as clearly as I can: I don't need musicians to speak for me. Period.

As head of our Strategy and Tactics department, she, of course, would have to be replaced with the utmost speed. Lucky for me I had someone on call who could take the job. Years before, when I first formed the ISS, I had asked The Beguiler to join up. He asked for a rain check of sorts. He was amenable to what we were doing and took a reserve membership in the organization, but said he was still "too young and wild" to join in a full-time management capacity. I decided at the time not to let the elevator break him down.

This is. . .oddly worded. Oh, it's another song lyric, isn't it? What if I sent you down an elevator shaft? How would that be?

Some twenty-five years later, I figured it was time to call in that rain check, and The Beguiler stepped up. He left Guam, where he was spending much of his time terrorizing those idiot fishermen, and became our head of Tactics and Strategy.

Among the other recruits we brought in were:

- Backstroke the Terrorswimmer, who had the power to create tidal waves with his mighty arm movements and kicks.
- Vahn-Dule, an alien warlord desperately searching the universe for a poem that could turn planets inside-out.
- KilloJulie, a super-hacker who could infiltrate the world's most secure computer

systems by transferring her consciousness into them via networking cables.

- Master of Puppets, an expert in mind control who also just really, really loved Metallica's West Coast brand of brash thrash rock, which pumped out through boom box and car radio speakers like raw, unbridled energy channeled into vibrations.
- Bubonia, a woman who could infect people with diseases by touch.
- Evil Sabledusk, a corrupt version of Sabledusk we brought in from another dimension.

With the new recruits in tow, we were staffed enough to carry out step two in the 150-part Super-Plan: Wipe out every last remnant of the Worldwide Conglomeration of Super-Criminals. Sure, we had already bombed their headquarters, but we had to be sure, right? Wiping out all the superheroes had created one hell of a power vacuum, and we sure weren't going to let those traitorous little snots who had done so much to set us back make any sort of move to fill it. We had come to a temporary truce to ensure that the heroes were scraped off the windshield of history, but that time had come and gone.

So here's what we did. We went and found Nicky Claws, who was somehow still kicking after all these years and who, for all intents and purposes, *was* the Conglomeration, much as I was (and am) the face of the ISS. We found him holed up in some makeshift operations center in a cave in Yellowstone National Park, giving a pep talk to three nobody lackeys. He was sure we would kill him, but we didn't. That'd be too easy. As they say, there's no easy way out. There's no shortcut home.

This is a line from the Rocky movie song. This was in a Rocky movie. What makes you think it's even slightly appropriate? Does it mean you want to be pummeled bloody? I can arrange that.

Instead, we made him pledge fealty to the ISS. We forced him to sign documents handing over any legal and illegal right to the name "The Worldwide Conglomeration of Super-Criminals" to us in perpetuity throughout the universe. We insisted, through force, that he wear a monitoring device at all times that would ensure he was not participating in any competing supervillain activity. How did we do this? All we had to do was tie him up and hang him over a pot of boiling water. The rest did itself.

From there, we had free rein to carry out a few dozen succeeding points in the Super-Plan at our leisure. I won't share each point here because I won't abide some copycat wannabe trying to replicate my accomplishments, but I'll list a few to give you an idea of what we achieved.

Point 6: Distract the world by sending Baby-Woman (a grown woman who has the power to look and behave convincingly like a toddler) to fall down a well in Texas, freeing us up to enact other world-changing plans.

Point 10: Work with our propaganda department to create *Full House* and *Saved by the Bell*, television programs designed to convince children to buy numerous hairspray products (which contained our carefully developed mind-control chemicals) and leave them highly open to suggestion via subliminal messages hidden in overbearing laugh tracks and "awwww" audience sounds.

Point 13: "Encourage" scientist Tim Berners-Lee to begin speaking publicly about technology that will eventually evolve into the Internet.

Point 16: Replace newly elected US President George H. W. Bush with a lifelike puppet solely designed to vomit on the Japanese prime minister at the most inopportune time.

Point 19: Organize the Woodstock '89 festival as a sort of victory lap for our greatest achievement, as well as try out a new ray on the youth of a new generation: a Disaffectation Ray designed to make them smug, indifferent, and standoffish.

This is definitely more album review talk, but I'll allow these words.

Point 21: Wrap all important books that could be construed as veiled interpretations of my life story in eye-catching holographic printing material and chromium to make them clearly evident as [monumental and momentous] literature.

Point 25: Precipitate the fall of the Soviet Union so as to eliminate the perception of more than one so-called "evil empire" (us) in the eyes of Western culture.

U2? We're mentioning U2 now? Oh, wait, we actually did this. Carry on.

Point 28: Activate laboratory-created synthezoid and U2 lead singer Bono's "Douchebag Matrix," further prodding the generation of the era not to care about anything because this weird jerk in sunglasses seems to care too much.

Point 30: Using the same reality-spanning technology we used to recruit Evil Sabledusk, find two alternate-reality versions of me and send us all back in time to the War of the Wicked, thereby ensuring our victory by faking my death.

Point 32: Take an active role in the ratings spike of *The Jerry Springer Show*, thereby normalizing violent, uncouth behavior so that what we do seems practically tame and safe by comparison.

Point 33: Facilitate and publicize the famous cloning of Dolly the sheep, convincing people the world over the cloning is some sort of nascent technology that is only beginning, giving us a massive head start in the field.

Point 35: Recruit gymnast Kerri Strug to compete on our behalf at the 1996 Olympic Games in Atlanta and *steal the world's hearts*.

Point 39: Send a brave group of henchmen and recruits off-planet, up to the passing Hale-Bopp comet, in hopes that they'll return with a report on what it's like up there when the comet passes by Earth again (sometime around the year 4380), after we have cemented our status as the planet's eternal rulers. We may build a base there in the future.

Point 41: Influenced by our teachings and run by many of our members, enable Microsoft to release Windows 98, the startup and shutdown sounds from which would later become gateways to hypnotizing any and all computer users into aggressively arguing with each other over the Internet.

Point 45: Encourage our acolyte, George Lucas, to release *Star Wars: The Phantom Menace*. The purpose is two-fold: It's a hilarious prank on everyone and a method for calibrating the Psychomonitor, a device I would later use to control the brainwaves of millions of readers of my guide, *The Supervillain Handbook*.

Point 46: Plan and organize Woodstock '99 to continue our tradition of influencing the youth of the day via "music." In this instance, we chose to draw everyone to the path of one of our top priorities: breaking stuff.

Point 49: Successfully fool almost everyone on the planet in believing the "Y2K" bug is a real threat, as if the calendars switching over to a "20" instead of a "19" would do anything to the computer systems of the world. In the midst of the panic, we set up radio transmitters to prepare for what we dubbed the "Y2K8" bug, which drives the world's economy to the brink of collapse and enables us to do our financial dealings with desperate negotiating partners.

Around the turn of the millennium, we took a brief break from the Super-Plan and reconvened the Villain High Council to update and revise a few points. Up until then, we had nailed everything, from the passing of the Hale-Bopp comet to the existence of *The Jerry Springer Show* to late-'90s computer operating systems. But as the century changed over, we looked to streamline a few things and plan some high-tech maneuvers.

I also started thinking, as I neared ninety years old, what a world without me might look like. As unlikely as that was to happen, I began wondering if there was even the slightest possibility of it. Every great artist, band, or leader must, at some point, set aside their instruments and allow a protégé to pick them up. "There I go. Turn the page."

Bob Seger. That may be the final straw, you worm.

These thoughts would guide my actions for many of the years to come.

Email Correspondence Between King Oblivion, Ph.D. and Christoph Robertau, Ghostwriter of "Villain Triumphant"

From: King Oblivion, Ph.D.
To: Christoph Robertau
Subject: Music quotes

Mr. Robertau,

I'd be the first to admit that I'm not the most plugged-in listener of music in recent years—after "O Fortuna" and "Night on Bald Mountain" why even bother making music anymore, to be quite honest—but I definitely noticed quotes from Prince, David Bowie, The Rolling Stones, Bob Seger, and that *Rocky* band in the text of the chapter, none of which I authorized or wanted.

And beyond that, there was all the stuff about "seminal work" and the like. What the hell is that? Is that what I hired you—that is, snatched your apartment out of the building—to do for me? I'd argue that it is not the case. Explain yourself or feel my wrath.

. . .

From: Christoph Robertau
To: King Oblivion, Ph.D.
Subject: RE: Music quotes

Maestro,

Though I have dabbled in novels and other writing, I have made my name in music criticism for various noted publications and I will say unequivocally that I have developed a number of habits over the years that have become very hard to break. A second nature, if you will. My hands hover over the keys and I simply compose without thinking. I construct the symphony.

I do not wish to offer rationalizations, but I suspected that this was the kind of writing you would want from me. You could have hired any number of writers to take on this job. I suspected that you would want me to write in my own voice as well as yours, given my pedigree. Some call me "the progenitor of modern rock criticism." If I was mistaken in my assumption, then I can only throw myself prostrate at your mercy.

. . .

From King Oblivion, Ph.D.
To Christoph Robertau
Subject: RE: Music quotes

Mr. Robertau,

I've got to tell you, I'm really, really getting sick of you writers. I'm continually disgusted by the way you speak to me. You know who I am, right?

I come to you with a legitimate complaint, and instead of saying, "Yes, sir. You are the emperor of my soul. I'll fix it," all I get are your justifications and explanations and apologies. Why can't I just get an affirmation that you'll do what I'm asking of you? Why the hell would I care what you did before this? You may have had some fleeting fame as a music guy before, but now you're writing for me. Your job is to replicate my voice. What you did before doesn't matter. Nothing you've ever done matters. Only I matter. I'm the only one who has ever mattered.

Why do you writers keep forgetting that?

. . .

From: Christoph Robertau
To: King Oblivion, Ph.D.
Subject: RE: Music quotes

Emperor of my soul,

Yes, sir. I'll fix it.

. . .

From: King Oblivion, Ph.D.
To: Christoph Robertau
Subject: RE: Music quotes

Oh, now you say it. I commend the effort, but it's too little too late.

Honestly, who could ever think that the words of a man named Prince could represent the thoughts, feelings, and ambitions of a king? *The* king! Of everything! Are you not capable of expressing yourself in your own words? Who ever thought you were a writer of any merit at all? Why did my decoys even kidnap you anyway?

Just to be clear, I don't actually wish for you to answer any of these questions. Instead, I'm commanding you to hide in the room you're occupying now, wherever you like. Find a secluded spot. It'll make it all the more satisfying when I arrive to hunt you for sport. It's the first time I've gotten to do that in a while, so I suppose I owe you at least a modicum of thanks for that.

On second thought, no I don't.

Transcript of Phone Interview with Connie Spiraci

Editor: Hello? Who is this? Can you send help?

Miss Spiraci: My name is Connie Spiraci. You may know me more readily by my stage name, Lillian Pemberton. I hear you've been calling some of my old associates, asking questions about King Oblivion.

Ed: Yes, that's true. I'm compiling his memoirs after what happened. The crash, I mean. I thought collecting some insight from people he knew might add color to the book. A little seasoning, if you will. I have a lot about what King Oblivion thought of himself, but not much about how anyone else regarded him.

MS: He is—was—a liar.

Ed: Oh, so—this is an interview? Okay, great. How so? What did he lie about?

MS: Lots of things. But here's one example: he said he loved The Blessing like a daughter. And I suppose he did care for her in some way, but more than anything he loved the power she gave him. He liked her being around. He got whatever he wanted because of her. It was his way of gaining more influence within the International Society of Supervillains and edging me out. The longer she stayed close, the more control he got. When I told him that we had to send The Blessing back to the League—which was truly the only way we were going to beat them—he pushed back. He tries to paint the picture of his fatherly love for the girl, but more than anything he knew that he'd have to actually compete with me for top leadership again as the connection waned instead of getting everything handed to him. He would never say it, but he was threatened by me.

Ed: Is that tension why you left?

MS: Partially. I didn't want to deal with the politics anymore. Dr. Blattarius had his fast-and-loose system for doing things, and I got out of that. Then King Oblivion had his approach, which was overbearing and micromanaging while still remaining . . . quite hands-off.

Ed: What do you mean by that? How could he micromanage and be hands-off?

MS: He left a lot of the real work to us, the department heads, but he was very concerned with how things looked. He wanted to come out of every scenario projecting as much power as possible. Not so much for the organization, but for him personally. He loved celebrity, infamy. Sometimes it felt like we were his personal publicity team.

Ed: Were there other reasons you left the ISS?

MS: I wanted to retire. I had been doing this a long time, even longer than he had.

Ed: Right. You were his teacher. I'm sorry if this is something you don't want to answer, but how have you lived so long? You have to be, what, 120? 130 years old?

MS: I'd rather not divulge my age. Certain . . . interests would prefer I didn't. But I can tell you that I've been around for a long time. Longer than you would probably even think. I have had a hand in many events, dating back quite some time. I still do. I may be retired, but I haven't stopped entirely.

Ed: Do you mind if I make a quick aside and ask a personal question for myself?

MS: I suppose I'll indulge your request.

Ed: Thank you. I've been stuck down here in the ISS headquarters for . . . let's see . . . three and a half months since I got the news that King Oblivion had died. It's getting dire down here. The food's running out. A lot of things are on fire. Would it be possible for you to come get me, or at least send someone?

MS: I'm not sure how much access I still have to the facility, but I can look into it for you. If it means a true account of King Oblivion's life will be published, then I definitely want you to liberate yourself from that place.

Ed: I'd be really grateful. Like you said, I want to publish a true account. I'm very interested in your characterization of King Oblivion as a liar. Any other examples I could possibly use?

MS: Well, he certainly has been insisting that superheroes have essentially been extinct since 1986. We absolutely crippled the League, but they're still out there. A whole bunch of them. And they've been causing him headaches with quite a bit of regularity.

Ed: Wow. I didn't even realize. How has he been able to cover something like that up?

MS: It's all just rhetoric. All you have to do is look and you'll see superheroes everywhere. They're active. They're at least somewhat organized. You've just heard him say that there are barely any left so many times that you begin to believe it. He does that to everyone, with everything. It was his most prodigious gift. Maybe his only gift.

Ed: So what are you up to now? How are you keeping busy?

MS: I'm a caretaker above all. You know, even after all these years, she still needs a lot of time and attention. She was never socialized to—

Ed: Wait, who?

MS: I have . . . an adopted daughter.

Ed: Are you talking about The Blessing? Is The Blessing alive? And with you?

MS: I've said too much and might've led you down the wrong path. I was simply talking about someone I took in—*(sound of another phone ringing)* And now I have to take this. I really must be going. I hope the book you're putting together lets people know who King Oblivion really was. They should hear the truth.

(click)

Villainspiration

The villain: Doctor Octopus
Key trait: Thought he is most widely known for committing crimes with the use of a harness that gives him the use of four mechanical arms, Otto Octavius's greatest accomplishment was taking over the body of his lifelong foe, Peter Parker.
How he uses it: In a brilliant stroke of planning, Doctor Octopus covertly switched bodies with Peter Parker/Spider-Man. At the time, Doc Ock was dying of complications from the punishment his body had taken from years of supervillainy, so by switching bodies he cursed Spider-Man to experience the death he was cursed to. Magnificent. Doctor Octopus used Parker's body to operate as his own version of Spider-Man in an attempt to show up his old nemesis.
The wrong takeaways: Doctor Octopus used the opportunity he made for himself to live inside the young, strong body of his greatest enemy to prove himself a more apt hero than Parker rather than shape himself into the greatest villain in known history. It was narrow thinking based on pettiness rather than seeing the big picture. Avoid that.

Chapter 16

LATE MISDEEDS

After the turn of the millennium, the 150-point world takeover Super-Plan continued, but I opted to slow down the pace while I focused my attention on something more important: legacy.

Not that I was—or am—particularly worried about how history will view me. My accomplishments, rhetoric, and inspiring actions all speak for themselves, are on-their-face impressive, and have been well documented. As you've seen, I have done more than just about any other human being, living or dead. I climbed every mountain. And then those mountains bowed down to me.

This is weak. Make it stronger, bigger, more triumphant.

It has long been my assumption that my face will be put on every nation's money in every denomination. That's why I've had myself photographed from every imaginable angle—straight on, 3/4, profile, from the back, 7/8, 1/4, from above, under the chin, 12/3, extreme ear close-up, inside the nostril, tooth x-rays, and so on—so that each note and coin can have a different image of me on it. I have carved my face on the side of every cliff I have ever come across, which must amount to hundreds if not thousands. Every building in Explosia is named for me. Tens of thousands of people live their day-to-day lives dressed exactly like me. And to top it all off, there's the memoir you hold in your hands. For anyone who somehow has managed to avoid news of my many achievements—by being born one thousand years in the future, perhaps—I expect that this text will be taught in every classroom on the planet at every grade. I predict it will become an academic subject, not unlike social studies or the sciences. Maybe it can replace something inessential, like math. I'm also assured that I will become the only person discussed on television news ever again.

Again: Could be stronger.

I'm not at all concerned about whether I'll be remembered. What I do want to ensure is that all the things I have built with these hands—and these hands alone—will last well beyond my years. I want these institutions to not only continue existing, but to hold sway over current events for hundreds of years. Thousands of years.

I have beaten death many times. By my count, it's 0–4. But someday, when I'm a lot older and little slower, there's a slim chance it may catch me off guard, one step behind. I'm a conqueror. I've defeated everyone who has stood in my way, no matter the price. But I must admit to myself that there will come a day when mortality will catch up to me. I must prepare for it. I must entrust my apparatus of power to someone.

Is there though? I have some serious doubts.

At one time, I believed I knew who that person would be. Some thirty years ago I made arrangements to bequeath my titles and holdings to The Blessing, a young woman I saved from the bile-soaked grasp and toothy jaws of a cabal of superheroes. She had a lot to learn. For one thing, she lacked the ability to speak, which may be the single most important skill that someone in my position can have. I am called on to rally and galvanize as much as I am to act and maneuver. To be a supervillain is to bloviate. Yet I saw a fire in her. She had a certain intangible quality; the same sort of quality I know I had in my own youth. I think it's what Dr. Blattarius saw in me that made him as fearful of me, even when I was a child.[71] I intended not to make the same mistake as my misguided old mentor.

I would nurture and teach The Blessing, reshaping her as my anointed, ready successor.

But then alternating acts of malice and incompetence led to her accidental death during an attempted space rescue, and I had to go back to the drawing board. As of this writing, the search continues. Not because there haven't been candidates. There have been dozens. Hundreds even. They have all lacked that intangible quality The Blessing had. Some have filed into the ranks of the International Society of Supervillains

With the "End of Heroism" chapter still unfinished—perhaps there's just no way to adequately encapsulate that grand story—we could stand to go into even more detail here.

71 Speaking of Dr. Blattarius, I found him upside-down and unmoving inside his jar on the morning of January 1, 2001. I'd assign some sort of significance to the date—leaving as the century he helped shape ended or some rubbish—but he tried to embarrass me before he tried to kill me. He spent the last several decades of his life in a jar. He doesn't deserve it.

as costumed criminals, while others have shuffled into our pool of decoy henchmen. Others I had no other choice but to throw to the sharks.[72] I've always had an affinity for sharks.

That's why, as a new millennium began, I ordered the Villain High Council to revisit the Super-Plan and make several adjustments. In addition to leaving our stamp on the world before ruling it, we would also plant seeds to facilitate our continued growth long after the Super-Plan was complete.

One such new step was the development of our first-ever International Society of Supervillains website in 2007. To the untrained observer, it would have every appearance of being some hacky young humorist's attempt at comedy, full of contrived jokes about pop culture and overwrought observations about comic books. But buried in that code and deep within the text of those pages were messages intended to activate new scions of villainy and nudge readers looking for a quick laugh toward donning a mask and hood. By 2013, the website was all but defunct, which was by design.[73] As former readers longed for our messages in their memory, their brains

I don't like this as a description of anything I've been involved with. Change.

72 In 2011, we started producing an as-yet-unaired reality series in the vein of *Shark Tank*. We called it *Supervillain Shark Tank*, and instead of four investors hearing business ideas, the show featured me—just me—hearing desperate contestants' pleas as they begged to become my protégé. If I decided I was "out," the floor would open up beneath the contestant, and they'd be instantly devoured by eighteen genetically enlarged sharks. So far, that's what's happened to everyone. Hoping to hear back from a network soon.

73 It had become a promotional tool for our supervillainy guides, which I'll get into shortly.

would shape closer to our image. This is what one of my newest recruits and advisers, Negmund Freud, told me. Specifically, he said, "Take something away from your target and they'll want you more than ever before. They do all the work for you, *bruder*!"

We also spent more than a decade developing the Psychomonitor, a device that was finally put to use with the publication of my 2012 guide to beginner's villainy, *The Supervillain Handbook*. I had a number of goals in mind with that particular book. First, I really did intend to serve as a teacher and mentor for the potential supervillains rising up among our impressionable youth. As you may have been able to surmise from previous plans I have enacted, this has been a particular driving force behind my actions for decades. I stand by the advice I provided in that volume, as well as its 2013 follow-up, *The Supervillain Field Manual*. I also thought it would be an appropriate cap to a full century as the most powerful being on the planet to cement my status as the top—and quite frankly, only—authority and thought leader in the realm of evil-doing.

Beyond those goals, however, I also truly, deeply wanted to take control of people's minds and bodies. The Psychomonitor facilitated that. Sure, many readers of those books were curious youngsters genuinely looking to find their place in the world, but just as many were voyeurs and looky-loos sadly aching for a glimpse into a world they didn't understand and never really could. Perhaps they even had an inclination to ridicule and look down on that world because they

Not insulting enough.

couldn't adequately grasp what it was about and had never truly felt the power of supervillainy.[74] I knew the former group would understand that I would have to take over their minds and bodies to ensure I did the same to the latter.

Most importantly, I knew that the truly powerful, those that genuinely had a future in the world of super-evil, would find some way to show their wherewithal and break the hold. It's what *I* would do. And they would find me. Indeed, some have. I have welcomed many into the fold here in the ISS, but none have proven that they have what it takes to succeed me.

I've been asked numerous times why I went through the "proper" channels to publish those books—as well as this one—when the ISS is a massive, global organization that could probably publish a book on its own or coerce a publisher to devote all its resources to me and my projects. And sure, I obviously could have done that. I considered it. I threatened it. But I ultimately decided that, much like with the Super-Plan, the harder path was the more satisfying and rewarding one. I wanted people to be able to trust the message I was delivering in these pages. Without question, everything I say is completely and verifiably true, but not everyone knows that. And forcing a company to publish by force creates a degree of doubt. It creates suspicion that what's being produced is

I'd say they do.

74 Despite my foremost efforts, I have not yet touched each of the seven billion-plus lives on this planet with supervillainy. I've affected many, but not all. There's still time. I know there's still time yet.

propaganda. That it's illegitimate and inauthentic. I wouldn't have that.

Aside from the new, specific points in the Super-Plan, I took it upon myself to make a few additional efforts to seek out the next Grand Commander of the ISS. For one, starting in around 2003, I sent a number of expeditionary teams to the places where I lived, the schools I attended, the institutions I destroyed to salvage any remaining evidence of my having been there in my younger days. I'm not above saying that nostalgia played at least a minor part in those seek-and-find missions to Dr. Blattarius's old network of igloos, the Oceania School for Mischievous Boys, the Madison Street flophouse I blew up in my teenage days, and so on. For example, we recovered the ceremonial knife that was used to cut my hand when I was admitted to the Oceania School. We determined that anyone worthy of my title should be able to take a stabbing from it.

Oh, but I'm above it all.

But that was far from the only purpose. It was also a forensic investigation. We took those remnants of my life up to now and brushed them for prints, then swabbed them for any DNA samples we could find. The idea was that anyone who had made the effort to touch everything I had ever touched might carry the proper amount of deference and respect to even attempt to step into my spiky boots.

We didn't find anyone who fit the profile, but quite shockingly did find that Eric Callum, a.k.a. The Air Terror, the pilot who flew me from the Oceania School to Chicago all the way back in

1928, had done more than fly me around that one time and offer me a card. He kept tabs on me for years, going where I went and touching my stuff along the way. It seemed pretty clear that Dr. Blattarius had tasked him with spying on me so that he could haughtily throw any and all of the announcements and pronouncements I wanted to make right back in my face. I had my decoys look up The Air Terror to see if I could go personally punch him in the mush, but as it turned out he died of heart dysplasia in 1957. So a group of us went out to his grave in Modesto, California, and kicked some dirt onto the headstone. Seemed to be just about what he was owed.

This is a lie. I look stronger younger more polished in every way.

Unfortunately for him, poor old Air Terror kicked it before all of us in the realm of super-powered adventuring—supervillains and superheroes alike—mysteriously stopped aging. As I write this in mid-2016, I look exactly as I did back in 1966. I'm unequipped to explain the whys and hows of it. Hell, I don't even know when this phenomenon took effect. If I did, I would have explained it at length in a previous chapter. All I know is that, aside from scarring brought on by accidents and/or various weaponized diseases we've come into contact with, every last one of us looks just as fresh as we did half a century ago.[75]

Another lie! I'm equipped for all tasks!

There's no solid way to explain it. Magic, perhaps? An unintended consequence of an Illuminarius or—less likely, since he was a fraud—

75 And, I guess I have to note, deaths. At least the deaths from which people didn't manage to recover, like I did multiple times.

Master Mysticism spell? The effect of some sort of heretofore undiscovered radiation we all encountered during one of our many battles? A child's wish? The result of us being the participants in a metafiction we're not aware of? It could be any of these. Frankly, I don't really care as long as I keep these youthful looks.

My point in all this is that I don't intend to bore you with what comes so often in these late chapters in so many other memoirs. The "oh, boo hoo, all my friends are dead and I'm still here" drivel. It's nonsense. Sure, some of the people I have come across in my life have passed on into our Great Supervillain Reward, a place where a throne awaits me to come lead everyone toward conquering the afterlife, but they all died in spectacular ways. They died through action. There is no shame in that.

For those of us left among the living, however, seeming immortality—or at least vastly decelerated aging—has proven to be a curse of sorts. On a number of occasions I have found myself looking for more and more ways to cheat death, to skirt by and only by the skin of my teeth avert the bony grasp of the Reaper.[76] Coupled with the fact that I have no real enemies to defeat anymore—*because I'll remind you that *I've already defeated them*—*I've spent a big chunk of the past decade or so engaging in what some might describe as a form of thrill-seeking.

Now, THIS is not a lie.

76 Who, I should note, I have met a few times before and he seems like a solid fellow. Lots of ideas I can get behind. I've got no real beef with him. More like a friendly rivalry.

In the meantime, we have continued to work through the various points of the Super-Plan as scheduled. For example, we just enacted point 97, which called for the film *Batman v Superman: Dawn of Justice* to sully the reputation of superheroes forever.[77] And, as I noted, I have devoted a lot of time to my protégé search. Plus, a few years ago, a consortium of world governments opened up a new anti-supervillainy unit called AGHAST (the Allied Governments Honorable Anti-Supervillain Taskforce). We've had a few tussles with them, but nothing we couldn't handle. Mostly they've taken down rogue agents, actions which have quite frankly helped us in terms of keeping competition at bay and in recruitment. They've been a bit of a nuisance in that they've required me to spend a bit of my time thinking about how to keep them from doing any serious harm to us, but they're bush league so they haven't taken up anywhere close to all my time.

Not sure I'm comfortable with this characterization.

To be candid, there has been lots of time to spare. So I've gone out on space expeditions to previously unexplored territories. I've dipped helicopters down toward whirlpools. I've taunted gigantic sea creatures in their own habitats. I've walked into the secret meetings of the "moral" and "upstanding" and taken bites out of the food on their plates, just to see what they'd do. I've made friends just to turn on them in the most

77 We are responsible for quite a few of the so-called "superhero" movies released over the past seventeen years or so—all part of the Super-Plan—but a few here and there are the work of a consortium of apparent hero lovers we have yet to fully identify. Finally, a new problem worth solving.

vicious ways possible to test whether they'd attack me back.

I'll give you one specific example. Back in 2009, I built a silver helium balloon, shrunk myself down to child size, and got in. I traveled nearly fifty miles across three counties in the Denver, Colorado, area at a shockingly high rate of speed. And I drew as much attention to myself as I could. I called local authorities telling them that I was a young child trapped in the balloon, and they, of course, alerted the news media. It all played right into my hands. Really I was just looking to strike a match and see what happened, but I couldn't help myself from at least partially covering my tracks. It's in my DNA. So I got Illuminarius to hypnotize a couple of local scam artists into thinking they'd created the entire hoax. In the end, I quickly teleported out of there with the help of Long Gone Sally, who was still hanging in there as a charter member of the ISS. Part of me hoped that the balloon might tumble down a cliff or through some nigh-impossible series of events I'd even be caught. But, of course, I executed the plan perfectly. What else could anyone expect of me? I'm too capable. It's my one flaw.

Get it right: I have no flaws.

Trouble is, after more than a lifetime of life-or-death struggles in graveyards and volcanoes, after "summer breaks" that involved death matches and university stints in the deepest reaches of the ocean, there aren't that many more thrills to be had. Short of doing something absolutely reckless and assuredly suicidal—diving toward the ground without pulling up, so to speak—what is left?

In every regard and in every arena, I've basically done it all. By the time the Super-Plan is complete in just a few short years and we will have conquered this measly planet after long-delayed gratification, I'll have beaten every challenge. But not just beaten. That's far too feeble a word. I'll have decimated these challenges. Manhandled. Slaughtered. Embarrassed.

I have a lot of life left to live, but when I leave it all behind, I'll only have one thought to share: "Everything was far too easy."

Letters Exchanged Between King Oblivion, Ph.D. and Jason Katzman, editor, Talos Press

King Oblivion, Ph.D.
Undisclosed Location
Deep Underground
Nowhere, XX 00000

August 13, 2011
Jason Katzman
Editor, Talos Press
307 West 36th Street
New York, NY 10018

Dear Mr. Katzman,

Most assuredly you know my name, but I'll reintroduce myself in case you didn't catch my pictures on the envelope and Explosian stamp. I am King Oblivion, Ph.D., the greatest supervillain, nay, human being, to ever draw breath. Be honored; most people who hear or read those words don't live long thereafter.

You get a reprieve, however, because I have chosen your publishing company—I assure you that you are the first and only publisher I have contacted—to bring my memoirs to the world at large. My hope is that the book will also serve as a guide—the tea leaves, so to speak—for a successor who will continue to wreak havoc on this planet.

Undoubtedly you know my accomplishments, so I won't bother to list them. But rest assured that my book will bring them to light in unprecedented, stunningly detailed fashion. These are details that no one else will have ever seen before. Just think about it: new information about one of the most important figures in all of history. You might as well be printing money (I, of course, will be demanding a 99.5 percent cut).

I assume that is the end of our business, and there is only the formality of signing the contract. Nonetheless, attached you will find a draft of the first chapter, detailing the astonishing, breathtaking story of my birth. Please, cry if you must.

Please review and respond as soon as you have dried your eyes. For the sake of courtesy, I'll say . . . within twenty-four hours.

Mwa-ha-ha,
King Oblivion, Ph.D.

. . .

Jason Katzman
Editor, Talos Press
307 West 36th Street
New York, NY 10018

August 19, 2011
King Oblivion, Ph.D.
Undisclosed Location
Deep Underground
Nowhere, XX 00000

Dear King,

Thank you for your letter and sample materials. I really appreciate you sending them along. I know a lot of work went into them.

In regards to publishing your memoir, my advice would be to hold off on that idea for a bit. While we're not totally against publishing "celebrity" memoirs, I think there's a much bigger audience at the moment for professional guides, and since you're clearly an expert in the field of supervillainy, maybe we should start a publishing relationship there, with a handbook of sorts for aspiring supervillains.

It can serve as a sort of introduction to readers, and then maybe somewhere down the road we can talk about an autobiography.

Let me know if you're open to the idea.

All the best,
Jason

. . .

King Oblivion, Ph.D.
Undisclosed Location
Deep Underground
Nowhere, XX 00000

August 22, 2011
Jason Katzman
Editor, Talos Press
307 West 36th Street
New York, NY 10018

Dear Jason,

Though I have to say I'm deeply insulted by the notion that there's any need to "introduce" me to anyone, you have once again bought yourself a momentary deferment from certain murder with this "handbook" idea. I do find the notion of cementing myself as the top authority in the field . . . compelling.

I do have some questions, though. For one, why would I give away all my secrets? This seems, quite frankly, foolish. And why delay publishing my memoir? I've already devoted several precious hours of my time to writing nearly half of it. What's the benefit of diverting my attention to this *other* project?

And if we do go through with this, can I be guaranteed that my memoirs will be published in the near future?

I'm reticent. But you have my attention.

Mwa-ha-ha,
King Oblivion, Ph.D.

. . .

Jason Katzman
Editor, Talos Press
307 West 36th Street
New York, NY 10018

August 29, 2011
King Oblivion, Ph.D.
Undisclosed Location
Deep Underground
Nowhere, XX 00000

Dear King,

To answer your questions:

- You won't have to give away all your secrets. Just stick to the basics. Most people aren't supervillains, so this will all be new to them.
- Don't worry about putting all your attention into this. You've worked with ghostwriters before, right? Come on, you're famous, so surely you have. Just hire someone to do all the work for you, then put your name on the cover. It's simple. We do it all the time!
- Rest assured, I will work to make sure we get around to your memoirs, as long as the sales on your how-to guides are within a certain range.

Let me know if you have any other questions.

Thanks!
Jason

. . .

King Oblivion, Ph.D.
Undisclosed Location
Deep Underground
Nowhere, XX 00000

September 1, 2011
Jason Katzman
Editor, Talos Press
307 West 36th Street
New York, NY 10018

Dear Jason,

My attorney will be contacting you about the financials, but for now . . . we have a deal.

Do not disappoint me.

Mwa-ha-ha,
King Oblivion, Ph.D.

. . .

Jason Katzman
Editor, Talos Press
307 West 36th Street
New York, NY 10018

March 2, 2014
King Oblivion, Ph.D.
Undisclosed Location
Deep Underground
Nowhere, XX 00000

Dear King,

Sales of *The Supervillain Handbook* and *The Supervillain Field Manual* have been steady, but I'm afraid I have to break the news that your memoir has been put on hold. Unless something drastic happens, we will be unable to release it. My apologies.

Best,
Jason

King Oblivion's Obituary as Published in the Blast Radius City Nitroglycerin

King Oblivion, Ph.D., our beloved leader, killed in tragic plane crash at 104

BLAST RADIUS CITY – King Oblivion, Ph.D., longtime ruler and monarch of Explosia, founder of the International Society of Supervillains, and winner of the title "Most Eligible Bachelor in the Explosian Peninsula" in all but one of the past seventy years was taken from us Sunday night in a tragic crash involving his personal supersonic fist-shaped plane.

According to official reports, King Oblivion had spent the evening engaging the latest of his many recent performance art pieces—some less respectful observers have called them "publicity stunts" or "acts of hedonism," but we would never dare. The great leader reportedly walked through the front door of the US National Security Agency headquarters in Fort Meade, Maryland, blasted through the metal detectors, and pushed aside a number of security guards to position himself directly in the center of the logo on the floor. He then said, "Come and get me, you imbeciles!"

Onlookers and official reports say that provocation led to a westbound air chase that crossed a number of states. King Oblivion's plane, piloted by one of his numerous "decoy" henchmen, doubled back and began a speedy trip across the Atlantic Ocean. Somewhere in the area above Bermuda, the multinational anti-supervillain agency AGHAST launched a new, experimental flying submarine out of the ocean, blasting out of the water like a missile. It collided with King Oblivion's fist-plane, destroying it on impact.

Authorities fished King Oblivion's body out of the water. He was later identified by his closest lieutenant, La Campeona. The pilot's body was not recovered.

Born just off the coast of Alaska on July 7, 1912, King Oblivion worked for every accolade and title he ever gained. After an already-eventful career that involved participation in the St. Valentine's Day Massacre, holding a key position within the now-defunct Western Association of Ruffians, and earning a doctorate in nefariology at a secret university he refused to name, King Oblivion became the undisputed monarch of Explosia in 1946 with a masterful, totally uncontroversial win at the nation's annual roshambo tournament.

He has won the tournament every year since with skill and ability that will never be matched.

In 1961, King Oblivion was the sole founder of the International Society of Supervillains, often shortened to ISS, after the ceremonious defeat of his mentor, Heinrich Misanthroach, a.k.a. Dr. Blattarius, and his Western Association of Ruffians organization. The ISS has become the world's most important institution in its five-plus decades of existence.

In addition to his geopolitical accomplishments, King Oblivion was incredibly influential on culture, whether he took name credit for his creations or not. Every statue in the nation of Explosia is of him, and he has written numerous books, though only two bear his name.

A snafu in the promotional schedule for the film *The Great Waldo Pepper* brought actor Robert Redford to Explosia for one day in 1975. A later voting error led to him, rather than King Oblivion, being named the "Most Eligible Bachelor in the Explosian Peninsula" that year. Redford was immediately vaporized and replaced with an android Redford controlled by King Oblivion. Thus, King Oblivion was the rightful founder of the Sundance Film Festival and director of the Oscar-winning film *Ordinary People*.

In recent years, King Oblivion deemed Explosia worthy of far more of his incomparably busy schedule than he had been able to allot in the decades prior. He could be seen riding around the various dunes and craters of the country in a dune buggy, doing donuts and jumping around on makeshift ramps. He proved that, even with his many achievements, he still knew how to have an incredible time.

King Oblivion is survived by his sons and daughters, each of us, the 212,000 residents of the nation of Explosia, many of whom chose to take up the mantle of dressing like him to serve as his henchmen in the ISS.

As our national motto proclaims, "We burst with pride." We were proud of our king. We will honor him forever. Fearsome fortune to him in the great unknown.

Email Correspondence Between Supreme Villainy *Editor Matt D. Wilson and the International Society of Supervillains' Attorney, The Litigatron*

From: The Litigatron
To: King Oblivion, Ph.D.
Subject: Memoir publication

Matt,

I understand from conversations with my associates that you have recently gained access to this email account, as well as any number of King Oblivion's private files. I'm also told that you have worked out a deal with a publishing company to finally get his memoir in print.

Nominally, I approve of these efforts. As the executor of King Oblivion's estate, I'm tasked with carrying out his final wishes, which include forcing someone to publish his memoirs. It would seem that you've done considerable work to bring that to bear, and I appreciate those efforts. It saves me the trouble of having to compile his mountainous notes into something readable.

However, I must warn you to be extremely cautious in gathering the materials to publish. I understand that you've already condensed a voluminous amount of material, but I'd advise you as King Oblivion's legal counsel to do a series of additional edits. Based on the draft materials I've been sent—and I believe it was only a sliver of what King Oblivion commissioned—there are numerous admissions of guilt and otherwise incriminating statements throughout the work.

King Oblivion insisted to me that he would be indemnified from legal culpability in these matters, but he's not here anymore. So I'm telling you to tone it down and scale it back. I won't have anything tarnishing King Oblivion's legacy or staining the reputation of the ISS.

I also insist I get final review on any materials published.

Fearsome fortune,
The Litigatron

P.S. I also heard from one of my associates that you're apparently trapped in the secret, hive-like ISS lair. I'll send someone to come and get you out of there in the next few days. There are actually a few things I require your assistance with. Keep an eye out.

EDITOR'S ADDENDUM

About two weeks after The Litigatron messaged me through King Oblivion's email, a field team of decoys found me scooping the last few sunflower seeds out of a jar as I tried to keep myself from starving. They came in the nick of time.

Once I finally saw the light of day—after nearly nine months of being stranded—the decoy team dumped me on a plane and took me to meet with The Litigatron in his New York office. I begged for some food once I arrived, and luckily one of the receptionists had some stale bagels I could gnaw on. To be entirely truthful, I didn't hear much of what The Litigatron had to say over my hearty chewing, but I did catch something about him wanting me to accompany him and The Malevolent ME, the ISS's resident medical examiner, to exhume King Oblivion's body from his gilded, diamond-encrusted sarcophagus buried underneath the now-decommissioned giant robot that bore his image. It had been bronzed and placed like a statue just next to Explosia Palace, on top of where some orphanages used to be.

Within a few short hours, I was back on another plane, now on my way to Blast Radius City. I was still pretty famished, so when I arrived I begged Litigatron and The Malevolent ME to get me something more substantial to eat. After a prolonged begging assault, they finally allowed me to pick something up—specifically, a pita wrap—from a food cart just outside the palace.

By the time we got inside the palace, the coffin had already been removed from the tomb. The Litigatron ordered a decoy to carefully open it while I stood by, voraciously eating my sandwich. At that time, everything seemed pretty normal. The body was in there—somewhat decayed but still immaculately dressed in an all-platinum version of King Oblivion's standard hooded cape, mask, and suit. I counted six crowns in there with him: one on his head, two on his hands, two at his feet, and one right at his crotch. The inside of the coffin was filled with televisions, all operating and tuned to different news channels—apparently this was a specific request in his will. There was also what had to be at least $500,000 in cash.

The Malevolent ME leaned down next to the coffin and extracted some fluid with a syringe. Then he opened up the mouth and took a look at King Oblivion's teeth and jaw. I also noticed Litigatron removing a folded-up piece of paper from King Oblivion's pocket and reading it over.

I should note that I can't exactly recount everything that was happening at this point because I was beginning to feel extremely woozy. My legs started to slip out from under my torso. I had no idea what was happening to me.

Litigatron and The Malevolent ME conferred for a moment. Then Litigatron walked over to me, slapped the piece of paper against my chest, and aggressively said, "This seems to be for you." That's the last thing I remember from that day.

I woke up in an Explosian hospital four weeks later. Apparently the meat in the pita wrap was marinated in a substance called Soothinal, a tranquilizing liquid invented by none other than King Oblivion himself. At least, that's what he told the Explosian people. It came as a shock that I had never heard of the stuff, considering that I had just spent months and months paging through every detail of his life, but according to the Explosian doctor who treated me, King

Oblivion developed Soothinal as an act of generosity toward the people of the country. I suppose he considered it one of his minor achievements.

It was intended to be a sedative to make a little more bearable the pain of having the dirt underneath your feet explode. The trouble was that the people of Explosia had built up a very high tolerance to Soothinal over the years, so they soaked just about everything they ate in it. I'm also told they drank it at meals. Not hailing from Explosia, this was my first exposure to it, and it was such a massive dose that it sent me into a month-long coma.

A day later, I was released as the first patient to ever be treated for something besides dirt-blast-related injuries at an Explosian hospital.

In a taxi on the way back to the airport, I was still wondering why King Oblivion never bragged about inventing Soothinal—maybe it was too nice a thing to do, so it didn't fit his image?—when my coat pocket started buzzing. I reached in and found a cell phone that Litigatron must have given me before he left the country. I answered, and before I could even ask who was calling, Litigatron hit me with a gut punch:

"It's not him."

I needed a minute to figure out exactly what he was saying.

"Who's not who?"

"The body," he shot back. "It's not his. We're thinking it's the pilot."

Then it hit me. Bringing The Malevolent ME. The fluid extraction for a DNA test. Checking the teeth. Something had them thinking they had buried the wrong body. And apparently they were right.

I tried to formulate a question. "So is he really dead or—"

The Litigatron cut me off. "You read that note I gave you?"

I hadn't. I'd totally forgotten. I told The Litigatron I'd call him back and began digging around in every pocket I had to find it. Had the hospital staff taken it? Just as I started to really worry, I found it folded up in one of my rear pants pockets. I unraveled it and started reading.

It was a jaw dropper.

Dear Matt,

Congratulations. You were never my first choice for editor/compiler of my memoirs, but necessity called after all my other editorial hires fell through, and you always do a . . . workable job.

Based on the reports I've been getting from inside the lair, you've nearly finished getting things together and, more importantly, news of my demise has spurred the publisher to finally give in and bring this extremely important part of our culture and world history to print.

I must express my disappointment that the chapters about the War of the Wicked and the End of Heroism were never realized in glorious prose, but I really should have known that no one's words but my own could have accurately described those monumentally historic moments. We were like the gods of Olympus. Nothing can be perfect, I suppose, myself excluded. I'm looking forward to publication, warts and all.

In the meantime, I'll be taking care of a few things. I've been monitoring your phone conversations and emails (as you might expect) and, believe me, I was very interested in the notion that The Blessing could be out there somewhere. I'll find Miss Spiraci and we will have words.

Nonetheless, point 100 in the Super-Plan—the publication of my memoir—is all but complete, and you had a big hand in it. Once I've completed some of the errands I must finish, I'll be around to collect you and bring you back home to the lair. Hang tight.

Mwa-ha-ha,
King Oblivion Ph.D.

After taking a few moments to let the letter sink in, I called The Litigatron back. He answered with a laugh. I asked him the only question I could think of.

"Where do I go?"

He leveled with me.

"Doesn't matter. Wherever you go, he'll find you. Just send off the manuscript and make the most of your freedom while you can."

* * *

As I write this from a hiding place I'd rather not reveal, mere moments before mailing it off to a publisher, I wonder if there's anything I can do to save myself.

I don't know if a word of this memoir is true. I don't know if King Oblivion, Ph.D. achieved even a tenth of the things he claims to have done in these pages. So many of the people closest to him call him a fraud, a liar, an egomaniac, a superficial and image-obsessed narcissist. They say he's so much smaller than he seems.

But I'll tell you this: Right now, I have never felt more terrified.

Matt D. Wilson
June 2017